THE ASYLUM WOMEN

THE ASYLUM WOMEN

ELAINE WHITEFORD

First published by Sterlini Publishing 2025

www.sterlinipublishing.com

ISBN 978-1-7384981-3-0

To my grandmother
Margaret Anderson
1897-1989

Scorned, spurned–naught ye have cared,
Raising your eyes to a wider morrow.

From 'The March of the Women'
Written by Cicely Hamilton (1910)

JESSIE

JESSIE PURDIE STEPPED into the recessed nook in the middle of Bayne's Bridge and peered over the parapet. The river, brown with recent rain, flowed steadily. With the incoming tide, it wouldn't be long until it reached the top of the cutwater.

She looked to her right for the grey heron that sometimes lurked in the reeds, then scanned across the swirling water to the trees and shrubs of the opposite bank. The spindly cherry blossoms were months away from blooming. Jessie longed for the day when the first splashes of pink and white would creep along their branches.

She picked at a brittle piece of yellow lichen and dabbed a tuft of velvety moss. She couldn't dally much longer; the foreman wouldn't hesitate to fine her a shilling if she was even a few seconds late. And when her father noticed her pay was short, he'd go into a rage if he was sober, a terrible rage if he was drunk.

There was a ripple in the shrubs. A figure in a hooded grey cloak crawled out and headed across the narrow grass strip. Jessie bit her lip, bemused. Surely they'd stop before the sloppy mud of the water's edge?

When they carried on, she put her hand to her mouth.

Between the cold and the current, they'd perish if they went into the river. She glanced around to see if there was anyone who might help. But there wasn't. It was down to her to do something. And quickly.

"Oi!" she screeched. Then louder. "Oi! Stop!"

The person looked up and the hood of their cloak slipped down, revealing long black hair.

"Oh my Lord!" What on earth was this woman doing? "Stop! Don't! It's freezing."

The woman pulled the hood back over her head and squelched on.

"No!" Jessie flapped her arms wildly. "Stop!"

The woman didn't.

There was a clatter on the cobbles. Thomson's Aerated Water cart was coming over the bridge. Jessie bolted in front of the two grey horses and waved Mr Thomson down. "Help! Please!"

He pulled on the reins and the cart came to an abrupt halt. "Good God, girl. What are you doing?"

"There's a woman down at the river. You have to help!"

He stood up and peered where Jessie was pointing. "Is she mad?"

"Quickly! She's going in!"

Mr Thomson cast the reins to the scrawny lad sitting up front with him, then leapt from the cart. "Come on then!" he yelled at Jessie.

She set off after him but stumbled on the cobbles. She put her hand out to break her fall and cracked down on her knees.

"Hurry up!" Mr Thomson shouted from the end of the bridge, before disappearing down the banking.

Jessie sucked the grit from her skinned knuckles and kicked off her clogs. Then she hitched up her skirt and hirpled on.

When she caught up, Mr Thomson and the woman were struggling on the grass. She was resisting him in a fierce tug-of-war. As he pulled one arm, she swung the other; as he caught one leg, she kicked the other. Jessie edged nearer the tangle of limbs, then hopped back as the two of them tumbled over.

Mr Thomson lay spread-eagled on the ground, clinging to the woman's ankles as she tried to crawl back to the river. "For God's sake, stop her!"

Jessie went to grab her arm but the back of the woman's flailing hand smacked her on the chin.

"Do something!" Mr Thomson bawled.

Jessie went from foot to foot, then skipped to the side to dodge another slap. "What?" she bawled back, exasperated.

Mr Thomson's face was red; there was saliva on his lower lip and snot on his upper one.

"Sit on her!"

"What?"

"Get on top of her!"

"Wh—?"

"Now!"

Jessie thudded down, knees first. The woman gave a deep growl as her chest thumped into the ground. Jessie shifted forward and forced the woman's shoulders down, until finally she was still.

Mr Thomson, out of puff, and smeared in sweat and mud, staggered to his feet. He put his hands on his hips, bent over and breathed deeply. His opponent remained motionless on the ground.

When he'd recovered, he took hold of the woman's wrist. "Right, lass. You get the other one and we'll drag her. And for God's sake, hold onto her. She's got the strength of ten men."

Jessie clamped on with both hands. But the woman didn't struggle as they dragged her up to the bridge.

The lad brought the cart over. The clip of hooves and the rattle of crates roused the woman. She began to weep.

Jessie stroked her matted hair. "Shush."

The woman closed her eyes and moaned. Shivering under her sodden cloak, she was slighter than she'd first appeared.

"Here, take this." Jessie undid her shawl and wrapped it round the wretched stranger. "It'll be all right."

The woman reached out and gently touched Jessie's cheek. Her fingers were freezing.

"Right," Mr Thomson said. The lad was fashioning a narrow space between some crates. "Let's get her up. The two of you will fit in there."

"What?" Jessie said, startled.

"And whatever you do, make sure you hold onto her."

"But I've got work to get to. I'm already late. I can't."

"You got me into this, lass, so you can help get me out of it. Once her majesty there comes to, she's not going to stay put, is she?" Mr Thomson nodded at the lad, who was climbing over the crates to the front of the cart. "And *he* won't be able to manage her on his own."

"But—"

"I've got deliveries to make. And I've better things to do than chase this mad woman round the county."

"Where are you taking her?"

"The state of her, it should be straight to the asylum. That'd save us all a lot of time and trouble. But that's the Inspector of the Poor's job, not mine. So I'm taking her – *we're* taking her – to the parish council. They can deal with her."

"But—"

"Right, m'lady," he said to the woman, "come on." He put his hands under her oxters and went to pull her up, but she clung to Jessie. He sighed. "Not this again."

"It'll be all right. Promise," Jessie said to her softly.

The woman got up slowly; Mr Thomson quickly lifted her onto the cart.

He turned to Jessie. "Right, lass. You next."

She supposed she was going to the parish council with Mr Thomson after all.

KATHERINE

With the medical superintendent attending the monthly meeting of the District Lunacy Board, and her fellow assistant medical officer Dr Dorsie dealing with an incident in the men's wing, it fell to Dr Katherine Forbes to receive the new patient.

She waited behind the ash writing desk in the middle of the Admissions Room, before taking her memorandum book from her jacket pocket, ready to note her observations on the patient's bodily and mental condition. She looked again at the soggy objects the police constable had found in the woman's possession: the return half of a ticket from Belfast to Glasgow dated three months prior, a few coppers and a cutting from *The Dublin Times. Delighted ... announce ... marriage ... daughter, Mary ...* were the only words legible on the smudged scrap.

At the brisk click of heels in the corridor, Katherine stood up straight and pushed a couple of stray hairs behind her ear. A dark outline appeared on the other side of the opaque glass door, then Matron Campbell entered, followed by a hunched young woman herded by Nurse Elliot.

"Good morning, Dr Forbes. The Inspector of the Poor's submitted this certificate provided by Dr Rennie in town. He says he'll return tomorrow to draw up the formal petition for committal for the Sheriff."

"Thank you, Matron."

The date and signature on the paperwork from the town's GP were in order but the woman's name was recorded simply as 'unknown patient – female'. Katherine looked up her. Lank hair covered her face and her mud-streaked hands were trembling.

"Just sit her there, Nurse Elliot." She nodded at the cane chair by the door. Then she angled the high-back desk chair towards the patient and sat down. "So – Mrs …? Miss …?" The woman slumped forward, her hair almost reaching the hem of her cloak. "I'm Dr Forbes, assistant medical officer. And you are? Mrs …?" Katherine opened her memorandum book. "If we're to help you, we need to know who you are." She wrote the date at the top of a fresh page. "So your name is …?"

The woman reached out and caressed the leaves of the potted palm next to her chair.

"Yes, it's a rather splendid specimen, isn't it?" Katherine said. She held up the newspaper cutting. "Is this about you? Are you Mary?"

When the patient lifted her head, Katherine performed a quick assessment. Beneath the grime her complexion looked healthy and her pupils were of equal size and reacting normally. She looked no more than twenty-five.

"So – Mary, is it?"

The corner of the woman's mouth twitched and a grin spread slowly across her face.

"Is this about you, Mary?" The suggestion was batted away with a tut and a shake of her head. "Did you come on the boat from Ireland, Mary? Hmm?"

The woman glared at Katherine. "No. I did not." She had a strong Irish accent.

"All right. So if it's not Mary, what is your name?"

"You know fine well who I am." She folded her arms and looked at the ceiling.

"I see a great many people each day. Sometimes I forget a name or two."

The woman wiped her index finger along the top of the dado rail. "It's very grand, this."

"It is, yes. Now, as I was saying … I see a great many people each day and I'm afraid I don't always remember everyone's name."

"Friends wouldn't have treated me this way." The woman stroked the crimson-flecked wallpaper. "Yes, very grand indeed."

"I'm sure they wouldn't," Katherine said. "In fact, I'm sure your friends will be missing you and wondering what's happened. So if you tell me your—"

"And my teacher told me I was working too hard." She clasped her hands together and jiggled her legs.

"Yes, that could be the case. And what does your teacher call you?"

"You know."

"Tell me again."

The woman dropped her hands to her lap and tilted her head. "I'm a lady. A relative of the Duke of Connaught."

Katherine noticed Nurse Elliot shift on the spot. The staff had heard that claim many times before. "All right. And how might we contact the Duke to let him know of your circumstances?"

The woman slumped over again and began to pull her hair.

Katherine put down her pencil and closed her memorandum book. Experience told her that she wouldn't get any useful information until the newcomer was settled.

"Matron Campbell, could you take the patient for a bath and then put her to bed in the observation ward, please?"

"Certainly, Dr Forbes."

"I'll see her on my rounds."

Nurse Elliot helped the woman to her feet and led her from the Admissions Room.

"Don't worry, Doctor, you'll find out who she is. It's just a question of time," Matron Campbell said. "If you need me for anything else, I'll be in the men's wing for the next while."

Katherine picked up her pencil and tapped it on the desk. The matron was right, of course – time did seem to be the best medicine for a great many patients.

The hall porter, Mr Johnstone, appeared at the door, holding a small white envelope and a larger brown one. "Ah, Dr Forbes. Two for you today." He gazed at the postmark on the white envelope. "Another one from Edinburgh, I see. Will that be … the *second* this week?"

"Yes, thank you very much. Now if you don't mind, Mr Johnstone …" Katherine snatched the letters from him. "… I must get back to my laboratory." She gave him the stare she normally reserved for male patients who tried to take liberties. "I'm sure the rest of those letters won't deliver themselves."

Mr Johnstone's ruddy complexion deepened. "Of course not. No." He patted the brown leather satchel that was slung across his chest. "A good day to you, Dr Forbes."

"And to you, Mr Johnstone."

Katherine closed the door. Then she sliced the white envelope open with the tip of her pencil and lifted out the embossed cream writing paper she had come to associate with Dr Andrew Cowan.

Royal Mental Hospital
January 1911

Dear Dr Forbes,

While it's just a few days since I last wrote to you, and only six weeks since I last saw you, it feels like many months. I

*could never have imagined the inspection tour would have
given me such a gift of friendship.*

*It's with great anticipation, therefore, that I await the reunion
of the 'Meerenburg Six' and our forthcoming meeting to
review our contributions to the journal. I'm very much
looking forward to reading your observations on the
employment of female nurses in male wards, which I'm sure
will be most erudite and illuminating.*

*I've been working hard on my own piece on pathological
protocols, which I pray will stand up to comparison and won't
diminish our collective effort. I'd very much value your
opinion on some technical matters and wonder if you might
agree to take tea with me at Miss Cranston's prior to the
meeting to go over them. I hope that—*

The door opened. Katherine thrust the letter into her
pocket.

"Dr Forbes?" It was one of the nurses from the men's wing.

"Yes?"

"Matron's asking if you might attend? Bummin' Jamie's
having one of his turns and she wonders if you could dispense
a sleeping draught?"

"Of course. I'll be there in just a moment."

Katherine lifted her memorandum book from the writing
desk. If only she could concoct a draught that would as easily
quell Dr Cowan's enthusiasm as the one for containing
Bummin' Jamie's excitability.

HELEN

Nurse Helen Elliot took the thermometer from the shelf and shook it, before dipping it into the bath water. Keeping an eye on her patient, she counted slowly to fifteen.

"Right. Let's have a look." She pulled out the thermometer. "Perfect. Ninety-six degrees exactly. Warm, but not hot." She wiped the thermometer on her apron and glanced at the 'Bathing Rules' plaque on the wall. She smiled. It had taken her a while to master, but now she could judge just the right volume of hot water to add to the cold so the temperature was always within the range set out in the regulations.

She put the thermometer back on the shelf, then guided the patient to the side of the bath. "In you get. I'll take this." She slipped the gown from the woman's shoulders and draped it over the dressing screen. "Come on now. In you get. You can't have all that mud still on you when Dr Forbes comes back. Matron'll have my guts for garters if I don't turn you out nice and neat and clean."

The woman slowly raised a leg over the bath. Helen eyed her body for any unusual marks. There were two perfectly level bruises the size of plums on her upper back. She'd need to report them in the daily returns book.

"What's happened here then?" The woman flinched when Helen gently dabbed the bruises. "They're going to be all shades of black and blue in a day or two."

The woman lowered herself tentatively into the water, and Helen lifted the bathing brush and copper pitcher from the floor.

"So ..." She rubbed the streaks of mud off the woman's hands. "... if you're not Mary, what are we to call you?" The woman stared at the water. "We're going to have to call you something. And if you don't tell me what, then I'll just have to make something up." Helen ran the brush up to the woman's shoulder and then under her armpit. "My granny had a cousin from Ireland whose name was Bridget. They called her Biddy. What about Biddy?"

The woman submerged a hand and waggled it to disturb the water.

"Biddy it is then. So, Biddy – what were you thinking, going into the river this morning? If Mr Thomson hadn't been passing, Lord only knows what would've become of you. A lovely young lady ... a lovely colleen like yourself." Helen brushed the soles of Biddy's feet. "Every single bit of you needs to be clean. And let me see your nails ... oh, they're just fine. Bathing isn't complete, you know, if your toenails are long. And mark my words, Matron'll be checking them later." Helen plopped Biddy's foot back into the bath and some water splashed up.

"Pah!" She grimaced.

"You're not scared of a little water, are you?"

"I'm a lady, you know?"

"Of course you are."

The bathroom door opened. "I thought I'd find you in here." Helen's colleague, Nurse Haggarty, was on the threshold with old Nellie Shaw, the asylum's longest-standing patient. "I heard you had a new admission."

"I do indeed."

Biddy folded her arms over her bosom and Helen poured water down her back.

"Have you heard about the meeting?" Nurse Haggarty said.

"No. What meeting?"

"Nurse Millar heard from her cousin at Mount Hope that they're thinking of drafting a petition."

"What for?"

"She thought maybe we could do one here too."

"Why?"

"That's what the meeting's about. To talk about whether we should do the same."

"But why?"

"*Why?*"

"Is this my bath?" Nellie said.

"No, you're going next door for your bath in a minute. You're having your own one, not sharing this one."

"Oh, my. I've never had that before," the old lady replied.

Nurse Haggarty laughed. "Except for last Thursday."

"No," Nellie said emphatically. "Six of us shared the same water last time. Because of the drought. And we had just one towel between us. Before that, we hadn't had a bath for six weeks. Though they sponged us down every day."

"That was in 1889, Nellie. You should think yourself lucky things have moved on in the last twenty-odd years and we've got proper plumbing now. Now just give me a minute while I speak to Nurse Elliot." Nurse Haggarty turned back to Helen. "So will you come to the meeting?"

Helen refilled the pitcher with bathwater. "Well, I usually do a bit of the Red Book in the evenings."

"Half an hour won't kill you. Anyway, I don't know why you're bothering with the Red Book. We've managed fine for years without needing a diploma."

"Well, it's—"

"I mean, what's the point in being qualified by your la-dida Medico-Psychological Association if you'll still be working eighty-four hours a week? Ninety-odd, if you count all the extras we do."

"Once I get it I might be able to—"

"And a fancy certificate on the wall won't reduce your hours or get you the same wages as the attendants. It'll just make them reduce the number of nurses even more."

"Dr Lockhart said in his lecture last week that once we've completed the course we'll be members of a 'highly trained respectable profession'. That we could go on and work in—"

"They even charge you for the pleasure, don't they? Two and six, isn't it?"

"—any hospital in the country. Look at Miss Sim, away to be assistant matron of that private asylum."

"What would you want to do that for? You'd be better finding yourself a nice gentleman to—"

"Is this my bath?"

Nurse Haggarty took Nellie's arm. "I'd better go. I hope to see you at the meeting tonight. It's in the Recreation Room after tea."

Helen gently brushed Biddy's back and shoulders. She wouldn't be going to the meeting and she would have no part in their petition. Nurse Haggarty obviously didn't have anything to lose if she was prepared to risk her job. She couldn't know what it was like to have so little you had to rely on scraps of food from the alehouse. And as for finding a nice gentleman? That was no guarantee of safety or security. If nothing else, Helen's mother had taught her that.

She put the pitcher and the brush down. "No one's ever happy with their lot, are they, Biddy?" She took a clean towel from the shelf. "Right, out you get. Let's get you weighed and find you some fresh clothes."

Biddy stared at Helen, then started to sing:

"The Lord's my shepherd, I'll not want;
he makes me down to lie in pastures green;

he leadeth me the quiet waters by.
My soul he doth restore again ..."

Helen opened the daily returns book at a new page and made a note: *Unknown female patient, two bruises on back, won't answer any questions. Has taken to singing Psalm 23.*

ISABELLA

MRS ISABELLA LOCKHART smiled when Tipper licked her hand. She put the latest edition of *The Vote* on the settee and scratched behind his ear. He was such a sweet little thing and, with those brown splodges on his white coat, cute as a button. She was certain he was a Jack Russell, even if Angus maintained he was just a mongrel that had strayed from the bottom end of town. Whatever Tipper's heritage, Isabella cared not a jot – a more affectionate companion she couldn't have wished for.

She glanced over to the mahogany mantel clock, the hands of which were about to strike eight. She didn't care much for the look of the timepiece, nor that it sounded every quarter hour. But it had been presented to Angus by visiting French physicians the previous summer and, as such, took pride of place in the drawing room of the medical superintendent's house.

She ought to feel fortunate living in such a stylish and commodious dwelling. It was a larger residence than she could ever have imagined for herself, a two-storey house with quarters for a housekeeper and maid. The ground floor alone was larger than her childhood home and the front porch was almost the size of the bedroom she'd shared with her sister. Yet this house would never really be hers and it would never be a home. It was only Angus's for as long as he remained the medical superintendent of Cappelmuir Asylum.

The clock struck the hour. Isabella sighed. Angus must have had supper with the staff and patients, as he sometimes did the day of a District Lunacy Board meeting. It was good for morale, he said, to present himself and reassure both staff and patients of the Board's continued support for the asylum. Hopefully, with him having had such a busy day, and with all the important things he had to consider, he might forget to enquire about the domestic detail of Isabella's day; more specifically, about her trip to town, where she was meant to have purchased a licence for Tipper.

It had certainly been her intention to do so. Even as she was getting into the horse-cab for the short drive, she was thinking of the two errands she had to run: a visit to Cree & Co. Ladies' Tailors to be fitted for a costume, and a trip to the post office for the licence. However, she'd paid a quick visit to the Suffrage Centre's Tea Room beforehand and the ladies had urged – practically dared – her not to purchase the licence. She'd explained that, as the wife of Dr Angus Lockhart, she couldn't be seen to be promoting tax resistance.

"But that's precisely why you must, my dear. You have a duty to because you *are* the wife of the medical superintendent."

The ladies were right about that, and with any luck, also in their supposition that Angus would be so pre-occupied with work matters he wouldn't realise her omission. So, in the end, Isabella had ordered a costume from Cree & Co for sixty-three shillings and had dropped the seven and six earmarked for Tipper's licence into the Women's Freedom League's donation box. If she were ever to be challenged by a Customs & Excise officer or a police constable for keeping a dog without a licence, then 'female feeble-mindedness' would surely be an acceptable excuse. How she was going to answer any direct question Angus might put to her on the matter, though, she'd yet to decide. She didn't want to deceive him, of course; on the other hand, as her mother often remarked about her own marriage, 'Least said, soonest mended.'

Tipper cocked his head when the door handle rattled. Isabella covered *The Vote* with one of the floral-patterned cushions that was a wedding gift from her aunt. Then she picked up her embroidery hoop, removed the needle from the linen and began to stitch.

"Good evening, my dear," Angus said, sweeping in. "I'm so sorry I'm late." He leaned over and kissed her on the cheek. "When I got back from the Board meeting – which went very well, by the way, I'll tell you about it shortly – I had all sorts to deal with. Mainly, a new admission who was brought in after Mr Thomson fished her out of the river, where apparently she was trying to drown herself."

"Poor woman."

"She refuses to give her name, other than to say she's a relative of the Duke of Connaught. I must say, that man seems to have a great many relations in institutions! The Inspector of the Poor wanted my support for a letter he's sending to detectives in the city to ask them to trace the young lady's actual relatives. He thinks she may be from Ireland. Certainly she does have a brogue. He's going to ask if they'll contact their counterparts in Dublin to ascertain if any young ladies – whether related to the Duke of Connaught or not – have been reported missing. There was a clipping from a Dublin newspaper in her pocket about the marriage of a 'Mary' – or some such thing – so they're speculating that our young lady may have been disappointed in matters of the heart. The Inspector's also hoping to get some coverage in the newspapers here."

"He's certainly taking his duties very seriously, going to all that trouble."

Angus laughed. "I fear it's more about knowing which parish to send the bill for the young lady's care to than concern for her well-being."

"Oh, that's not fair. He was always most solicitous about the pupils when I was at Park School."

"Yes indeed. But they said at the Board today that the number of disputes about payment is increasing month on month and that we need to be conscientious in making sure we're prompt in finding out who to send the invoices to. The Chairman was so good as to mention, however, that our balances remain healthy due to my prudent management of institution finances."

"Very good of him."

"Indeed. And they've also agreed now to the terms of the visit from the American Psychiatric Association. The Chairman was very taken with the prospect of Cappelmuir being held up as an international model. And the APA's most interested in our use of female nurses on the male wards."

"Excellent."

"Isn't it? Right, my dear. I'll just change and then I'll pour you a sherry."

Isabella secured the needle in the linen again. "Thank you, dear."

"Oh …" Angus stopped at the drawing room door. "How was your trip to town? Did you attend to the licence for that mongrel?"

Isabella smiled at the licence his question offered her. "Yes dear, I attended to it."

JESSIE

Jessie was clearing away the last of the tea plates when her father came back into the cottage, tucking his shirt into his trousers.

"Before you settle down for the night, give it a sweep out there. It's running like a slurry pit. I don't want to be stepping through that in the morning."

"It was probably you that caused the shit river to start with," her oldest brother James said.

"With more than enough help from you pair." Her father kicked out at Jessie's other brother, Robert, who had his foot on one of the stools. "And get your mucky boot off that. Your sister's got enough to be doing without you making the place look untidy. If you want to live like a pig, move out to the midden."

"Pigs'd be better neighbours," Robert said, ducking to avoid a slap from his father as he moved to the front door. "Hurry up. They'll have drunk the alehouse dry by the time we get there."

Jessie watched from the window as the men pushed and shoved their way along the lane. When they turned onto the road to town, she went through to the back room and lifted the hessian drape, made from two discarded mill sacks, that separated her bed from her father's and brothers'. She slid her hand under the mattress for her cloth bag. Taking her Band of Hope medallion out, she caressed it with her fingertips. She never imagined she'd find comfort in the group, in its slide shows about the evils of drink and its songs about the joys of abstinence. Then again, she never imagined her father and brothers would turn into such drunkards.

She recited the Temperance Pledge: "I promise by divine assistance to abstain from giving or partaking of all intoxicating liquors and I will discountenance all the causes and practices of intemperance." She hadn't signed it officially like others, in front of everyone at the meetings. That would be too risky. The men would find out. But she'd taken it silently, and that was good enough for now.

She licked her finger and wiped a smear from the crown symbol on the medallion's red enamel. Then she checked that the ribbon's pin clasp would still hold. It would probably do another few outings, but when she next saw the tinker she'd ask if he had a replacement in his barrow.

She pinned the medallion to her blouse, then shook her cloth bag to gauge how many pennies were in it. By the dull clinking, enough to buy bread and oats, should the men spend the household's wages before the end of the week. She took out a penny and stuffed the bag back in its hiding place. Then she reached under the bed for the pair of black Oxfords that had belonged to her mother. Jessie's feet had only grown to fit them in the last few months but she'd worn them to every meeting since. She pulled them on, careful not to stretch the leather.

The town clock struck the half hour. She tutted. She'd already missed the first part of the evening. But arriving late would still be worth it for the cup of tea and bun at the end. If she hurried, she might still make it to the Temperance Hall in time for the Magic Lantern show and to see any newcomers sign the Pledge.

~

Mr Turner, the hall caretaker, was sitting at his little table just inside the storm doors reading a newspaper. Jessie put her penny down in front of him.

"Thank …" He looked up. "Oh, it's you."

"Hello. I hope I've not missed too much."

"Well I daresay anything you've missed you'll have seen before and you'll see again next time. Anyway – what's this I've been hearing about you?"

Jessie gave a little start. "Eh?"

"That you witnessed a bit of excitement last week with Mr Thomson and some mad woman in the river. It says here …" He prodded the newspaper. "… she's been admitted to Cappelmuir and they don't have any idea who she is. They're asking the police in Ireland if they can help find out."

"Really?" Jessie grinned. "*I'm* in the … I mean, *it's* in the paper? Am I mentioned?"

Mr Turner looked puzzled. "Why on earth would you be mentioned? No. But it does say—"

Jessie's shoulders dropped. "Oh."

"—how brave Mr Thomson was, going into the water and saving her from certain drowning. And Mrs Thomson told me she had the strength of ten men. And right enough, it says here … now, let me see … yes, here we are … 'She is well-educated, speaks with a strong Irish accent, and appears to be in good physical condition'. Mind, I don't know how they can say she's well-educated if she was taking herself into the river and now won't say who she is. Sounds more like an imbecile to me. Although word has it some of them are better off in Cappelmuir than they are out of it. Three square meals a day, kept safe, warm and dry, no need to work for a living. Maybe we're the mad ones, eh?"

"Maybe. Anyway, I'd better get in or the meeting'll be over."

Just as Jessie turned to enter the hall, the storm doors burst open.

"What in hell's name are you doing here?" Her father loomed over her, furious. "I didn't believe them when they said they'd seen you go in. But ..." He cracked his knuckles then planted his hands on his hips. "... you've made a liar out of me."

Jessie put her hands in her pockets and took a step back. "I—"

"You're meant to be sweeping the back green."

"I was. I will. I was just ..." She pressed her chin into her chest.

"And what's this?" Her father ripped the medallion off her blouse.

"Give that back!"

He held it out of Jessie's reach. "How long have you been sneaking in here to listen to all this nonsense?"

She glanced at Mr Turner in case he was about to betray her. But he remained studying his newspaper, with the concentration of someone determined not to become involved.

"Not long."

"*Not long?* It's obviously been long enough to get one of these." Her father thrust the medallion in her face. Then he turned and threw it out into the street.

Jessie pushed past him and ran to pick it out of the gutter.

"Now get yourself home and get to it like a respectable daughter would! *Should.*"

She spun on the heels of her Oxfords and started to run.

Her father yelled after her. "That's it. Go on. Hurry up! Your mother would be turning in her grave if ..."

Jessie stopped dead.

"... she could see you now, if she knew what you were doing, how you were sneaking about. Yes. Turning in her grave."

In that moment, Jessie hated him. She gathered all her strength. "You'd know all about that!" she roared. "It was you who put her there!"

KATHERINE

KATHERINE TIPPED a few drops of the unknown female patient's blood from the vial onto a glass slide, which she carefully positioned on the stage plate of the microscope. A test had already shown no signs of anaemia – but what might this show?

She turned the knob and the familiar kaleidoscope pattern came into focus, giving her the same sense of wonder she'd experienced as a student on first seeing cellular structures.

She raised her head from the eyepiece and jotted down on a piece of graph paper the number of the various types of cells in the blood smear. They were all in regular proportion and didn't display the disturbance in the balance of lymphocytes and eosinophils that was observed in some mental conditions.

Satisfied, she removed the slide from the stage plate and slotted it into the wooden case built into the drawer on the underside of the bench.

There was a place for everything in the Cappelmuir pathology block: a room for microscopical, bacteriological and chemical investigations; a mortuary; a post-mortem room; a photography room; and a room for research, where she kept the guinea pigs that provided the blood and livers she needed for her research.

It was a far cry from the draughty, cramped laboratory of her university days. Indeed – and as Dr Lockhart was always keen to remind her – the Commissioners for Lunacy had assessed the facilities at Cappelmuir as 'highly satisfactory, placing the asylum in advance, in that respect, of every asylum in Scotland'. Inevitably, this pronouncement of his had a coda: 'And remember, Dr Forbes, it is not just in this respect, but in every respect, that we wish our establishment to be in advance of every asylum in Scotland.' A lofty ambition, which Katherine hoped one day to contribute to from a more senior position.

She pulled the gold chain from under her laboratory coat and looked at her watch. The attendants would be bringing Mr McGee's body from the hospital block at any moment. He'd been isolated with consumption. Such was his age and general feebleness, his was not an unexpected death. Nevertheless, a study of the condition of his organs and the constitution of his bodily fluids might inform future medical developments.

The post-mortem room was already prepared for the arrival of the body and the necessary equipment set out. Katherine stored her instruments in a small wooden box, no bigger than a pencil case, that her father had given her for her first human dissection. While the scalpels, forceps, probes, scissors and hooks she'd used back then had long since been replaced, and doubtless would be replaced many more times, she kept the box as a reminder of the sacrifices her parents had made for her to go to university like her brothers.

Her father didn't say much these days but she knew he was proud of her. The only disappointment he occasionally voiced was that she'd seldom gone to church while working towards her degree. So he was very content now she was required to attend Sunday service at the asylum's chapel. As for her mother, she remained adamant that Katherine was competent to fill the highest posts in the medical world, whether partaking of Sunday worship or not, and ought to reap the fullest rewards for such labours.

In return for her father's faith and her mother's conviction came an obligation to repay their investment. Any potential distraction to that had to be dispelled. So Katherine couldn't allow the recent flow of letters from Dr Cowan to derail her ambition.

Not that Dr Cowan was without appeal. Indeed her enjoyment of the inspection tour of Meerenburg had been greatly enhanced by his attendance. But she couldn't encourage his overtures – combining a career and love was an impossibility.

However, of all the letters that had arrived for her this week, the most troublesome was the one nestling in the pocket of her laboratory coat. If Mr Johnstone had known what it contained when he'd handed it to her, he'd surely have been unable to contain himself. *I see you're being sued for professional misconduct, Dr Forbes. Dr Lockhart won't like that one bit. If I were you, I'd start packing your trunk.* News of her predicament would've spread round Cappelmuir in minutes.

Katherine looked in her pocket but didn't remove the envelope. Her duty was clear: she must inform Dr Lockhart of the unfortunate circumstances before anyone else did.

The laboratory door opened and Matron Campbell waited as usual on the threshold. (The odours of chloroform, formalin and carbolic were rarely to anyone's taste.)

"The attendants are waiting with Mr McGee at the mortuary door. Dr Lockhart asks if the preliminary results might be conveyed to him at your earliest convenience."

"Certainly. Mr McGee will have my immediate attention." Katherine got up from the workbench. "Are you aware, Matron, if Dr Lockhart is free of commitments away from the asylum for the rest of the week? There's a matter I'd like to discuss with him."

"I'm not aware of any external appointments. Although, of course, he'll be busy with his regular meetings with the house steward, the clerk of works and the store keeper, going over their books. Do you wish to make a personal request to him for leave?"

"No, no." Katherine tapped the pocket of her laboratory coat. "It's just that there's something I'd very much like to discuss with him."

"And it can't wait until he summons you for some other matter?"

"Not really. You see, em … I've learned of some research that might benefit our patients. Yes. The Central Laboratory's seeking an establishment to work with to test out a thesis and I wanted to put to Dr Lockhart the possibility of Cappelmuir offering its services. The techniques being pioneered are of considerable interest and may be of great significance."

"Indeed?"

"Oh yes. There's a method in development of making autogenous vaccines from a patient's own blood serum that may be of use in acute mental illness, particularly where there's evidence of infection. It's thought … yes, it's thought …" Katherine continued, her tale gathering momentum, "… this technique might one day be efficacious in treating general paralysis of the insane which, as I'm sure you're aware through your long experience, appears to be characterised by a specific bacillus."

Matron Campbell stood even taller. "Of course."

"And you know as well as I do how keen Dr Lockhart is to promote Cappelmuir as being in advance of every asylum in Scotland."

"Indeed I do."

"So this opportunity may be of great interest to him."

"Well …" Matron Campbell checked that the cuffs of her stiff black dress were level. "… it's possible that if I were to enquire of the house secretary, he might be able to find a few minutes for you to discuss the matter with the medical superintendent. If it's for the advancement of Cappelmuir, of course."

"Of course." Katherine headed to the adjoining door to the mortuary. "There's certainly every possibility that it might be."

HELEN

THE SUBJECTS of Helen's first year of study were anatomy and physiology, and she'd read the forty-one pages devoted to them in the Red Book several times. When the exams came around, she'd know the contents of the *Handbook for the Attendants of the Insane* by rote.

She put the book down and looked at the two framed photographs commemorating the opening of the Nurses' Home which hung side by side next to the French doors leading from the Lecture Room to the gardens. One was of the splendid white building, which, with its decorative gables, windows and chimney stacks, was said to have been modelled on the Turnberry Station Hotel; the other showed the order of proceedings and the list of dignitaries in attendance, Lord Beattie of Cappelmuir taking pride of place at the top.

It must have been exciting to have been on the staff when the Home had opened. The nurses and attendants had been given an extra afternoon off for the celebrations and His Lordship had chatted to some of them. Not only that, but the medical superintendent and Matron Campbell had even been seen sharing a pleasantry or two with the staff.

The splendour of the Home seemed to have diminished none in four years, and the comforts the nurses enjoyed, such as individual bedrooms, had been very well considered. In that respect, as the medical superintendent often remarked, Cappelmuir was 'very much superior to most other asylums in the country'.

How fortunate Helen was to reside in such a grand place.

She gave a little shiver as images of the hovels she'd lived in as a child suddenly bombarded her mind's eye. The damp single room of the city slum. The crowded dormitory of the poorhouse. The chilly rooms of the orphanage. The dusty attic rooms above the fancy office buildings her mother used to clean. Helen hadn't imagined then ever living in a palace like Cappelmuir.

She glanced at the wall clock above the chalkboard and closed her Red Book. The meeting would be starting soon. If she wanted to avoid getting caught up in it, she should head to her room before someone came to seek her out.

Just as she got up from her desk, however, the door to the Lecture Room opened.

"Are you coming?" Nurse Haggarty said.

Helen put the Red Book under her arm. "Well, I …"

"Everyone's gathering."

"… suppose …"

"Get a move on then. We don't have long before lights-out."

"… so."

Against her better judgement, Helen followed her colleague out of the Lecture Room, head bowed.

~

Every seat was taken and it looked as if most of the asylum's fifty nurses were in attendance. Helen lurked just inside the

Recreation Room, then shuffled behind the tallest of a group of four.

"Ladies, ladies," Nurse Haggarty said. She picked up the poker and tapped it against the fireplace. "Can I have your attention, please?"

Helen hunched to remain out of her eyeline.

"We're keeping a lookout in case we're discovered, but as you know, our house matron isn't always, shall we say, as *meticulous* as our beloved Matron Campbell. So I don't expect we need concern ourselves until her after-dinner schooner of sherry is dry. Nevertheless, I'll be quick."

Nurse Haggarty put a finger to her lips to quell the giggles. "Shush! Let's not tempt fate. Now, the reason for this meeting is to discuss the recent reduction in the number of nurses and the increase in hours for the rest of us. We're working – officially – eighty-four hours a week. But if you take on board the extra duties we're obliged to do, it's actually ninety-one. In those ninety-one hours, we're expected not only to do everything and more for our patients but also to do everything and more to keep the wards clean and tidy. And all for just a few pounds more than the kitchen and laundry maids get. The hall porter gets twice as much for half the work. Less than half the work. They're gathering signatures at Mount Hope to present to their medical superintendent in protest about the same matters. The question is, should we do the same at Cappelmuir?"

"Mount Hope's different," someone (who Helen didn't break cover to see) piped up. "You wouldn't want to be a nurse there. When I was there, we had to sleep next to the wards. We were never off duty. And the stuff they fed us … Dr Lockhart wouldn't let the farm animals eat it. So I'm happy as I am, thank you very much. Mount Hope's not my problem. Some of you don't know you're born."

Helen muttered in agreement, then glanced around in case anyone had heard her. She didn't want any of this unrest.

She'd worked hard to be at Cappelmuir and all she wanted was to get on with her job.

"That's not the point," Nurse Haggarty said. "Just because it might be better here doesn't mean it's good." There were a few nods. "Nurse Millar says they're talking about refusing to do any more than eighty-four hours at Mount Hope if their medical superintendent doesn't listen to them. See how he gets on trying to keep order on the wards without any nurses."

"And where is Nurse Millar?" It was the same voice as before.

"She's trying to shake off a nasty headache. She was slapped across the face by the new Irish patient." Helen keeked around the group so she could see Nurse Haggarty. "She was trying to leave the observation ward and Nurse Millar asked her to go back to bed. The next thing she knew, she was blind-sided. Her cheek was still throbbing when Matron Campbell gave her a ticking-off for making the woman excitable. Can you believe it? Anyway, she's taking the evening air."

Helen looked at her feet; more likely Nurse Millar was taking a stroll with Mr Kennedy, senior attendant of the men's wards. Never mind a ticking-off – if she was discovered consorting with him by Matron Campbell, dismissal would follow. That's what'd happened to the last nurse who'd been flattered by such an invitation. Mr Kennedy, though, had avoided censure and continued to enforce discipline on his wards as if still an infantryman in the Scots Guards.

"What we're talking about isn't just one person," Nurse Haggarty continued passionately, "it's about all of us! Whether we're willing to put our heads above the parapet and make a stand." A few of the nurses nearest the door started to leave. "We won't be the ones getting a pension after twenty years' service," she called after them. "We'll never make twenty years' service!" The room was emptying. "Think about it. Let's support the Mount Hope nurses to improve things for us all."

Helen wasn't going to think about it and she hoped none of the other nurses would either.

She fell in behind the group of four as they made their collective move, then broke away to return to the Lecture Room. There was still some time to read before the house matron began to scour the building for curfew-breakers.

There was a final, fading, rallying cry from behind: "All for one … and one for all!" If not for her folly, Nurse Haggarty must surely be commended for her sincerity.

Helen sat back at her desk in the Lecture Room and opened the Red Book at a random page. She liked to read gobbets, little by little – it was a good way to learn new things.

There are certain other terms besides 'insanity' in common use to express the same idea. One of the commonest is 'lunacy'. This is a very old word, and is based on the idea that changes in mental state occur in sympathy with the change of the moon (luna). This idea is not now accepted.

She gazed out at the sky but thick cloud was obscuring the planets and constellations.

The French doors opened. Nurse Millar came in, and flushed when she saw Helen.

"Oh! Nurse Elliot. It's you."

"Yes. Good evening."

"Em, good evening. I've just been … em …" Nurse Millar closed the door quietly.

"Taking the night air?"

"Precisely, yes. I had a bit of a headache and—"

"So I believe. I trust the night air has offered you some … relief? Your cheeks certainly look … rosy."

Nurse Millar touched her face then smoothed down her pinafore. "Um, yes."

"It's a pity, however, you didn't hear Nurse Haggarty's call-to-arms, since I believe you were instrumental in encouraging her to take up the cause."

"No, no. I only mentioned what my cousin told me about

Mount Hope and speculated what might happen if we did the same. I wouldn't say I was *instrumental*. No. Well." Nurse Millar sniffed. "Anyway. Yes. I'd better get to my room before the house matron starts her rounds. I expect she'll just be finishing off her sherry. Goodnight, then."

"Goodnight." Helen smirked as Nurse Millar squirmed by. So much for 'all for one and one for all'.

ISABELLA

Isabella looked at her eight of clubs, anticipating that it wouldn't be enough to win the final trick. Although she wasn't an expert in counting cards, she was sure the nine was still in play. If her partner Effie wasn't holding it, the hand would be lost and they'd remain at the same table by the window when the whist drive resumed after the refreshment break.

Mrs Inglis, on her left, cast down the six. Effie put her card on the table face down, slowly revealing it to be the seven of clubs.

Isabella grimaced as she turned over her eight. "Well done, you two. Well played."

"Mrs Huntly-Sykes still has to play," Effie said.

"Yes, but I have the nine, my dear," the League's branch president said, slapping it down triumphantly. "Thank you, ladies. That was a close hand."

"Although we didn't quite manage to beat the experts," Isabella said. She gathered the cards from around the table and palmed them into a neat block ready to be shuffled when the session recommenced.

"It's nothing to do with expertise, Mrs Lockhart – it's

experience. And once you and Mrs Buchanan have been playing together as long as Mrs Inglis and I have, you'll be just as expert as we are, I can assure you."

"Oh, I'm sure there's more to it than that," Isabella said.

"You're very kind. Now, tea awaits." Mrs Huntly-Sykes got up and went with Mrs Inglis to the counter.

Effie giggled.

"What is it?" Isabella said.

"D'you think that'll be us in another thirty years? Doling out advice on whist?"

"No. We'll have moved on to much more important things by then. And you'll soon be too busy to play whist, once you produce all these children you're hoping to have."

"We're certainly trying," Effie said, patting her belly. "And I'm sure it won't be long for you and Angus either."

"Perhaps." Isabella glanced out the window at the double-decker Corporation tram trundling by.

"It's still hard to believe it's hardly any time since we were standing in front of our classes at Park. It seems such a distant memory. Did you ever think," Effie said, glancing around the room, "we'd be sitting in surroundings like these?"

Isabella straightened the green tablecloth, then ran her index finger over its neat white and yellow embroidery. Her time at Park School didn't just seem like a distant memory, it seemed like a different lifetime. Before marriage, she'd been Miss Izzy Muir – daughter of Willie and Anna – who'd done well for herself becoming a teacher. Now she was Mrs Angus Lockhart, who'd done even better for herself by becoming the wife of an eminent doctor. She looked at Effie – Mrs Robert Buchanan – and smiled. "No, I did not. Now let's get something to eat before the game starts again."

As Effie swithered over the Victoria sponge and the iced fruit cake, Isabella perused a selection of silver hat-pins which were on display.

Mrs Russell, a regular volunteer at the Suffrage Centre Tea Room, appeared at her side. "They're rather nice, aren't they? Popular with those ladies who prefer, when the occasion demands it, a more, shall we say, *discreet* display of support."

"Quite so," Isabella said, rolling one of the hat-pins in her palm and admiring its enamel decoration in the green and white of the League.

"And they're also of a length that would be unlikely to project beyond the brim," Mrs Russell said, studying Isabella's purple felt hat. "After all, you wouldn't want to be like that unfortunate girl who was convicted after her pin scratched a man's nose as he walked by."

"Surely not?"

Mrs Russell cackled. "Yes, it's true. It's reported in the newspaper today. She was apparently given the choice of a fine of one and six or twelve hours' arrest. Have you ever heard the like?"

Isabella put the hat-pin back on the shelf. "Where was this?"

"Vienna, would you believe?"

"Oh, I thought you meant here."

"No. Well, not yet, anyway. Though with the way things are going, it might be sooner rather than later. Ha! But tell me, Mrs Lockhart – I see it's not only Vienna in the headlines."

"I beg your pardon?"

"The young Irish woman at Cappelmuir. The one in the river. Has the mystery of her identity been solved?"

"I'm sure you'll appreciate, Mrs Russell, I—"

"I wonder how she ended up here?"

"I'm sure I couldn't say." Isabella hid her frown by inspecting some of the marquetry and painted china on display.

"Maybe she didn't like what's going on in Ireland and thought she might fare better here."

"I really couldn't say. I don't have anything to do with the patients. There are over seven hundred. Three hundred of them are women. I wouldn't know her if I bumped into her in the grounds. And even if I did, I certainly couldn't—"

"Oh, I'm not asking you to break any confidences, Mrs Lockhart."

"Of course not."

Effie was returning to the table with their tea tray.

"Ah, Mrs Buchanan has our refreshments. Please excuse me." Isabella turned away without waiting for a response and sat next to Effie with a tut.

"What?" Effie poured the tea.

"Mrs Russell was asking about the woman at Cappelmuir who was rescued from the river. The one who's been in the papers. She wanted to know if she'd been identified yet."

"And has she?"

"Well, not that I'm—"

Glimpsing a sudden movement, Isabella lurched to the side to avoid the object that came smashing through the window. As she looked up, glass shards hanging on the frame crashed to the ground. She hauled Effie out of the way as splinters blasted in all directions. They both fell to the floor, landing inches from a red brick, the edge of which had crumbled on impact with the glass.

Mrs Huntly-Sykes hurried over and knelt beside them. "Ladies! Are you all right?"

Effie gave a little groan. "Yes, I'm fine."

"As am I." Isabella got to her feet and went into the street.

Two gentlemen in bowler hats were kicking pieces of glass into the gutter, while three ladies looked on, gloved hands to their mouths. The tram was coming back down the line and passengers on both decks were gawping at the scene.

Isabella looked one way along the street, then the other. "Did you see who it was? Did anyone see who did it?"

Effie came outside and took her arm. "Izzy?"

"Well? Did anyone see anything?" she screamed.

"Izzy! Please! Come inside."

"Did anyone see who—?"

"Izzy! Come in! You're covered in blood!"

JESSIE

JESSIE LOOKED along the row of machines to check the foreman was still heading out to the yard, then reached under her apron for the hunk of dry bread. She took a sly bite. She'd missed breakfast as her father had knocked the pan of porridge off the stove. At least it wasn't on purpose this time.

But once Jessie had wiped away the mess, there'd been no time to make toast in the fire. She'd already been locked out of work once this week for being late, and the household couldn't afford to be another sixpence down. Granted, she could've bartered with the gateman to let her in, for he'd only just closed the gates when she'd arrived at the mill, but his price would've been greater than she was willing to pay. Her reputation was worth more than the sixpence foregone.

She took another bite of the bread then nearly dropped it when someone nudged her elbow.

"What?"

Her co-worker shot Jessie a glance then quickly stared back at her loom. When Jessie looked round, the manager was behind her, glowering. She let the bread fall into her lap, wiped the crumbs from her work surface and began to wind some yarn around the bobbin. What was he doing there? She'd never seen him on the floor before.

"Don't you know the rules?" His voice was high and whiny, not at all how she'd imagined it would sound. She fumbled with the thread. "Well?"

The foreman came running back along the row of machines, puffing. "I'm so sorry, sir. What can I do for you? I was just—"

"Whatever you were doing, it wasn't supervising. This girl is eating at her machine. Haven't you made the rules clear to her?"

The foreman glared at Jessie. "Of course, sir, I—"

"What am I paying you for, if not to ensure the rules are followed?"

"Sir, I can only apologise that—"

"Just deal with it. Then I need to see you about an urgent matter." The manager pushed past the foreman and headed to the door to the upstairs.

"Of course. I'll be there directly, sir."

Jessie fidgeted with the yarn and bit the inside of her lip in anticipation of a scolding.

"Gather your belongings and go," the foreman said.

"What?"

"You've demonstrated of late that you cannot, or will not, abide by the rules."

"But I was just—"

"You have one minute, Miss Purdie, before I send for the gateman to escort you off the premises."

"But I didn't—"

"Go!"

Jessie flinched at the foreman's roar. She put the remaining bread in her pocket and scurried out to the yard. How was she going to explain this to her father?

She leaned against the wall and covered her face with her hands.

"You'd better not let the foreman catch you out here."

Jessie looked through her fingers at the gateman. He was stroking his straggly grey beard as he leered at her.

"Haven't you been in enough trouble of late?" He was so close she could smell the stale tobacco on his breath. "Is there anything I can … *help* you with?"

When he put his hand on her arm, she shrugged it off. "Yes, you can. You can let me out of here."

"All right, all right. Keep your hair on."

He rushed ahead of Jessie as she strode towards the gates. While he fumbled with the padlock, she tapped her foot on the gravel. As soon as he raised the shackle, she heaved open the wrought iron gate and squeezed through the gap.

"Don't think you'll get a job at another mill. I'll make sure they know you're trouble!" he shouted after her.

Jessie bolted along Mill Street and turned into the first lane she came to. Anywhere to be out of his sight. She squatted and put her head between her knees, breathing heavily. What was she going to say to her father and brothers? They'd have no truck with her excuses.

Maybe she should go straight to the rubber factory to see if there were any positions there. If she set off now, she'd make it in time for the dinner break. Or perhaps she could find a position as a shop assistant. She'd heard there might be a vacancy soon at the grocer's just down from the factory, since the shop girl was getting married; although, more likely than not, one of her relatives was already in the frame.

Jessie stood up, straightened her skirt and sorted her shawl. There were plenty of shops in town and she would go into every one of them until she secured a position.

Turning out of the lane, she spotted Thomson's Aerated Water cart making a delivery at the alehouse in Bell Street. Perhaps Mr Thomson would know of a vacant position, given he supplied most of the town's shops and hostelries. She approached the horses, nodded at the lad holding the reins and waited until his boss had finished unloading a crate.

"Hello, lass," Mr Thomson said. "You've not been rescuing anyone else from the river, have you?"

Jessie smiled. "No, no. I haven't."

"Just as well. We couldn't be doing that every day, eh? I don't think my heart could stand it." He tapped his chest.

"She was very strong, wasn't she? The woman."

"She was that." He hauled the crate along the pavement.

"Mr Thomson?"

He wiped his hands on his overalls. "Yes?"

"D'you know what's become of her?"

"The last I saw of her was when we dropped her off at the parish council. And if I never see her again, it'll be too soon. I bet she's giving them no end of trouble at Cappelmuir."

"Mr Turner at the Temperance Hall said some people are better off at Cappelmuir because they get three square meals a day, have a nice dry bed to sleep in and don't have to work for a living."

"Well that's not what I hear. I know a lass who's just started with a very nice family in town. She was a laundry maid at Cappelmuir and said they had her working all hours. And that she wasn't allowed out without the express permission of the medical superintendent, no less."

"Really?"

"Yes. Mind you, from what I've seen of the place – which granted isn't much, only the store and the Visitors' Tea Room – it's very pleasant. And I'm not just saying that because they're consumers of Thomson's Ginger Beer and I deliver a few dozen crates to them every week. Actually, I'm going there this afternoon. But it does seem very … yes, pleasant. But you know what they say? One man's palace is another man's prison."

Jessie looked back at the mill, then ahead in the direction of her father's cottage; whether the asylum was a palace or a prison, either would be better than her current arrangement.

"Mr Thomson? Might I hitch a ride with you this afternoon to Cappelmuir?"

KATHERINE

KATHERINE GLANCED at the oak long-case clock that stood outside the Blue Room. Five minutes remained until she was due to report to the medical superintendent's office and there was no point in presenting herself at the Administrative Wing any earlier because she wouldn't be permitted access in advance of the appointed time.

She checked her collar to make sure her necktie hadn't come loose, then centred the buckle of her belt. If these were to be her last moments as assistant medical officer, she wanted at least to look the part.

Even though she'd always carried out her duties at Cappelmuir with the utmost conscientiousness, and although her legal matter pertained to a previously held position, the medical superintendent had the authority to dismiss her if, in his judgement, her conduct had compromised the character of the institution. And such was his passion for the promotion of the asylum, Dr Lockhart might consider the merest suggestion of malpractice, however unwarranted, too much for its reputation to endure.

She went into the Blue Room. Its customary late morning tranquillity prevailed, with every one of the soft couches and easy chairs taken by patients. The more capable ladies were sewing window valances and cushion covers for other parts of the asylum, while those ladies with senile insanity were knitting indeterminate creations, consuming one ball of wool after the other.

Nurse Elliot was sitting on the cushioned bench in the window nook, supervising a group of patients whose chairs she had organised in a semi-circle on the red and blue floor rug. She'd been an excellent addition to the staff complement, serious about her role and one of the new breed encouraged into asylum work by the prospects for self-improvement Cappelmuir offered women of her class.

"I see the head gardener's paid a visit," Katherine said, noticing an impressive cascading ivy on the little teak table at the side of the nook.

"Yes. And he's also been so kind as to bring another rubber plant to replace the one that was damaged," Nurse Elliot said.

The unknown female patient was at the far end of the room, standing next to the new plant, stroking its shiny green leaves.

"Am I to take it that needlework isn't to her taste?" Katherine said.

"She's certainly not been keen to apply herself to the craft."

"Has she said anything that might shed any light on her identity?"

"Nothing."

"Well, Dr Lockhart may be a bit closer."

"Oh?"

"Yes. The police in Ireland have got back to say they're following a few leads and that they're going to send over some clippings from the marriage announcements that mention a Mary. Dr Lockhart hopes to match one up with the scrap of newspaper that arrived with our patient."

Nurse Elliot glanced over at Biddy, who turned her back on

them. "Perhaps she might be usefully employed in the laundry," she suggested. "I think she needs to be active."

Katherine laughed. "Certainly! Pounding clothes may make her less inclined to pound the nurses!"

"Well, quite. Yes. But I have to say, there's been no hint of any such behaviour from her since then. Any excitability she may have had at first seems to have settled."

"Excellent."

"Having said that, it would be no bad thing for her to do some physical work. And ... " Nurse Elliot smiled. "... I'm sure the head laundress wouldn't turn down the offer of another pair of hands."

"Then let's try that."

"Certainly, Dr Forbes."

The clock chimed the hour. "Thank you. Now I must leave you to it. I trust your day continues as present."

The closer Katherine got to the Administrative Wing, the stronger the smell of beeswax on the pitch-pine floor became. She pushed the double doors and the house secretary's voice came from the half-open reception window on the wall to the right.

"Please go in. The medical superintendent's expecting you."

Dr Lockhart, standing behind his roll-top desk, waved her forward. "Good day, Dr Forbes."

"Good day, sir. It's most kind of you to see me, particularly as I know you'll be anxious about Mrs Lockhart. I do hope she's recovering well from what must have been a very traumatic experience."

"Thank you. She's naturally very shocked, but fortunately her wounds aren't severe."

"I'm relieved to hear that. As I'm sure are the gentlemen of the hospital ward."

"Oh?"

"Yes. While taking the air on the verandah, they've become

accustomed to seeing Mrs Lockhart pass by. They tell me they've sorely missed her appearances."

"Well, her cuts are healing and Matron Campbell has kindly released one of her charges to attend to the dressings. So I expect it won't be too long before Mrs Lockhart resumes her activities."

Katherine raised her eyebrows and gave a slow nod. Dr Lockhart wasn't usually one to engage his inferiors in unnecessary pleasantries. "That's excellent news, sir."

He pulled down the tambour top-slide of his desk. It cracked shut.

"However, I'm sure you didn't ask to see me to discuss Mrs Lockhart, Dr Forbes."

This was more like him. "No, sir. I didn't."

"Matron Campbell tells me the Central Laboratory has a research proposition which may be of interest to us." He went over to the window and peered out at the ornamental gardens.

"They do … but … that's not what I wanted to speak to you about."

"Oh?" He took his pipe from the top pocket of his jacket and put it in his mouth.

Katherine hesitated. Perhaps she should wait until things were more certain before briefing Dr Lockhart on her legal matter. But if she did that, and he were to find out about it by another route, that would be unforgivable. She cleared her throat. "Dr Lockhart, it's possible that I'm to be sued for unprofessional conduct."

The medical superintendent spun round on his heels. "Unprofessional conduct?"

"Well, *alleged* unprofessional conduct. It was before my employment here, when I was a locum in general practice. I can assure you that I consider the allegation to be completely unfounded and that I'll robustly dispute it. However, it's my duty to share the matter with you, as I do not under any circumstances want the reputation of Cappelmuir to be besmirched in any manner whatsoever by—"

"What is the nature of the allegation?" He went over to the desk and retrieved a box of matches from one of the pedestal drawers.

"I'm accused of the wrongful granting of a certificate stating that a patient was of unsound mind, thereby causing his admission to Mount Hope."

"I see." Dr Lockhart struck a match and lit his tobacco. "And was the patient subsequently detained at Mount Hope?"

"He was. For some four months. And I can assure you, sir, that my certificate was the result of a carefully weighed and well-considered judgement of the facts of the case. And taken under the fullest sense of my professional duty for the safety of the patient and his family."

"And your judgement was corroborated at the time, I assume?"

"It was. By a colleague also in general practice."

"I see." Dr Lockhart turned back to the window and puffed on his pipe.

"If you wish me to, sir, I'll—"

"Dr Forbes." He blew some smoke into the air. "If I had a guinea for every patient who said they'd been wrongly detained, I'd be a wealthy man indeed. A very wealthy man."

"Yes, but a patient saying he'll sue you is a bit different to him actually contacting a solicitor with the intention of suing you."

"Dr Forbes, that you might be sued is possible. That you will be sued is unlikely. That you'd be sued successfully is highly unlikely." He turned round again and balanced his pipe on top of the desk. "Did you know that some years ago I was also sued?"

"I'd heard something of the like."

"Yes. For ten thousand pounds, if you can believe it. By a fellow who made a similar allegation against me to the one made against you. He even threatened to shoot me! William Noakes was his name. He was a river pilot whose behaviour drove his wife and family from their home. He called on me to provide him with a medical certificate so he could take a month off employment to pursue his suspicions about his wife's infidelity. After examining him, I had no hesitation in providing a certificate stating he was suffering from mental excitement and was unfit for duty. Later that same day he attempted to strangle his wife and expressed homicidal intentions towards several men who he believed she had, at some time or another, looked at in the wrong way. I was called back to see him, and it was clear he was suffering from sub-acute insanity and that, in the course of that excitement, certain delusions had arisen in his mind. Thus I had no hesitation in certifying there and then that he was a person of insane mind and a fit and proper person for treatment in an asylum. Like your fellow." Dr Lockhart stroked his chin. "I presume it's a man?"

"It is."

"Yes. Noakes was detained for three months and as soon as he was released, I received the indictment. The decision of the court was, of course, that the certificate wasn't granted wrongfully, nor without due inquiry and examination. In fact, His Lordship confirmed that Noakes had been insane and had been a proper patient for admission and detention. So you see, Dr Forbes, with the doctors and the judges in such agreement, far from diminishing the reputation of each profession, the lawsuit enhanced it. So if this action is pursued and is heard in a court of law, you must trust the system, for the system surely trusts you."

Dr Lockhart raised the lid of his desk and opened one of the small docket drawers.

"Take this." He handed her a white business card. "If you don't have legal representation yet, this gentleman has my personal recommendation."

Katherine looked at the embossed black writing on the card, not sure what to say. Of all the responses she'd anticipated from Dr Lockhart, professional pride wasn't one of them.

"Now – will there be anything else, Dr Forbes?"

Katherine backed towards the door. "No, sir. Nothing at all."

HELEN

HELEN HELD Biddy's elbow and gently steered her to the first of the long tables set out in the communal dining hall, where Nurse Millar's male patients were already sitting at alternate places. There was a setting of cutlery at each one and a side plate of bread, with two slices for the male patients and one for the females.

Biddy gazed at the high ceiling in the same way most new patients did. After the intimacy of the observation ward, the crowded, cavernous hall could be unsettling.

"We have the weekly dances here, too," Helen explained. "The carpet's rolled up and we move the tables to the side." She pointed to the other end of the hall and the painted drape in front of the raised stage. "The orchestra sits up there and Dr Dorsie and Mr Johnstone play most of the music for the dances. We have cakes and cookies, and on entertainment nights we set the chairs out in rows just like at the theatre. We have cinematographs, theatrical performances and concerts. It's the staff concert soon. Dr Forbes will be playing the piano, Nurse Millar the mandolin and the Reverend Fulton will likely give us one of his recitations. I've even heard that the medical superintendent himself might grace us with a song or two."

She gave Biddy a nudge. "Now, plonk yourself there, opposite Mr Smith.

Biddy stared at the male patients, who, in turn, were eyeing the newcomer. She'd certainly scrubbed up well. Fresh-faced, in a smart blue dress and with her hair in a neat bun, she was a far cry from the banshee who'd first presented at Cappelmuir.

"This is Mr Smith and Mr Allan and Mr Robertson. Mr Smith helps Dr Forbes in her laboratory. And this," Helen said, addressing the men, "is a new lady, who I hope you'll all make welcome."

Mr Allan and Mr Robertson peered at their place settings, while Mr Smith grinned, making his thick, ginger moustache spread across his face.

"Delighted to make your acquaintance, madam. King Robert Smith VI, Lord of All, at your service." He took a handkerchief from his breast pocket and flourished it at Biddy.

"Mr Smith's also well-known for the wonderful gatherings he organises, particularly the gentlemen's At Homes. If you're lucky," Helen said, "you might be asked to take to the floor with him – he's a fine dancer. And if you're *very* lucky he might even write an ode to you, for he's a fine poet too."

Mr Smith pushed his shoulders back and cleared his throat:

"I would ride my grand chariot to dine with Nurse Alliot,

I would sell my fine cheviot to sup with Nurse Ee-lliot,

I would be a fair idiot to fool with Nurse Illiot,

The lovely and delicate, the splendid Nurse Elliot."

Mr Allan gave a loud belch and flapped his hand in front of his mouth. "I do beg your pardon, ladies."

Mr Smith stood up and raised his arms as if giving the benediction at a church service. "I am God and can give you a free pardon."

Biddy banged her fists on the table, then stood up too. "And I am a relative of the Duke of Connaught!"

"Well, Duchess," Mr Smith said, "I shall write to him

tomorrow and petition on your behalf that you be allowed to go immediately from this place."

"Ah, here we are now," Helen said. Thank goodness the kitchen maids were coming with the food. Biddy might be less excitable but she was still unpredictable. "It's Thursday, so it'll be broth and bread, then roast pork and potatoes."

"Broth and bread, then roast pork and potatoes," Biddy repeated in a very passable Scottish accent. A bowl of soup was put in front of her and she leaned over to sniff it.

"It's very tasty, I can assure you," Helen said, annoyed. Anyone who'd tasted the slop of the poorhouse or the stale rations of the orphanage would appreciate what a banquet it was.

"Although not what you'll be accustomed to at the palace, no doubt, Duchess," Mr Smith said. "I'll write to my fellow monarch, King George the Fifth, to advise him of your plight."

"Now, Mr Smith," Helen said. "Don't let your soup get cold. You'll—"

Biddy's chair squealed on the floor as she pushed away from the table. "I am a lady."

She lifted her knife and, brandishing it as a conductor would a baton, began to sing the national anthem.

Helen shifted in her seat but didn't get up. Nurses weren't supposed to interfere unless a patient was a danger to herself or to others. Biddy was singing, not threatening. She would probably put the knife down at the end of the song.

"Thy choicest gifts in store, on him be—"

Mr Kennedy grabbed Biddy's wrist from behind, took the knife from her and spun her round. "Enough!"

"Oh!" Biddy studied Mr Kennedy's face, then smiled.

"Now … sit … down," he said, quietly.

Biddy followed the instruction, picked up her spoon and began to sup her broth.

Helen got up from the table. "Thank you, Mr Kennedy, but there was no need. I was just about to—"

"Use gentleness and patience against a knife, Nurse Elliot?"

Helen stepped away from the patients and lowered her voice. "She was acting. She wouldn't have used it. I could see it in her eyes."

"Yet you didn't see in her eyes that she was about to yield a weapon, and stop her?"

"I—"

"I think, Nurse Elliot, you'd be better served studying your Red Book less and your patients more."

"My patient was—"

"It's as well there are still – although who knows for much longer? – some male attendants in the asylum. As I intend to make clear in my report to the medical superintendent on the matter, your patient is muscular and I doubt any nurse would've had the strength needed to restrain her, had it proved necessary. So while you and your colleagues are colluding to replace us, think on that. Even if you nurses don't find it degrading to be in the men's wards, where indecent men throw off their clothes, and worse, perhaps you'll nonetheless accept that attendants, given their greater strength, still have a role to play."

Helen put her hands on her hips. "And I will also make it clear in my report, Mr Kennedy, that—"

"Extending the nurses' sphere of influence may yet come at a grave cost to this establishment." Mr Kennedy shook his head. "And to society."

Helen glowered at him, then looked back to the table, where all remained peaceful.

"Anyway. Now that matters appear to be under control, I must return to my own duties, Nurse Elliot. I suggest, however, that you carefully count the knives when you leave. And that your patient should perhaps take her meals in the ward dining area until you're more able to anticipate and control her urges."

Mr Kennedy swaggered back to his post at the hall exit.

When Helen took her place again at the table, Mr Allan was regaling Biddy with one of his tales. "I'm on a special diet of eggs, you know? I eat them shell and all. D'you know why?"

Biddy shook her head.

"D'you not know that eggshell is good for your insides?"

"No. What does it do for them?"

Helen leaned in; it was the first time she'd heard Biddy engage in conversation with another patient.

"Well, there are usually hairs in the pudding and eggshell is a grand thing for scraping them off!"

When Biddy started to laugh with Mr Allan, Helen looked over to the doors to check if Mr Kennedy was watching. This should surely show him that her patient wasn't a danger to anyone.

But when she caught his eye, he turned away and set off along the corridor – although not before winking at her.

ISABELLA

Isabella sat at the dressing table in her bedroom waiting for Nurse Elliot to finish scrubbing her hands at the sink. She dabbed the gauze on her cheek, hoping that the nicks underneath had healed sufficiently and wouldn't need further attention.

Nurse Elliot dried her hands with a cloth and approached Isabella. "May I, madam?"

"Please do." Isabella tilted her face and the nurse lifted one side of the gauze, then slowly peeled it back. "How does it look?"

"It all looks very clean now, madam. There's nothing at all on that." Nurse Elliot turned it over to show that it was free of blood and pus.

"That's wonderful. And no small thanks to your excellent care. You must be highly regarded to be recommended by Matron Campbell."

The young woman beamed. "Thank you, madam."

"So tell me – how did you get into nursing?"

"Beg pardon, madam?"

"Nursing. Why did you become a nurse?" Isabella looked in the mirror and thought she saw a hint of panic in the nurse's face. "I became a teacher because I wanted to try and give girls an education, to help them get on." Isabella hoped her openness would encourage Nurse Elliot to speak freely.

"Well, I ..." She cleared her throat and looked down at the gauze again. "My mother was ... well, one day we – my mother and I – we were in a reading room and I saw this book and ..."

"Ah!" Isabella gave a little clap. "The power of books! Read everything you can whenever you can. That's what I used to tell my pupils if they wanted to get on." Though how the mother of a young Miss Elliot might have spared fifteen shillings or so for the annual fee to a subscription library, Isabella couldn't fathom.

"Yes, madam."

"So – this book?"

"Yes. While my mother was ..." She rubbed her chin. "... when I opened it, there was a drawing of a human heart. I flicked through the pages and there were all these other drawings."

"Goodness."

"Yes. My mother told me not to look at them. Said they weren't suitable. But I did anyway. I was only about twelve or so. I didn't really understand what was written but I was fascinated by all the drawings. Just the thought of all that under your skin and inside your body, the bones and the organs and the muscles and nerves."

"Well indeed," Isabella said. "It must have been enthralling."

Nurse Elliot gave an enthusiastic nod. "Then one day a gentleman came in and saw me looking at the book. He told me I could never be a doctor but that nursing would be a very respectable thing for someone like me. And so—"

"Someone like you?" The nurse didn't take up Isabella's invitation to say more about herself. "And you've never looked back."

"No, madam, I haven't." Nurse Elliot flushed and took on a more serious demeanour. It was clear from the studied look on her face that their conversation about her path into nursing was now over. "Now …" She ran her fingertip over Isabella's wound. "… it's important that the healing's complete to avoid the possibility of infection."

"And is it complete?"

Nurse Elliot scrunched the dressing up and placed it in the pouch of her white apron. "I believe it is."

"That's excellent news." Isabella leaned towards the mirror and smiled. There was no lasting damage. Her cheek looked the same as it always did, slightly coloured against her otherwise pale complexion.

"But …"

"But what?"

"Nothing, madam."

Isabella stood up and pushed the stool underneath the dressing table. Nurse Elliot clasped her hands behind her back and stared at her boots.

"Do you have further instructions from Matron Campbell or Dr Lockhart regarding my care?"

"Em … no, madam."

"Good."

"Only that …"

"Only that what?"

Nurse Elliot hesitated, then looked up. "Only that I'm to ensure that you're *completely* healed."

"You just said I was. That my wounds were completely healed. Are they not completely healed?"

"Yes, I would say they are, madam."

"Then we're agreed. Thank you for the care and attention you've provided. I'll be sure to inform Matron Campbell and Dr Lockhart that their faith in you was well-founded."

"Thank you, madam."

She accompanied Nurse Elliot downstairs, where Mrs

Drummond, the housekeeper, was waiting in the hall. "I'll take some tea once you've shown the nurse out, thank you, Mrs Drummond."

"Certainly, Mrs Lockhart."

Isabella went into the drawing room and Tipper trotted over from the fireplace. As soon as she sat on the settee, he jumped up and plodded onto her lap. "Tipper!" He pressed his snout against her nose and licked her face. She rubbed his head with both hands, then settled him by her side. "At least *you* think I'm completely healed."

She picked up the mail from the side table and selected the envelope addressed to her in Effie's neat handwriting.

My dearest Izzy – I'm so relieved to learn that your injuries aren't serious. I've informed the ladies at the Centre, all of whom are enquiring most solicitously about your well-being. They, like I, hope it won't be long until we see you back.

The broken window's been replaced and Mrs Huntly-Sykes, who is missing your presence at the whist table, is in daily contact with the police. She's informed them in no uncertain terms that she expects them to pursue the perpetrators with as much vigour as they have any women who might have undertaken similar acts. She's also started a door rota for the ladies to keep watch for any potential miscreants. Heaven help any poor fellow who catches the eye of Mrs H-S!

I've enclosed a copy of the latest organ to keep you informed of developments since the King's Speech on Monday. The League's resolution to boycott the census has resulted in great activity and the branch has arranged a meeting to discuss what might be done. Mrs H-S hopes our ladies will take up the idea of the boycott very heartily and has already offered to open her house to evaders on the night.

Isabella folded the letter, then flicked through *The Vote*,
scanning for details of the forthcoming meeting in the 'Branch
Notes' section. Now that she no longer needed her wounds
dressed, perhaps she could resume her former activities.

The door opened.

"Just put the tray on the table, please, Mrs Drummond,"
she said without looking up.

"And would madam also like me to pour?"

"Angus! What are you doing here? With that?" He put the
tea tray on the table. "And at this time of day?"

He pushed Tipper off the settee and sat next to Isabella. "I
was passing by the house and I thought, 'How nice would it be
to pay an unexpected visit to my dear wife?' So here I am."

"How flattering. There can't be many things you'd abandon
work for."

"Indeed not." He took her hand and kissed it. "You're the
only one."

Isabella reached for the teapot. "Since there's only one cup,
I take it you're not staying long?"

"No. As you know, I've a very busy diary."

"And so?" She poured herself some tea then sat back,
inviting Angus to speak with a tilt of her head.

"There's something I'd like to put to you."

"And it couldn't wait until this evening? I'm perfectly fine,
Angus. You don't need to check up on me. Nurse Elliot says
that my wounds are completely healed."

He stroked her cheek with the back of his hand. "Yes. And your face is as perfect now as it's always been."

"Ha." She took a sip of tea.

"Well, you see, I heard today of an innovation which I consider might be of value to us. The asylum. I've discovered there's an institution which publishes a quarterly magazine to interest and amuse its patients. I'm told it contains lively notes of events in the social life of the asylum – letters, poems, anecdotes, short articles, interviews, even jokes. The patients are also encouraged to make contributions, whatever their age, sex or condition."

"That sounds very progressive."

"I believe it is. In amusing the patients, it may enable them to forget their sorrows and troubles, or at least pass an hour or so without weariness. Not only that, if the magazine were to be offered to benefactors on a subscription basis, it might even turn over a small profit."

"That sounds very promising."

"It is. However, the house secretary and his staff are far too busy with the serious business of the asylum to produce a magazine."

"Of course."

"So I wondered, my dear, whether, given your previous occupation and your love of the written word, you might perhaps be amenable to drafting some pieces."

"What?" Isabella felt a rush of delight.

"For my consideration as editor-in-chief, of course."

"Of course! Obviously."

"I think you could craft some excellent articles. And be a fine interviewer."

"Perhaps." She blushed at the unexpected compliment. It was the first time Angus had taken such an interest. "Although I fear I'd have to rely on others to provide jokes and anecdotes."

"I wouldn't anticipate there being any shortage of anecdotes, dear."

Isabella ran her hand over her hair. "I could consider it, I suppose …"

"Excellent. A worthwhile diversion might also aid your convalescence."

"My convalescence is over, Angus. My wounds are completely healed."

"The wounds on your face may be healed but you've had a terrible shock and you'll need time to recover your composure before you venture back to your … usual habits. In any case, until the maniac who did it is found, it's not safe for you to be out and about. Had you not been so quick in noticing what was happening, I could've been widowed."

"Don't talk like that, Angus. It wasn't me he was trying to hurt – I just happened to be there."

"Anyway, there's no need for you to go out. There's plenty for you to do here with the new magazine." He kissed her on the cheek and got up. "I must get back to the office now. The Chairman of the Board's visiting. See you later, my dear."

Isabella invited Tipper back up beside her with a pat on the settee. "Did you hear what he said?" She nuzzled the dog. "We're not to leave the house." Tipper licked her cheek where the laceration had been. "We'll see about that, won't we?"

JESSIE

BEHIND THE MAIN BUILDING, unseen from the azalea-lined track that led up from the asylum's decorative iron gates, was the sandstone laundry block. With its grey slate roof and crow-stepped gables, it reminded Jessie of her school.

The office of the head laundress was just inside the front door, at the start of a whitewashed corridor that led to a series of halls and rooms. Miss Wilson pushed a thick leather-bound book to the side of her desk and read to Jessie from a sheet of paper.

"Miss Purdie. You will be engaged as a domestic servant. You will receive your instructions from me, be under my control and direction, and will obey all orders. You will be paid sixteen pounds annually and will receive board, meals and two uniforms. You will obey the rules of the institution and promote its objects. You will be careful of its property, avoid gossiping about its patients or its affairs, and endeavour, by your conduct and demeanour, to sustain its respectability. The medical superintendent has the right to discharge you, without warning, if, in his opinion, you have shown any want of kindness to the patients, or committed any act of intemperance, disobedience to orders, or any transgression of the rules – for all of which the medical superintendent shall be the sole judge. So far as any patients may be entrusted to your care, you will be regarded as a nurse, subject to the rules laid down for them, and may be dismissed or punished for neglect of duty or breach of these rules. If anything improper is done in your presence or to your knowledge, you shall consider yourself bound to report it to the physicians or other superior office-bearers." Miss Wilson looked up. "Do you understand?"

Jessie nodded and attempted a small curtsy.

Miss Wilson dipped the gold nib of her pen in the inkwell then handed it to Jessie. "Sign this agreement, please."

Jessie wrote her name at the bottom of the sheet of paper without reviewing the text. Although she was holding the pen tightly, its mother-of-pearl barrel was so smooth that it almost slipped from her fingers.

Miss Wilson took a pile of clothes from the chair behind her and handed them across the desk. "Here are your uniforms."

Jessie ran her hand over the plain blue cotton dress on top.

"Are they not to your liking?"

"No, not at all. I mean, yes, they're to my liking," Jessie said, admiring the white apron and matching cap underneath. She'd never had a uniform before, or anything other than a sturdy skirt for school and work, a tweed one for Sundays, two blouses, her jumper and her shawl. "They're lovely."

"Make sure you look after them. The tailor doesn't want to waste his time mending your things. He's got enough to be doing."

"Yes, Miss Wilson." Jessie held the uniforms against her chest and breathed in the fresh smell. "I'll take great care of them."

"Very good." Miss Wilson pulled back the starched cuff of her blouse and consulted her rose-gold bracelet watch. "Miss Anderson will show you round the laundry then take you to the dormitory. You'll share her accommodation. You'll take dinner in the servants' tea room and commence work immediately afterwards. Miss Anderson will instruct you in what is required. Do you understand?"

"Yes."

Miss Wilson looked to the open door. "Miss Anderson?"

A plump girl of around Jessie's age stepped into the office, tucking some strands of ginger hair back under her cap. "Yes, Miss Wilson?" She wiped away some sweat from her ruddy cheeks with the back of her hand.

"Show Miss Purdie the laundry rooms and then the dormitory. She'll share your accommodation. After dinner, explain to her her tasks."

"Yes, Miss Wilson."

"That is all."

"Thank you, Miss Wilson." Jessie backed out of the office, then trotted to catch up with her guide, who'd already set off along the corridor.

Miss Anderson stopped at the first room on the left, where four uniformed girls sorted bedding and items of clothing into large baskets.

"This is the receiving room. Everything comes here. If it doesn't come here, it doesn't get washed. There's an inventory listing everything. If it's not on the list, it doesn't get washed. Soiled things are washed separately and everything's sorted into baskets, labelled and taken to the wash house."

Miss Anderson set off again. Jessie could feel the heat coming from the next room before she reached its doorway.

"This is the wash room. The items are boiled in those," Miss Anderson said, pointing to a row of large coppers, "and then you thump down on them with the dollies."

Jessie waved away some steam as she watched the girls pound the linen in the tubs. It wasn't going to be cold in the wash house, that was for sure.

"Then they're taken for drying in there," Miss Anderson said, continuing past the next room, giving Jessie only the briefest glimpse of the large rails suspended from the ceiling and the clothes horses on the floor. "And then they go in here." She stopped at a bright room with a glass-panelled roof. There were two long tables, each lined with girls starching and ironing. "Then they all go to the dispatch room at the end of the corridor, where the list's checked again. And that's all there is to it. Just make sure there's nothing missing. Heaven help you if you have to report something missing to Miss Wilson."

Jessie glanced at Miss Anderson to see whether or not she was smiling. She was not.

"Don't worry. It won't take long to get the hang of it. Once you've done everything a few times, you'll be an expert. Come on. I'll take you over to the dormitory. The room's not up to much. Just a couple of beds with—"

"It's just the two of us in the room?"

"Yes. It's just two beds with a nightstand between them. And there's a chest with a couple of drawers for each of us."

"Sounds fine."

"Depends what you've been used to, I suppose."

"How long have you worked here, Miss Anderson?"

"Call me Mary."

"And I'm Jessie. So how long have you worked here?"

"Just a few months."

"Oh, I thought it must be much longer. You seem to know everything."

"It doesn't take long. You'll see. I was a domestic with a lovely family before. The gentleman was a bank manager. They had a big house with a garden, and three nice children. I had my own room. They were very generous with time off at weekends."

"So why did you come here?"

Mary's cheeks turned a deeper red. "Let's just say that the master of the house wasn't always the gentleman he made out to be."

They went outside to the courtyard and waited while a

gleaming black brougham passed by. The lad leading the black horse tipped his cap at Mary.

"That's Duncan. He helps with the horses. He'll be taking the carriage round for the medical superintendent. Some of the nurses and attendants say Dr Lockhart's all right but it doesn't make any difference to us – the linen will still need washing whether he is or he isn't. And what about you?" Mary said as they continued through the yard. "Where were you before?"

"North Mill."

"What have you come here for? Weren't the wages better there?"

Jessie looked away. Now it was her turn to flush.

Mary put her hand on Jessie's arm. "It's all right. None of us ends up here without good reason."

"Well … my father and brothers were …"

"Say no more. A few of the girls have been in the same boat. I don't suppose he'll be too happy you've come here."

Jessie bit the inside of her cheek. When he found out, he surely wouldn't.

KATHERINE

KATHERINE PAUSED outside the white-fronted building and gazed up at the neighbouring tenement block. The last time she'd visited this part of the city was during her midwifery training in the summer break following her fourth-year study of obstetrics and gynaecology.

She'd been called to a fetid basement a few streets away to deliver a baby to a mother of six. They all stood round the bed at the birth, while her husband, worried by his wife's suffering, took himself off to the public house.

Despite the surroundings, the child was born seemingly healthy and well-nourished. After she'd cleaned his eyes, Katherine wrapped him in a blanket she'd brought to offer some protection from the jumping fleas and slithering lice on the mattress.

That last excursion had certainly been a world away from her present one – tea at Miss Cranston's with Dr Cowan.

She peered through the leaded windows to the interior of the tea room, then pushed the entrance door.

A waitress, all in white, with a smooth pompadour and wearing a necklace of large pearls, led her past a long screen topped by glass panels. As Katherine approached the table in the Front Salon, Dr Cowan stood up and pulled out one of the dark oak ladder-back chairs. He was immaculate in a grey suit, his perfectly knotted light-grey silk necktie precisely positioned under his wing collar.

"Dr Forbes. Wonderful to see you again. I trust this room meets with your approval?"

"Yes, it's most elegant." Katherine settled herself on the rush seat and admired the pastel pink and green panels of the stained-glass windows.

"Although I hear it doesn't compare to the Ladies' Salon upstairs, which I believe is most lavish. Have you had the pleasure of visiting it?"

"No. This is my first time here."

"Well you really must come back and visit the *Salon de Luxe*, even if it will cost you an extra penny."

"Oh, I don't think Dr Lockhart would consider attendance at a tea room – even one such as this – of sufficient import to grant additional leave."

The waitress returned and placed a two-tier plate stand, crammed with a selection of cakes and scones, in the middle of the table. "I'll be back in a jiffy with your pot of coffee."

"I took the liberty," Dr Cowan said, "knowing how much you enjoyed it in Amsterdam and Meerenburg, of ordering coffee."

"Thank you." Katherine turned her blue willow-patterned cup in its saucer. It couldn't be more different to the rough, brown pottery mugs of the dim coffee shops the group had frequented in Holland. She expected, too, that the coffee at Miss Cranston's would be more delicate than the bitter Dutch brew she'd quickly become partial to. "I did take quite a liking to it."

"You were certainly the bravest in trying out the local fare."

"I was just making the most of the experience."

Nobody had said as much, but Katherine knew she'd only been invited to join the visiting delegation of the Scottish branch of the Medico-Psychological Association to ensure that Dr Alice Strachan wouldn't be the only woman in the party. And there was no doubt Dr Lockhart had put her name forward more to promote the name of Cappelmuir than the name of Dr Katherine Forbes. But an opportunity was an opportunity irrespective of its origins, and, if nothing else, the trip had introduced her to five experienced colleagues who had not only been generous in sharing their expertise but also most open to her contributing to lively supper-time discussions on the treatment of the insane.

"It really is good to see you again," Dr Cowan said, clasping his hands together. "You look …" He smoothed down his neat brown moustache with his thumb and index finger. "… very well. Very well indeed."

"Thank you. As do you." Katherine glanced at the black-handled cutlery on the table. There was a tiny square motif, similar to the one on the floor rug, on the blade of the silver-plated side knife. Below the motif was engraved 'Miss Cranston's'. "My goodness, they've thought of everything. How charming." She tilted the knife for Dr Cowan to see.

"Indeed."

The waitress came with the coffee and Dr Cowan offered Katherine a cake from the stand, before manoeuvring a scone onto his own plate with the tongs.

"I've been very much looking forward to our meeting today, Dr Forbes."

"I'm looking forward to seeing everyone too. Unfortunately, though, I can't stay as long as I'd like, as I've another appointment that I simply can't miss."

Dr Cowan's moustache twitched. "Oh," he said flatly.

"Yes. It's regarding a legal matter, I'm afraid. So if you'd like to discuss your piece on pathological protocols, it might be best to do it now."

"Of course, yes." He reached into the inside pocket of his jacket and took out a sheet of paper. "It's disappointing, though, that I ... that *we* ... the group won't have the pleasure of your company for the entire afternoon. But I trust your legal matter will be resolved soon. And that when we meet again to review the final article there might be time for some lighter conversation."

"I hope so too. But I have to confess, the prospect of it not being resolved without recourse to the courts is of great concern."

Dr Cowan leaned forward. "It must be, yes."

"I wish now I'd paid more attention to my lectures in medical jurisprudence. One thing I do remember, though, is that we were told that even a doctor who knows his subject well can be made to look a fool in the witness box. I think I'd rather be the chloroform clerk telling the surgeon his patient's breathing has stopped than be in the dock as the accused."

"I'm truly sorry. If there's anything I can do to assist, I'll gladly do so."

"Thank you. But I've been referred to a solicitor. I must trust he'll resolve things without the need for an appearance before the judge."

"Quite so." Dr Cowan lifted the sheet of paper from the table. "Perhaps, though, Dr Forbes, I shouldn't burden you with my piece at the moment."

"No, please do. That's the reason I came, after all."

"Of course, of course."

He removed his pince-nez from the breast pocket of his jacket, secured the loop around his ear and positioned the clip on the bridge of his nose. He'd told her in Holland that it was crooked due to a childhood accident with a cricket ball. If anything, the imperfection added to his appeal.

He began to read. "*Observations on the Pathological Protocols followed in the Dutch Asylums for the treatment of the insane. The pathological protocols ...*" He put the paper down on the table and unhooked his glasses. "Dr Forbes – since you won't be spending the whole afternoon with us, there's something I must ask while we have this time alone. As you know from my letters, I immensely valued the time we shared on the inspection tour."

"Dr Cowan, I—"

"Please," he said, holding up his palm. "I know we've not known each other long and that the circumstances of our meeting were professional. It would, however, be a great honour if you'd consider accompanying my sister and me to the theatre in the coming weeks. As I've previously mentioned, my sister is also a doctor and I'm sure you'd have much in common. She might even be able to offer you some advice on broadening your medical experience."

"I'd certainly be most interested to engage with someone as accomplished as your sister." Katherine shifted in her seat. "She, on the other hand, might be less keen to engage with me. Given my legal matter."

"All the more reason to join us, Dr Forbes. As a colleague, she may be able to offer some assistance."

"You're very kind."

"What are friends for?"

He raised his cup in a toast and Katherine took a sip of her coffee. Her expectation was correct – it was insipid compared to the Dutch concoction.

She watched Dr Cowan take a piece of Madeira cake from the rack and put it on his plate. He was a generous man, a handsome man, a gentle man. A man who, if she were to lose her career, she might consider marrying.

"Thank you, Dr Cowan. I accept your invitation. As a colleague. I would very much like to meet your sister. Very much indeed."

HELEN

THE LADIES WENT in pairs along the tree-lined walkway that had been constructed by some of the male patients the previous autumn. South-facing and offering splendid views of the surrounding countryside, it was a favourite excursion for those patients for whom exercise was a possibility.

Helen, at the rear of her group, kept a close eye on Nellie Shaw and Biddy, who for different reasons were lagging behind the others. Nellie was generally apt to dawdle, not least on account of her age; while Biddy was taking time to survey every part of the asylum estate. Helen speculated she was plotting an escape.

In that, Biddy was unusual. For, despite the ward doors remaining unlocked during the day and some of the more trusted patients being allowed free access to the grounds unaccompanied, escape attempts were few.

The last one to give it a go was Margaret Morton, who, after some twenty months at Cappelmuir suffering from melancholia, slipped away from a walking party. She was discovered two hours later hiding in an adjacent cornfield, her intention being to wait until darkness to flee.

On returning to the ward, she cried ceaselessly for two

days. But within two weeks she was bright, cheerful and rational, and so markedly improved that after a further week she was discharged.

Helen glanced over to the cornfield, which lay fallow. If Biddy were to make a run for it, she wouldn't find cover there. Nor was she likely to reach the estate's boundary without being apprehended. Any escape attempt was almost certainly doomed. Indeed the most successful escapee of recent times had been a sow that had fled from the newly constructed piggery, getting three miles distant before being recovered.

Biddy and Nellie were falling even further behind. "Come on, you two," Helen said. "I know you're enjoying the fresh air but you need to keep up."

Biddy gazed around the expansive grounds. "Where's the lake?"

"The lake?" Helen laughed. "There's no lake here."

"No lake?" Biddy tutted. "It's no Bagshot Park. And where are the horses? I'd like to go riding in the grounds."

"Oh, you would, would you?"

Biddy folded her arms and pouted. "I'm a lady, you know?"

"Yes, I know." *And I'm the Queen of Sheba*, Helen thought as she took out her daily returns book. She noted her patient's remarks, then guided Nellie from the lawn and back onto the walkway. "And you too. Come on, Biddy."

Four male patients, supervised by Mr Kennedy, were preparing the ground by the old drying green, where Dr Lockhart's latest initiative, a 120-gallon water tank for fire-extinguishing purposes, was soon to be installed. The pipes supplying the tank had already been plumbed in, as had those that would deliver water to the recently purchased steam pump, which was parked at the boiler house pending completion of the asylum's own fire station.

'There will be no repeat of Colney Hatch here.' That's what Dr Lockhart told those gathered in the recreation hall the day he secured funding from the Board for the new equipment. 'Once again, Cappelmuir will lead the way.'

Helen had even heard that the asylum's electrician had invented a system of alarms, where turning a switch in any building would set off a loud bell and register the position of a fire. She shuddered at the thought of it. Over fifty had died at Colney Hatch, all women. But she could sleep safely in her bed knowing that Dr Lockhart was keeping everyone safe – staff and patients alike. How Nurse Haggarty could complain they weren't well looked after at Cappelmuir, Helen didn't know.

Biddy suddenly screamed and leapt back from the grass verge. Helen hurried over to her. "What on earth's wrong?"

"It's a bird," she said, recoiling. "There's a dead bird on the ground."

Helen stared at the pigeon lying on the soil. It cocked its head and looked at her with a bright orange eye. "I don't think it's dead. It's maybe just—"

"D'you want me to kill it, Nurse Elliot?" One of Mr Kennedy's patients was standing behind her, holding a spade in the air.

She put her arm out to stop him bringing it down on the bird. "No, Roddy! No. But thank you all the same."

He dropped the spade by his side. "I can easily kill it for you, Nurse Elliot. It'd be no bother."

"Yes, I know, Roddy, but—"

"I got a shilling yesterday for killing two rats at the store. I'm going to buy a new dickie to wear to next week's dance with it." He raised his chin – even in work attire, he was dapper, colourful neckties being a favourite accoutrement. "I'm an expert, Nurse Elliot. That's why Dr Lockhart made me 'the rat catcher'. He told me it would 'put my natural proclivities to a useful purpose with no detriment to my character and no small gain to my pocket'."

Helen tried not to smile at the boy's expert mimicry of the medical superintendent. "And he was undoubtedly correct."

Roddy The Rat Catcher might only be four-feet-eight tall and weigh six-stone-ten, but his wholesale destruction of farmyard fowl, cats, dogs and small livestock lay behind his expulsion, at age fifteen, from the orphanage, and his admission a few days later to Cappelmuir, where his mother was already a patient.

With his father boarded out as a lunatic and his two sisters deemed idiots, it was unlikely that Roderick McMillan would be released any time soon. But he was much improved in habit and conduct since his admission. He was even becoming quite sensible and manly. So it was possible that he might, in due course, leave recovered. Not everyone who spent time in an orphanage need be ruined for life. Helen was testament to that.

"Thank you, Roddy, for your kind offer of assistance. But perhaps we should allow some time for the bird to recover. And if after a suitable period it seems that there's no hope, then we'll call on you to do the kind thing."

"Listen to what Nurse Elliot's telling you, Mr McMillan. Her advice is wise."

Helen turned to Mr Kennedy, who was standing close behind her. "You agree with my proposal then?"

He regarded her from top to toe. "Most heartily. Now, Mr McMillan – while I'm sure Nurse Elliot and her ladies are most grateful to you, you should return to work. I fear the others will toil without your strength and enthusiasm."

"Yes, Mr Kennedy, sir." Roddy took his cap off, bowed to Helen, then jogged away.

Mr Kennedy squatted by the verge and gently cupped the pigeon in his hands. "It may simply be exhausted." He stood up slowly, cradling the bird. "Or it may have a fatal injury to a wing or leg." He stroked the top of the pigeon's head. "Perhaps Mr Smith could find a box for it to rest in and put it with the guinea pigs in the laboratory until the likely outcome becomes clear. I'm sure Dr Forbes wouldn't object. If there's still a chance, then we must see what can be done for it." He beckoned Mr Smith and gave him instructions for the bird's care.

"Thank you, Mr Kennedy. The ladies and I are most grateful to you," Helen said.

"My pleasure, Nurse Elliot. I assume …" He glanced at Biddy. "… that your recent charge has begun to settle, given she's trusted to participate in the walking party?"

"Indeed. She's doing well and is to start work in the laundry."

"Good. She seems to me to be someone who'd benefit greatly from directing her energy into physical activity."

Helen raised an eyebrow, then waved at Biddy and Nellie to continue along the path. "Well, thank you again, Mr Kennedy. We must get on."

"Before you do, Nurse Elliot – I thought you'd like to know that I'm about to submit my report on the recent incident in the dining hall. Perhaps—"

"I've already passed mine to the medical superintendent," Helen said sharply.

"Before I do, I thought we might meet to discuss it to … ensure my interpretation of events is consistent with your own." He looked up at the sky. "It's to be dry this evening. Perhaps we could …" He smiled at her. "… take the air."

Helen folded her arms. Talk about sleekit. She wouldn't 'take the air' with him if he was the last man alive. If he thought she was another Nurse Millar, he had another think coming.

"I've no doubt, Mr Kennedy, that if you tell the truth, your report will say exactly the same as mine."

She turned on her heels and marched after Biddy and Nellie.

"I think he's got a notion for you, Nurse Elliot," Biddy said when Helen caught them up.

"Don't be ridiculous."

"But just remember poor Dublin Mary. Don't be like her.

She got in tow with a handsome man who fooled everyone too and look what happened to her."

Helen got out her notebook again in case Biddy was about to reveal something.

"Why? What happened to—"

Biddy burst into song.

"Mistress Mary, quite contrary,

How does your garden grow?

With silver bells, and cockle shells,

Sing cuckolds all in a row."

Mr Smith began clapping. "Oh, brava, Duchess! Encore! Encore!"

Biddy raised her hands in thanks to an imaginary audience and bowed deeply.

"Are you Mary?" Helen asked. "Dublin Mary?"

Her patient crossed her arms and tilted her head coquettishly.

Helen opened her notebook. "Well?"

"Ah now. Wouldn't you like to ..." Biddy turned her head. "Would you look at that now ..." Then she set off towards nothing in particular.

"Come back!" Helen shouted after her charge. But she was already skipping ahead, waving her arms in the air and laughing at the top of her voice.

ISABELLA

ANGUS HAD SUGGESTED MR GILLIES, the gatekeeper, would be the ideal choice as the first 'Cappelmuir Character' to be profiled in the magazine. Discreet and loyal, he had served the asylum for almost thirty years.

As Isabella approached his wooden sentry box just inside the gates, she cleared her throat to alert him to her presence. There was a shuffle and a thud before he appeared in the gloomy doorway.

"Mr Gillies, good day to you."

"Mrs Lockhart!" He quickly put his cap on and stepped outside. "I didn't know you were leaving, madam. Is the carriage coming?" He peered up the long driveway, then started towards the gates. "I'll open up."

"No, it's quite all right, Mr Gillies. I'm not in need of your gatekeeping services at the moment. However, there is something I'd like to speak to you about."

His face coloured. "Speak to *me* about, madam?"

"Yes. But it's nothing of concern. Quite the contrary. You see, Dr Lockhart is considering publishing a magazine for the asylum, which he hopes will—"

"A magazine?"

"Yes ... to provide entertainment and amusement to both the patients and the staff."

"A magazine for the asylum?" When Mr Gillies pouted, his nose gave a little twitch.

"Yes. Isn't it a wonderful idea?"

It had certainly become a more engrossing project than Isabella had anticipated. Learning about asylum life was enjoyable. And, once staff and patients overcame their initial reticence about speaking to the medical superintendent's wife, they were most willing to suggest items for inclusion. So much so that already there was material on the weekly dance, the forthcoming staff concert, the visit of the travelling representative of the London Bioscope Company, Dr Forbes's study visit to Holland, celebrations for the King's coronation, and the recent inspection by His Majesty's representative of the General Board of Commissioners in Lunacy for Scotland. As well as that, there might be forthcoming a pastoral contribution from the Reverend Fulton to lift the spirits and a 'Queries' section where patients could seek the opinions of others on everyday problems.

"And Dr Lockhart's keen to include profiles of some of his most able and trusted staff," she said.

"Oh?" Mr Gillies shifted on the spot and wiped his lapel.

"Yes. And you were the first he mentioned."

A broad smile spread across the gatekeeper's face. "Really?"

"Yes."

"Well, I don't know what to say, Mrs Lockhart."

"My husband tells me that over a great many years your conduct has been exemplary and that you're a fine example to every member of staff."

"Well, I ... thank you, madam. It's very kind of Dr Lockhart to say so. Very kind indeed."

"So if you'd consider sharing some matters regarding your employment, I'd very much like to hear them."

Mr Gillies stroked his chin. "And these matters would appear in this magazine?"

"If Dr Lockhart decides to proceed with the notion, yes."

"And the magazine could be read by everyone in the asylum?"

"Yes. And by those outwith. Dr Lockhart's considering making it available on subscription."

"Well … my word," he mused.

"So would you be willing to offer some insights into your work? Dr Lockhart and I would be most grateful."

Mr Gillies looked over to the front window of the gatehouse cottage, where his wife was watching from behind the net curtain. "Most certainly, Mrs Lockhart. If it's for the entertainment and amusement of the patients."

"Thank you, Mr Gillies."

"Thank *you*, madam."

"Excellent." Isabella clapped. "We have our first Cappelmuir Character."

The gatekeeper put his hands behind his back and smiled. "And what's it to be called, this magazine?"

"It hasn't been decided yet. But I think *The Passing Hour* might be appropriate."

"Well, if it helps the patients pass the time, that would be a very worthwhile thing, madam."

There was a clang behind the sentry box, and Mr Gillies looked over to the asylum entrance. A man in muddy brown boots, trousers tucked into his socks, was shaking the gates.

Mr Gillies rushed over. "Oi! What do you think you're doing?"

"I want to see my daughter!" the man bellowed. "Let me in."

"Visiting day's Wednesday. Visitors aren't admitted at any other time unless they have special permission." Mr Gillies looked the man up and down. "Do you have special permission?"

The man let go of the bars. "No." He straightened his cap. "How do I get special permission?"

"That can only be issued by an office-bearer of the institution, medical superintendent or one of the matrons."

"Then let me see one of them."

Mr Gillies puffed his chest out. "You can't see them because they're in the asylum building."

"How can I get special permission from them if I can't get in to see them?"

"That is, indeed, a conundrum."

The man kicked the ground, then shook the gates again. A bottle fell out of his jacket pocket, spilling what Isabella presumed was alcohol onto the road. "Is my daughter here?"

"You don't know if she's here?" Mr Gillies said.

"She needs to come home!"

"And who might your daughter be? Is she a patient or—?"

"Jessie Purdie!" he snarled.

Isabella cocked her head – there'd been a pupil of that name in her class at Park School. A bright girl, with lovely fair hair and blue eyes, who'd had the potential to go up to the high school. The grubby, uncouth lout haranguing Mr Gillies surely couldn't be that girl's father.

"Tell me if she's here!" he shouted.

Mr Gillies stepped forward so that his nose almost touched the gate. Then he thrust his hand through a gap in the bars and grabbed the man by his stained neckerchief.

"I will tell you nothing, sir, while your conduct is so unseemly. Now, I suggest you go back to where you came from. And if you intend to return here, only do so when you're sober. Otherwise, I'll be forced to take certain actions which, I can assure you, won't be to your benefit. Do you understand?" When Mr Purdie nodded, Mr Gillies let him go. "Now – on your way."

Mr Purdie stepped back from the gate, picked the bottle up

and took a swig. Then he coughed, bent over and spat on the ground.

"Mrs Lockhart, I must apologise," Mr Gillies said, returning to Isabella. "You shouldn't have to witness such behaviour."

"Very ably handled, Mr Gillies. I can see why Dr Lockhart thinks so highly of you."

"Thank you, madam."

Mr Purdie slunk away along the perimeter railings in the direction of town.

"Tell me," Isabella said. "Is there someone of his daughter's name at Cappelmuir?"

"There is, madam." Mr Gillies went into his sentry box and brought out the passbook which contained the names of every person who'd entered or left the grounds in recent times – or, quite possibly, in the past thirty years, judging from its thickness. He ran his finger down a page. "Yes, here she is. Jessie Purdie. She came seeking employment and is now a domestic servant in the laundry under Miss Wilson."

"Is she a girl of around fifteen? Fair hair and blue eyes?"

"She is indeed, madam."

Isabella looked up to the asylum.

"But with a ruffian of a father like that, Mrs Lockhart, I doubt she'd make a good subject for one of your profiles."

JESSIE

IT WAS SO quiet Jessie couldn't sleep. So used was she to the snoring and moaning of her father and brothers that the silence of the dormitory room was unsettling. And so attuned had she been to the individual sounds within the cacophony, that when her mother died, the absence of her light breathing was so discordant that Jessie began to inhale noisily so she couldn't hear its omission.

Mary Anderson, lying on her back in the other bed, wasn't much of a snorer, only occasionally sighing when she changed position, and sometimes giving a short yelp if she inadvertently pulled on her long hair as she did so.

Jessie sat up, clasped her hands behind her head and leaned back. The full moon was shining through a slit in the curtains, casting the room in a silvery light. She looked across to the chest of drawers, imagining her uniform neatly folded in the bottom drawer and the rest of her clothes bundled in the one above.

The top two drawers were Mary's and, as well as clothes, they housed her copies of *Jane Eyre* and *The Channings*, since the only book allowed to be displayed was the Bible. A copy of that lay on the nightstand between the two beds. Mary said

Jessie could read her books if she wanted, but as of yet all Jessie wanted was to sleep.

Working in the laundry was hot and physical but she loved that each day she transformed dirty, smelly rags into clean, fragrant garments, banishing muck, stains and odours in a way she hadn't known possible. Even when her mother had spent all day cleaning the floors, airing the rooms, doing the washing and wiping the surfaces, their cottage had never been – never would be – as fresh as any of the rooms at Cappelmuir. The cottage seemed to have a permanent layer of grime that could never be removed, no matter how much her mother, and then Jessie, toiled.

What sort of state would the place be in now? Her father and brothers would be wallowing in their own filth. *Your mother would be turning in her grave.* She probably would – although not just because of the men, but also because of Jessie, who'd abandoned them.

The sound of hooves in the lane made Jessie turn her head towards the window.

"It's Duncan walking the horses," Mary said.

"Oh … did I wake you?"

"You and them both. It's all right. I need to relieve myself anyway." Mary rolled out of bed then reached underneath for the white tin chamber pot. It was the third time that night she'd done so.

"You all right?"

"Fine."

Jessie kneeled on her pillow and looked outside. Although their clip-clopping was resonating along the lanes of Cappelmuir, she couldn't see the horses. "What's he doing walking them at this time of night?"

"They're not very well. The veterinary surgeon's been coming a lot. One of them's not been able to pull the carriage for a few weeks now. Sometimes when it's bad, Duncan sleeps in the stables to comfort them."

"He must be very fond of them to do that."

"He is." Mary pushed the chamber pot back under the bed and sorted her nightdress. "If it's not about horses, he doesn't want to know. But he's nice enough. He comes into town with us sometimes on our days off or when we go for a walk in the woods. He doesn't say much, though."

Jessie got under the covers again. "How did he end up here?"

"Don't know. He's never said and I've never asked." Mary returned to bed and pulled the sheets up to her neck. "That's me. See you in the morning."

Jessie lay down, picturing the horses pulling the medical superintendent's shiny carriage and wondering how its interior might look. For a man of Dr Lockhart's standing, there would surely be leather and satin. Whatever the upholstery, it would certainly be a lot fancier than Thomson's Aerated Water cart. Still, even with its bare wood and splinters, it had carried Jessie to Cappelmuir just the same.

She closed her eyes and thought of the poor woman she and Mr Thomson had rescued from the river. She'd been admitted to the asylum. If she was still here, she'd be sleeping in one of the wards nearby. It was said she was Irish but Jessie hadn't heard her speak. On the journey from Bayne's Bridge to the parish council she'd only whimpered. But no words had been needed; Jessie could tell from her eyes she was grateful for being saved.

She turned over on her side and exhaled slowly. What would make someone wade into the river like that? According to the newspaper, the woman was well-educated. And she'd been well-dressed, so presumably she came from a nice home.

What if Jessie hadn't spotted her? Or if Mr Thomson hadn't been passing by? Jessie wouldn't have been able to get her out of the water on her own. Likely the woman wouldn't have ended up at the asylum but in a box in the ground. It didn't bear thinking about.

What type of madness would make someone put herself in danger like that?

Was it even madness? Jessie had sensed gratitude. And fear. But madness?

Still – the woman had been admitted to Cappelmuir, so she must be mad.

And what did Jessie know? She was just a laundry maid who got a fair day's pay for a fair day's work. Who had a roof over her head and a nice room to sleep in.

She gave a little snort and snuggled in bed. She was safe and the woman was safe.

That's what mattered.

KATHERINE

KATHERINE WENT into the laboratory's research room and inhaled the musty smell of straw, sawdust and small animals.

"How's our most recent patient, Mr Smith?"

"She's grand, Dr Forbes." Mr Smith returned the cooing pigeon to the cage he'd crafted from a wooden crate and pulled the chicken wire back over the top. "Just grand." He smiled as he watched the bird settle. "She'll be ready to go home tomorrow. I don't mind saying, I've become quite attached to her."

"What do you mean 'go home'?"

Katherine went to her workbench and touched the bottle of ox blood the butcher had delivered to check if it was still warm.

"Well, once it had regained some energy, I examined it and found an address under its wing. When I mentioned it to Matron Campbell, she sent word to the owner that it was here."

"Oh, I see. It's a homing pigeon."

"Yes. Seems the owner sent twelve birds out but only ten returned due to high winds. Matron's arranging to have this one forwarded to him."

"'Forwarded' to him? Can't it … *fly* home?"

Mr Smith shrugged earnestly. "It's maybe still in shock."

"I suppose that's possible. Anyway … all's well that ends well."

"I'd say so, Dr Forbes."

Katherine stifled a grin. If only human patients could be as easily treated and dispatched as the pigeon. Heavens, they'd even managed to trace its family, which was more than could be said for some of Katherine's patients. Perhaps people should be made to wear inscriptions with their names and addresses on them – it would make life much easier for the physicians of Cappelmuir.

She lifted a specimen jar containing minced guinea pig liver from the shelf above the bench. Once it was strained, it would be ready for use as an antigen. She gave the jar a shake.

"And that's not all." Mr Smith opened the flap of one of the guinea pig runs. "This one's given birth again. That's her second litter. There's five of them. I'm going to move the first litter to another run so they don't mate with the new ones. You've got to be careful of inbreeding, Dr Forbes. I don't want you to have any abnormal ones for your research."

"Indeed not," Katherine agreed, although it was unlikely there was any scientific requirement for such precautions given she needed only the animals' blood for her serum.

Mr Smith gently removed the guinea pigs from one run and placed them in another, stroking each animal as he set it down. "I've been thinking, Dr Forbes …" He closed the latch on the run. "… since we've a surplus of animals, maybe we could make some money by supplying them to other laboratories."

"What do you mean?"

"Well, I could breed them and then we could ship them to other places for, say, a guinea a crate. I'd arrange all the transactions and organise dispatch. And I'd maintain the accounts, of course. You wouldn't have to do anything. And

I'd still help in the laboratory. I wouldn't let any of my other duties fall by the wayside."

"I'm sure you wouldn't, Mr Smith."

"I could do it, Dr Forbes," he said, going from foot to foot.

"I've no doubt you could."

"And I think it would very much please Dr Lockhart if it were to prove a success."

"That's no doubt also true."

"Shall I put a proposal forward with all the details?" He tugged his waistcoat, then straightened the handkerchief in the breast pocket of his jacket.

"Well, I suppose there's no harm in putting forward a proposal. After all—"

"Thank you, Dr Forbes. I'll do it immediately." Mr Smith clicked his heels, saluted and dashed out of the research room.

How different he was to the man admitted over a year ago with sub-acute mania. That man was hardly able to walk due to scratches on his feet sustained from jumping through the window of his lodging house. Weak, underweight, with trembling muscles and a ruddy face, he looked much older than his thirty-four years. Restless, excitable and unable to take care of himself, he was suffering from religious mania and delusions, claiming to be in communication with the spirit world. But now, here he was, muscular, with clear skin and sparkling blue eyes, an excellent worker and a patient to be trusted. It was time she discussed his discharge with Dr Lockhart.

Katherine put the specimen jar back on the shelf then felt the bottle of ox blood again – it was cooling nicely.

There was a knock on the door and it was pushed open a few inches. "Dr Forbes?"

"Oh. Mrs Lockhart, it's you."

"May I come in?"

"Better that I come to you." Katherine headed outside so

the medical superintendent's wife didn't have to contend with the laboratory odours. "Good day. Is there something wrong?"

"Not at all."

"It's just that we don't usually see you in this part of the asylum."

Mrs Lockhart glanced over her shoulder. "I wanted somewhere discreet to speak to you."

"Oh?"

"Yes. I'll come straight to the point. Dr Lockhart tells me you've a spot of legal trouble."

"I—"

"Please don't be offended he told me. You can be assured it'll go no further. He's concerned for your welfare and sought my advice – as a woman – as to how best he might assist you."

"He's already assisted me by recommending a solicitor, for which I'm most grateful. I've had a brief meeting his clerk."

"I know. That's what I'm here about. Don't get me wrong, the solicitor he's recommended is a fine man. Very professional, very solid. And very, well … traditional."

"That sounds just what I'll need."

"Yes, and I'm sure he'd do a fine job. However, *this* gentleman, on the other hand …" Mrs Lockhart opened her embroidered blue purse and took out a little white card. "… may be more suited to your particular case, if you've not engaged Dr Lockhart's man …"

"Not formally." Katherine read the name on the card. "Mr Charles Huntly-Sykes."

"Yes. I know his mother. She's most supportive of the suffragist cause and—"

"Mrs Lockhart, thank you. But this isn't a matter of sex, it's a professional matter. A scientific matter."

Mrs Lockhart gave a little smile. "Am I correct that it requires two physicians to certify someone as insane?"

"You are."

"And tell me – was the other physician who certified your patient a man?"

"He was."

"And is he being sued too?"

"Well …" Katherine shifted on the spot. "… I'm not really sure."

"And what about the medical superintendent of the asylum your patient was sent to? Is he being sued?"

"Well, I assume so but—"

"Assuming isn't knowing, Dr Forbes. Perhaps you should make some enquiries. And until you know for sure, keep the card. It may be that Mr Huntly-Sykes will be a more apposite choice than you currently imagine."

HELEN

"Nurse Elliot, I've assigned your patient to Mary Anderson," Miss Wilson said. She pointed to the chubby red-headed girl who was thumping her dolly so enthusiastically that water was slopping over the rim of the copper. "She's most conscientious and has a very sympathetic nature. A load's just arrived from the men's hospital ward so there will be plenty to keep your patient occupied until dinner time."

"Thank you, Miss Wilson. Occupation will be a great boon to my patient's health. I think she'll be better suited to physical work than to the more sedate activities of the ward." Helen turned to Biddy and gave her a white apron. "Put that on over your dress."

Miss Wilson took a notepad and pencil out of the pocket of her black dress. "And what's her name?"

"I call her Biddy." Helen lowered her voice. "She's the young woman from the river. We don't know her identity yet."

Miss Wilson raised her eyebrows, then wrote in her notepad – *unknown female patient*.

A fair-haired girl came in and went over to the steaming copper next to Miss Anderson's. Biddy suddenly took off and threw her arms around her.

Helen rushed over to them. "Do you know this patient, miss?"

The girl tried to prise Biddy off. "No, Nurse. Not really. Well, sort of."

Biddy leaned her head on the girl's shoulder and nuzzled her.

"She certainly seems to know you," Helen said.

Miss Wilson appeared beside them, hands on her hips. "Miss Purdie – explain yourself to Nurse Elliot at once."

"Well … I … I was there when she was rescued from the river. Then I went with her when Mr Thomson took her to the Inspector of the Poor."

"And did she explain anything of her circumstances to you? Or her reasons?"

"No, Nurse."

"Or offer her name? Did she say anything about a wedding? Or a man?"

"No." Miss Purdie shook her head. "She never spoke. All she did was cry and moan."

"Nurse Elliot, are you sure your patient is ready for employment?" Miss Wilson said in a tone which suggested she was finding the matter tiresome.

"I am." Helen folded her arms. "As is Dr Forbes, on whose recommendation I'm here."

Miss Wilson sniffed. "Do you think she can begin work then? Miss Anderson has much to do."

Helen glowered at the head laundress. She might have attended the Edinburgh School of Domestic Economy but she'd never make a nurse, not with that sort of impatience.

"I'm sure, Miss Wilson, my patient will—"

Biddy stood up straight. "I want to work with Miss Purdie." She tied her apron at the back. "I'll work hard. But only with her."

"Miss Purdie's only recently started in the laundry. You'll

work with Miss Anderson, who is more experienced," Miss Wilson said.

Biddy glanced at the girl, who looked as if she wanted the floor to open up and swallow her. Then she stamped her foot. "If I can't work with Miss Purdie, I won't work at all."

Miss Wilson's eyes narrowed. "You'll work with whoever I say you will."

"Em, might it be possible," Helen said, "if it weren't too inconvenient, of course, to have my patient work alongside Miss Purdie while being *supervised* by Miss Anderson? I'm sure you know the importance Dr Lockhart attaches to employment for the patients' well-being and recovery."

Miss Wilson drummed her fingernails on the rim of the copper and scowled at Biddy. "Very well, Nurse Elliot. We'll try it for this morning."

"Thank you."

"But if it causes any inconvenience to the efficiency of the laundry, I'll have no hesitation in reconsidering the situation."

"Of course."

Biddy grinned at Miss Purdie, who looked as perplexed as Miss Wilson did annoyed.

Helen made her way back to the ward through the gardens. The progress Biddy had made under her care was gratifying. Even if small, and sometimes imperceptible from one day to the next, improvement was evident. Biddy was less fearful and more communicative, although sometimes still as recalcitrant as when she'd arrived at Cappelmuir.

If Miss Wilson had seen her that day, she might've been impressed by, rather than dismissive of, Biddy's steps towards recovery. Still, Miss Wilson couldn't be blamed for not having such insight. She'd doubtless led a sheltered life. She hadn't studied the Red Book or attended Dr Lockhart's lectures. All she had to concern herself with was making sure the linen that came in dirty went out clean.

Sheets and trousers didn't shout, scream, cry, swear, spit, obsess, accuse or hit. Yet the head laundress was probably paid twice as much as a nurse, if not three times. *You don't know you're born*, that's what Helen would really like say to her. She kicked some pebbles to the side of the path – perhaps there was something to Nurse Haggarty's petition after all.

As she passed the male hospital ward, some attendants were moving the bedridden out onto the verandah, where a couple of able-bodied patients were re-painting the wooden railings. Sunlight, fresh air and occupation were so important to patients, whether chronically sick or mentally incurable. And for those like Biddy – temporarily insane – the most important aspect of their recovery was often simply time.

Helen entered the main building and turned into the long corridor that led back to her ward. As she approached the Admissions Room, the door opened.

"Ah, Nurse Elliot," Matron Campbell said, "the very person. The medical superintendent and I were just talking about you. Would you come in for a moment, please?"

Dr Lockhart was standing behind the small desk. "Come. And close the door, Nurse Elliot."

Helen did as instructed then stood before her superiors.

Dr Lockhart put his hands behind his back and swayed back and forth. "I've received the reports of the incident involving the unknown female patient you've been caring for."

Helen glanced at Matron Campbell, who was staring into the distance.

Dr Lockhart opened his briefcase and took out a Red Book with some pieces of paper sticking out of it. "It seems that it could've turned into a very serious incident indeed had Mr Kennedy not intervened."

"No, sir, I don't think it would have. She was just—"

"Was there not a knife involved?"

"Yes, sir, but it wasn't—"

"As a keen student, Nurse Elliot, you'll know that when it comes to suicidal tendencies ..." Dr Lockhart opened the Red Book at a place marked by one of the pieces of paper and read aloud. "... *impulse is readily begotten by the sight of means to gratify it.*" He lowered the book and peered at her.

"Yes sir, I know that but I didn't believe she was a danger to herself or to others."

He raised the book again. "And that ... *a want of constant vigilance may be the cause of some dire calamity.*"

"I *was* being vigilant, sir. The circumstances were jovial and she was singing. As I'd seen a steady improvement in her mood, I didn't consider there should be any interference. In fact, just this morning the patient has—"

"A good nurse must always be on watch. You have to think for your patients. And newly admitted patients require constant care to ensure they—"

"I've given Biddy constant care," Helen protested.

"Don't interrupt the medical superintendent, Nurse Elliot."

"Biddy? Is that her name? Why have I not been informed of this?" Dr Lockhart said.

"No, it's not her name. It's just what I call her."

"Nurse Elliot, this establishment can only operate if its rules for discipline and the guidance set out in the Red Book are paid due attention. In this case, I find that you haven't done that."

"And the Red Book also says that an establishment's rules can't provide for all emergencies that may occur, which must be left to the common sense and judgement of those directly engaged with the patient."

"Nurse Elliot!" Matron Campbell warned her, moving closer to Dr Lockhart. "I'm terribly sorry, sir. Nurse Elliot doesn't normally behave in this manner."

Helen took a half-step forward. "And that a good nurse knows her own mind, takes a personal interest in the welfare of those placed under her charge, perseveres in promoting their recovery and well-being in every possible way and—"

"Nurse Elliot!" Matron Campbell said sharply. "Enough."

"—that in order to do this she must observe—"

"Nurse Elliot, you must desist from speaking to the medical superintendent in this way!"

"—their peculiarities and conduct."

Matron Campbell grasped Helen's arm. "That is enough!"

Dr Lockhart slammed his Red Book shut. "Nurse Elliot."

Helen looked at the floor.

"Your wages will be docked in the amount of the standard fine." He thrust the book into his briefcase. "Now return to your duties at once before I consider imposing a more serious sanction."

ISABELLA

Isabella linked arms with her good friend as they strolled along the perimeter path. When they came to a wooden stile, they stopped to take in the expanse of the asylum grounds.

"It's very extensive," Effie said.

"Yes. Most people don't realise. I thought you'd be interested in seeing it. I also thought Mrs Drummond was getting a bit fed up with me being in the house and that a long walk would do us both good."

Effie surveyed the scattering of buildings. "It's like a little town."

"Yes. We get vegetables and fruit from the farm, fresh bread every day from the bakery. Our washing's done at the laundry. There's a service in the chapel on Sundays. And entertainment in the evenings. Well, after a fashion. I could probably get most things I need without ever leaving." Isabella sniffed. "In fact, I think Angus would prefer that."

"Talking of Angus," Effie said, as they walked on, "have you broached the matter of the census with him?"

"Not yet. But I can't imagine he'd agree. Any sympathy he might have for women getting the vote likely won't extend to them refusing to provide information for the census return. And most certainly not to harbouring those who wish to evade it. I'm not sure I should ask him."

"You must, Izzy. You know what they're saying – if women don't count, why should we allow ourselves to be counted? And it's not as if we're talking about breaking windows or setting postboxes on fire. It's a great way to raise the profile of our cause. A clever way. Best of all, an irksome way. I'm not suggesting you have a house party but you could take in quite a few ladies in that house."

"I know. But it might come as a shock to him if I were even to ask. He isn't really … well, he isn't really aware of the extent of my involvement."

Effie stopped in her tracks. "But he knew you were involved with the equal pay campaign when you were teaching, didn't he?"

"Well …" Isabella looked past Effie towards the house. "… perhaps not the full extent of my activities."

"All the articles you wrote?"

Isabella shook her head.

"Izzy! I confessed all to Robert."

"Yes, but Angus isn't Robert. Though I did tell him I'd made the occasional lighthearted contribution to fill a few column inches."

"*Occasional? Lighthearted?*" Effie laughed. "It's just as well you used a pseudonym."

They continued towards the house.

"But Angus must surely support the principles we believe in?"

"Well, in theory, of course," Isabella said.

"I mean, look what he's done with the matrons and nurses here."

"Yes, he's fine with the principles. It's just in the domestic sphere he's less comfortable with the practice."

"But surely if you talk to him, sweet-talk him, he'll have no choice but to support his beautiful young wife in her campaign."

"We'll see."

"And if that doesn't work, just send in Mrs Huntly-Sykes to berate him."

Isabella laughed. "She'd definitely be more persuasive than me. She'd probably talk him into submission."

"Or now that you're back wielding your pen, perhaps you could slip a short piece into the asylum magazine."

"I couldn't do that. It's for the amusement of the patients not the promotion of our cause."

"I thought you said it could contain articles?"

"Yes, but not those sorts of articles. Articles about the life of the asylum."

"And aren't there women in the asylum who'd like to hear what's happening in the wider world? Who deserve to hear what's going on in the wider world?"

"Perhaps. Although from what I hear about the plight of many of them, I think the matter of the franchise may be the least of their worries, whether they're in the asylum or not."

When they arrived back at the house, Isabella hung their jackets and hats on the coat stand in the hall, then checked her appearance in the mirror above the little oak table where Angus liked the day's mail to be left. She flipped through the envelopes that were propped up against the lamp in case there was anything from the Suffrage Centre ladies, who'd all been so kind writing to her during her recovery.

"There's nothing for you today, madam," Mrs Drummond said, appearing from the kitchen, out of breath. "And if it's all right with you, I'll bring the tea once I've dealt with the laundry maid. She's just arrived at the back."

"Is it the girl I asked them to send over with the clothes?"

"I don't know, madam. Who did you ask them to send?"

"A Miss Purdie."

"I don't know. I didn't ask her name."

Isabella exchanged a glance with Effie, the way she used to when one of them was on the verge of scolding an insolent pupil. "Well, do you recognise her? Or is she someone new?"

Mrs Drummond shrugged. "There's always someone new in the laundry. It's hard to keep up."

"I'll come and see for myself," Isabella said. "Effie, take a seat in the drawing room. I'll be with you shortly."

Mrs Drummond's head jerked back. "You're coming through to the back, madam?"

"Yes. Is that all right with you?"

"Of course, madam. It's just that, well, I haven't had time to—"

"It's quite all right, Mrs Drummond, I'll avert my gaze from everything but the girl," Isabella said, smiling only once she'd passed by the housekeeper.

The laundry maid stood in the middle of the kitchen, gazing at the crockery on the shelves of the Welsh dresser. With her head tilted, some strands of fair hair had escaped from under her cap. Although she looked a bit older than when Isabella had last seen her, there was no doubt this was the Jessie Purdie from Park School.

"So it is you."

The girl looked round. "I beg your pardon, madam?"

"It's Jessie, isn't it? Jessie Purdie?"

"Yes." The girl rubbed her brow, then gasped. "Miss Muir?"

"It's Mrs Lockhart now. I married last year."

"Oh, I beg your pardon, madam," Jessie said, bobbing down.

"I thought so. I always remember the bright pupils."

The girl blushed. "Oh."

"So what brings you here? I thought you'd be going on to the high school? Didn't you want to go after all?"

"No, I ... well ... I did, but, you see ..." Jessie cleared her throat. "... my mother died and my father took me out of school to get a job and to look after him and my brothers and the house. So I couldn't go to the high school anymore."

"Oh. I'm sorry to hear about your mother. That must've been very hard for you. And your father. For all of you."

"Thank you, madam."

"And, em, how is your father now?"

Jessie looked at her feet. When Isabella thought back to the man who'd turned up at the asylum gates, she could understand why.

"Anyway, I'm sure he must be very proud that you're gainfully employed now. If you do as well here as you did at school, you'll soon gain promotion. Of that I've no doubt. Miss Wilson is very lucky to have you."

"Thank you, madam." Her former pupil glanced up, stifling, Isabella was sure, a sob. "Now, if there's nothing else ..."

"No, there's—"

With that, Jessie Purdie fled from the kitchen.

JESSIE

JESSIE AND MARY sauntered along the cobbled lane towards the store to get the extra packets of soap flakes needed due to an incident in one of the men's wards. Although an unexpected chore, Miss Wilson said it would be a good opportunity for Jessie to learn how to procure supplies.

Where Jessie went, Biddy went, and she was sandwiched between the two laundry maids so that if need be they could exercise control over her. If Jessie hadn't witnessed Biddy's deranged behaviour that day by the river, though, she'd never have believed the docile woman walking in step with her and Mary was the same person. She was behaving impeccably, listening carefully to instructions and doing each task asked of her without complaint.

"That's the tailor's," Mary said as they passed an open doorway with rolls of cloth stacked outside. "The print shop's up at the end. And the stables are there." She pointed down a passageway off the lane which opened into a recessed yard. Duncan was leading one of the horses round it.

"Can we go and see the horses?" Biddy asked.

"No, we're going to the store."

"Actually," Mary said, "you two should maybe wait

outside. There are things in the store that …" She nodded in Biddy's direction. "… sharp things."

"Of course," Jessie said. Not only were they under strict orders that Biddy mustn't be left unaccompanied, they were also not to allow her near dangerous objects. "Well, maybe we could look at the horses while you go inside."

"All right. I need to go in anyway," Mary said. "I need some balsam." She put her hands on her hips and arched her back. "It's killing me. And my legs are aching too."

Jessie laughed. "You shouldn't beat the clothes so hard."

"That's why everything I wash is so pristine. I'm not the one whose shirt was sent back because there was grime left on the collar."

"I'm still learning."

"Well, you'd better not do it again. Miss Wilson won't be so understanding a second time." Mary took the order sheet from her apron pocket. "Right. Won't be long."

Jessie walked Biddy down the short passage and into the courtyard. As Duncan approached them on his circuit, he tipped his cap.

"Is it all right if we watch?" Jessie said.

He stopped and wound in the rope, standing aside for Biddy to pet the horse. She leaned in and nuzzled it.

"You like horses, then?" Jessie said.

"Yes. My uncle had a farm and when we visited him, I'd get to ride one."

Jessie jerked her head at the accent Biddy had just spoken in. Not exactly local, but from not too far away either. Certainly not as far away as Ireland.

"What did you just say?"

Biddy bit her lip, then scuttled behind the horse. Jessie followed her.

"Biddy?"

She bent over and stroked the horse's flank, her back to Jessie.

"Are you really Irish? Or are you—?"

Biddy whirled round. "Shush!" Then she whispered in her Scottish accent, "My name's Matilda."

Jessie pulled her closer. "Matilda?"

"*Shush.*"

"Matilda what?

"Please. You can't tell anyone." Biddy cleared her throat, grinned and started to hum.

"Is Matilda really your name?"

"Ach, no. Away with ya," she said, switching back to her Irish accent. "I was just pulling your leg, so I was." She patted the horse again.

Jessie took a deep breath and looked up at the sky. What if this was just part of Biddy's madness? Patients said all sorts that weren't true. And if they were excitable, they could distort their voices like the devil himself. Just think what Biddy had been like with Mr Thomson, with all that crying and moaning. How was Jessie to know whether she was joking now? In any case, it wasn't for Jessie to know. It shouldn't matter to her whether the patient was Biddy, Matilda or someone else entirely. Jessie was a laundry maid and all the rules required of her was that she report the incident to someone else.

"I'm going to have to tell Nurse Elliot."

Biddy grabbed her arm. "You can't! Please. If they find out I'm here, they'll come for me and they'll kill me."

"Who'll kill you?"

"I can't tell you. I can't tell anyone."

"All right. But I'll have to report it. Otherwise—"

"You've saved my life before. You have to do it again. Please."

Jessie pulled Biddy into the passage. "Right. I want the truth. Now. Otherwise I'm going straight to Nurse Elliot."

"All right. Shush! "

"So what's your name?"

"Matilda."

"Matilda what?"

"Matilda White."

"Are you Irish?"

"No."

"Why did you go into the river?"

Matilda glanced along the lane, then back to the yard.

"If you don't tell me, I'll have no option but to—"

"All right. Shush, I'll tell you. I needed to get away. Somewhere they wouldn't find me. I was waiting for someone to come onto the bridge and when I saw you looking out, I—"

"What do you mean, waiting for someone to come onto the bridge?"

"Waiting for someone. Anyone. So they'd see me and come and help. I wasn't really trying to drown myself. It just had to look like I was."

"Why?"

"So they'd take me away somewhere."

"Where?"

"Anywhere. It just turned out to be here."

"And who are the *they* who're going to kill you?"

Matilda shook her head.

"Tell me who they are."

Mary came out of the supplies store. "Right, you two. Come on. I've got everything."

Matilda immediately trotted over to her. "Did you get your balsam, then?" she said in her thickest Irish accent.

"Yes, thank you. I did."

"That's grand. My relative, the Duke of Connaught, swore by it, so he did. Used to rub it on his legs. Did I tell you I was related to the Duke of Connaught?"

"I believe you've mentioned it before, yes." Mary handed Jessie a box of soapflakes. "Here, you can take this. I've got the receipt. And that's all there is to getting an order from the store. You'll know what to do if Miss Wilson sends you next time."

"Yes, thanks," Jessie said, somewhat befuddled, as Matilda took up position between the two maids for the return walk.

Miss Wilson was waiting for them at the front door of the laundry. "Finally. I thought I told you not to dawdle?"

She snatched the box of soap flakes from Jessie. "Good. Now get back to your positions. You've things to catch up on."

The three of them stepped inside.

"But not you, Miss Purdie." Miss Wilson tugged Jessie back. "I need a word."

She waited until Mary and Matilda were far enough along the corridor to be out of earshot. "For some reason, I can't think what, Mrs Lockhart has…"

Jessie felt a thud in her throat. Had Mrs Lockhart complained about her?

"… asked if I can spare you one afternoon this week to assist her with something."

Jessie's leg began to tremble. "With what?"

"I wouldn't know. But it's most irregular. However, as she's the medical superintendent's wife, I don't suppose either of us has any choice in the matter."

KATHERINE

MR CHARLES HUNTLY-SYKES looked like a schoolboy who'd been allowed to sit behind the desk while his father momentarily stepped out of the wood-panelled office. Yet, hard as it was to believe, this slight fresh-faced fellow, talking on the phone and shifting inside the light-grey suit he didn't quite fill, was the man recommended to Katherine by Mrs Lockhart.

He held the receiver in one hand and a pen in the other, drawing lines on the ink pad on his desk with every 'uh-huh'. For one so youthful, he had a surprisingly mellow baritone voice.

"Uh-huh. Yes. Uh-huh. I see. Very good. Uh-huh. Thank you. Goodbye." He replaced the receiver on the stand and wound the pleated cable neatly around its base. "Well, there's bad news and good news, Dr Forbes." He put his pen down. "The bad news is that you're the only doctor being sued."

Katherine twitched. "And the good news?"

"You're the only doctor being sued. As you know, a single opinion isn't sufficient to consign someone to the asylum. So it doesn't make sense for just one of the certifying doctors to be targeted. One opinion is only valid in conjunction with another of the same." Mr Huntly-Sykes grinned at her like a child hoping to impress his mother.

"Why is that the good news?"

"Because it doesn't make sense. There's something else at play here. And, if it comes to it, I shall use that fact in court to prove that the case against you is ill-founded, as it is based not on the fact that your opinion was incorrect, but on the fact that … you're a woman."

Katherine sat forward and tapped her fingers on the desk. "The other doctor who backed up my opinion was a man. And you're saying that if my opinion was wrong, then his opinion must've been wrong too."

"Correct."

"And if that's the case … why isn't he also being sued?"

"Precisely. This case is so feeble, I doubt it'll even make it to court. I'm surprised my colleague's willing to represent the plaintiff in the matter. But sometimes, of course, despite best advice, clients are so adamant that nothing will deter them from pursuing their grievances. And no matter how weak a case might be, the legal representative still receives his fees. Much though we'd like, we can't always be choosy about who we represent."

"I'm glad I'm a doctor and not a solicitor." Katherine folded her arms. "No offence intended."

Mr Huntly-Sykes laughed, leaning back in his leather-padded swivel chair. "None taken."

How could he behave with such levity when her professional and personal integrity was being challenged in such an unfair manner? She was about to remonstrate with him when he composed himself and looked her in the eye.

"Dr Forbes, I'll fight this matter for you to the best of my abilities. Not because I'll receive a fee but because I believe the case against you to be egregious and that you deserve the best representation possible. You're an excellent professional and it's only your professionalism that should be of concern to a patient, not your sex."

"Oh." Katherine shifted in her chair. "Thank you. It's a pity not everyone has such an enlightened outlook."

"Indeed. I'm sure neither of us would have to look far to find men – *medical* men – who don't like the idea of women joining their profession."

"But surely they wouldn't go as far as to … would they?"

Mr Huntly-Sykes cocked his head and raised his eyebrows. "I'm afraid they might, Dr Forbes. But as I said, we will fight this, and I'm hopeful we will win."

"Thank you."

"Oh, don't thank me." He laughed. "I'm a product of my mother."

"Then please pass my thanks on to her."

Mr Huntly-Sykes got up and went over to the door. "My mother also says that no woman needs a man to speak for her. So if you'd like to thank her in person, you'll find her at the tea room across the road. Among her many roles, she's president of the local branch of the Women's Freedom League. I'm told their Victoria sponge is the best in town." He offered Katherine a handshake. "Leave matters with me and I'll contact you with an update soon. And, please, Dr Forbes, don't worry. This will come to nothing, I assure you."

Katherine looked across at the Women's Freedom League Suffrage Centre, a narrow two-storey building with a large glass-panelled white frontage. (Mrs Lockhart was lucky not to have suffered more serious injuries given the size of the pane that had shattered.) She glanced towards the railway station and pulled out her watch. Quarter of an hour until the next train to Cappelmuir. There were still a few moments to spare.

She crossed the road and stopped to look at the pamphlets,

books, flags and 'Vote' placards in the window. Then she put her face against the glass and peered inside, where a number of ladies were taking tea.

A middle-aged woman came out and stood in the doorway. "Could I ask you not to linger there, please, madam?" She had the same eyes and nose as Mr Charles Huntly-Sykes. "We've had some trouble with vandals recently and we're asking people either to come in or move on."

"Of course. Yes," Katherine said. "The recent incident was quite appalling. Mrs Lockhart's extremely lucky to have escaped relatively unscathed."

"You know of the incident?"

"Yes. I'm Dr Forbes, assistant medical officer at Cappelmuir Asylum. Mrs Lockhart's husband is the medical superintendent."

"Of course he is. Well, it's very good to meet you, Dr Forbes. I'm Letitia Huntly-Sykes, local branch president of the Women's Freedom League. Do come in for a cup of tea."

"I actually have a train to catch and ..." Katherine looked back towards the station again – she should really return to her duties as soon as possible, given Dr Lockhart had granted her leave to attend to business. Bad enough she'd chosen his wife's recommendation for a solicitor over his; if he found out she'd also taken advantage of his generosity to visit a tea room, he'd not only be insulted but angry. And if she didn't get the next train, Dr Dorsie would have to undertake rounds on her behalf.

"We do an exquisite Victoria sponge," Mrs Huntly-Sykes said.

"So I've heard." Katherine consulted her watch. There would be another train in an hour. And Dr Dorsie would only be seeing a few more patients, which would be no great hardship. It wasn't as if *he* was being sued.

Yes – given her travails, why shouldn't she have a little

time to gather her thoughts? "Thank you, you're most kind. I will. A cup of tea sounds just the ticket."

After only a short time in Mrs Huntly-Sykes' company, it was clear from whom Katherine's young solicitor had inherited his conviction, optimism and loquacity. The words gushed from her like water from a tap.

"And I don't know if you're aware, but my husband is a man of, well – there's no other way of putting it – significant means. He's helped me establish a number of initiatives to assist those less fortunate than ourselves. This centre isn't just about the vote, it's about so much more – fair pay, improved educational opportunities, health advice, medical treatment. What we're trying to do isn't simply charity, it's about changing the structure of society so that charity isn't needed."

Katherine dabbed the last crumbs of her Victoria sponge. "That's very commendable."

"But you must tell me – what are *your* ambitions, Dr Forbes?"

"My ambitions?"

"Yes."

"In what sense?"

"Well, if things follow their normal pattern, Dr Lockhart will either remain at Cappelmuir for another twenty years or he'll leave to take up a more senior position elsewhere. If he leaves, you won't be considered for the post of medical superintendent. And you're unlikely to secure a post in the male preserves that are our hospitals."

"There are some women in senior positions," Katherine said. "In fact, Dr Alice Strachan, with whom I travelled to Holland, is—"

"Yes, dear. I'm acquainted with Dr Strachan. She's a great supporter of my work with girls. But do you have the same connections she has?" Mrs Huntly-Sykes gave a pained smile.

"Well, no. But—"

"Do you want to spend your entire career as an assistant

medical officer? Or are you just biding time until you succumb to matrimony? Forgive my plain speaking, but I've found over the years that it's the best way if you want to get things done. I'd venture you're not one for unnecessary small talk either, Dr Forbes."

"Well …"

"I thought not. You know, we're always looking for intelligent and principled women to support our initiatives."

"Oh, I'm afraid I don't have time to commit to voluntary activities."

"I'm not talking about voluntary effort, Dr Forbes. I'm talking about paid employment."

"Oh. I see."

The Tea Room door opened and two mature ladies came in.

"But I'm afraid I must leave you." Mrs Huntly-Sykes stood up. "I've a meeting now about the forthcoming census. But think about what's important to you and where you see yourself. There might be alternatives you haven't considered. It was lovely meeting you, Dr Forbes. Goodbye now."

And before Katherine could say as much as a 'thank you', the local branch president of the Women's Freedom League had gone from the table.

HELEN

TEA WAS SERVED on arrival at the gentlemen's At Home at seven thirty precisely. Helen herded her patients into the day room and directed them to the small tables arranged around the perimeter. On each one was a large platter with a fine selection of cakes and cookies freshly made by the asylum's baker.

Nellie Shaw, who needed no encouragement when it came to sweet treats, grabbed Biddy's wrist and led her to a couple of vacant seats at the table next to the piano, where Dr Forbes was reviewing some sheet music and Dr Dorsie was tuning his violin.

Helen nodded a hello to the assistant medical officers as she waited for her ladies to settle. Dr Dorsie would no doubt be treating them to some solos, as well as playing alongside Mr Allan on the accordion when the jigging started. As for Dr Forbes, she'd be providing the accompaniment for the communal singalong, as well as for the national anthem, which would close the soirée at exactly nine thirty.

Seeing the doctors take part in the regular social events lifted the patients' spirits and contributed greatly to their well-being. The male patients in particular relished the company and always made sure they were well turned out. In fact, more

116

often than not, the stylishness of their attire and general appearance exceeded that of the ladies.

Mr Smith was working the tables, greeting each lady with a bow and a compliment. Roddy The Rat Catcher, meanwhile, sporting a splendid pair of red dancing slippers and matching bow tie, followed a few paces behind, no doubt hoping that some of Mr Smith's charm would rub off on him.

Once he'd completed his rounds, Mr Smith bounded over to Helen. "Nurse Elliot! How splendid! Your cheeks are like cherry blossom."

"Good evening, Mr Smith. Once again you've excelled yourself. Your organisational skills are second to none. I think when you leave us, you shouldn't return to plate-laying but instead find an employer who'd benefit more from your many talents."

"Nurse Elliot, you're most kind. But I've found my métier at Cappelmuir. Did you know I'm working for Dr Forbes exporting guinea pigs now?"

"Really?"

"Yes, I am indeed in that business. And in so doing, I'm contributing to scientific endeavour. Isn't that right, Dr Forbes?" he called over to her.

She put her sheet music on the piano and came over. "Isn't what right, Mr Smith?"

"That I'm now working with you in the business of exporting guinea pigs."

"Indeed you are."

"Goodness," Helen said.

"Yes. And Mr Smith has today secured his first order – a crate of live guinea pigs to an asylum in Edinburgh – and has earned a guinea for Cappelmuir."

Mr Smith clapped and chuckled. "A guinea for the guinea pigs. Very good, Dr Forbes, very good. Ah. Now, if you'll excuse me, I must go and prepare the ladies and gentlemen for the first of the dances."

"He's certainly in good form," Helen said, once he was out of earshot. "I was just telling him he's wasted on the railways and should think about another line of work when he leaves here. D'you think it'll be soon?"

"By any measure, he's much improved. However, the question I'm pondering is … whether or not he'll be able to thrive outwith the asylum."

Mr Smith took a seat at the table alongside Biddy and Nellie.

"He calls her the Duchess," Helen said, "on account of her relative. The Duke of Connaught."

Dr Forbes smiled. "Of course." She leaned into Helen and lowered her voice. "Speaking of Biddy … you might like to know that Dr Lockhart's received some cuttings from *The Dublin Times* and a list of all the Marys who recently married there. He's narrowed it down to a couple who are about the same age and description. And one of them can't be traced. So you never know, we might soon learn who she actually is."

"She's certainly a queer one. Not like any patient I've ever had. Just when you think you've got the measure of her, she does something that wrong-foots you."

"Whoever she turns out to be, she's making progress. You're doing well with our Biddy, Nurse Elliot."

"Thank you, Dr Forbes." Though it was a pity Dr Lockhart hadn't thought the same when he'd fined her. Her exemplary record and all her studying seemed to have counted for nothing.

"And there haven't been any further incidents of the kind reported in the dining room. That's a good sign as well."

"Yes, she …" Helen bristled as she spotted Nurse Haggarty and Mr Kennedy approaching.

He smiled broadly at Dr Forbes. "I trust you'll be treating us to some tunes on the piano this evening, Doctor? You play so well and I know my patients enjoy these evenings that bit more when you're in attendance."

"Yes, I will be. Thank you, Mr Kennedy. You're most kind."

"Oh, it's not kindness, Dr Forbes, it's simply honesty. And, if nothing else, I'm an honest man."

Helen exchanged a glance with Nurse Haggarty.

"Well, now that you've set me up on such a pedestal, I should return and study my music." Dr Forbes gave a little snort that verged on a giggle. "After all, I wouldn't want to disappoint you or your patients, Mr Kennedy."

"There's nothing you could do to disappoint me, nothing at all. Now, after you, Doctor." He gave a little bow and followed her to the piano.

Helen and Nurse Haggarty folded their arms at the same time. Nurse Haggarty was the first to laugh. "I think you and I must be the only women at Cappelmuir immune to Mr Kennedy's charms."

"*Pff.*" Helen scowled. To see him gadding about and posturing, insinuating himself with those above his station – it was infuriating. "Not if he were the last man on earth."

"It's so unfair that he's as handsome as he is immoral."

"That's a matter of opinion."

"I think yours might be a lone one on that matter, Nurse Elliot."

Helen sighed. "Probably."

"You'll not be getting anything done on your Red Book tonight."

"No. But these events are very useful for assessing patients' progress. It's helpful to see them in a different setting."

"Your devotion to your patients is commendable."

"And you're no less devoted, Nurse Haggarty, even if your views on our workplace, and our colleagues, sometimes differ from mine."

Nurse Haggarty smiled. "Thank you."

"Although … it may even be that our views don't differ as much as you believe."

"Oh?"

"Yes." Helen leaned into her colleague so that their elbows touched. "How are things with the petition?"

"Many of the nurses have expressed their support in principle – but they fear repercussions. Especially now that one of Mount Hope's assistant matrons has been dismissed. She apparently refused an order by the medical superintendent to sign an obligation saying she wouldn't strike. Some of our nurses fear Dr Lockhart might instruct us likewise."

"He wouldn't do that, surely?" Helen said. "We haven't even submitted a petition."

"And he'll want to keep it that way."

"It wouldn't be fair of him to ask that of us."

"Fair? Has there ever been anything to lead you to believe that anything about Cappelmuir is fair?"

Helen pursed her lips. Being fined by Dr Lockhart, that wasn't fair.

She put her hands on her hips and turned to Nurse Haggarty. "If you'll allow me, I'd like to help with the petition."

ISABELLA

ISABELLA COULD TELL by the scowl on Mrs Drummond's face that the housekeeper didn't approve of the visitor who'd been sent round to the back door and consigned to wait in the scullery.

"Please show Miss Purdie into the dining room, Mrs Drummond."

"The dining room, madam?"

"Yes." Isabella got up from the settee. "And I'm sure she'd appreciate a cup of tea, having worked since six this morning. Could you bring some for us, please?"

"Tea, madam? Miss Purdie's in her maid's uniform and—"

"Yes, Mrs Drummond," Isabella said, forcing the housekeeper to step aside. "If you wouldn't mind, thank you. I'd be most grateful."

She crossed the hall and went into the dining room, where the black Royal typewriter she'd persuaded the house secretary to lend her sat on the mahogany table. Isabella jabbed the 'I' key with her index finger and a typebar rose, striking the cylinder with a firm click and putting a bold, black mark on the paper.

She pulled two chairs out from under the table and moved

the vase of flowers from the middle to the corner. Then she went over and straightened the painting of Cappelmuir which hung above the sideboard and which had been donated by the asylum's first medical superintendent in 1869. Although the building hadn't changed in forty-two years, more blocks had been added and the grounds had matured from the barren land of the original surroundings.

It was such a drab painting, predominantly black, brown, beige and grey. Were it up to Isabella, it would be taken down and replaced with something more cheery.

"Your, em, *visitor*, madam," Mrs Drummond said from the hall.

"Ah." Isabella turned away from the painting. "Thank you for coming, Miss Purdie. Come in." The girl shuffled in, swivelling her head as she took in the surroundings. "Please take a seat."

Mrs Drummond put the tea tray on the table rather heavily.

"Thank you, Mrs Drummond, that'll be all." Isabella poured two cups of tea and sat down. "Would I be right in thinking that you took shorthand and typing at school, Miss Purdie?"

"Em, yes. I did." She looked at the cup of tea and then to the door, as if the refreshment was for someone who was still to arrive.

"Pitman's?"

"Yes."

"Good." Isabella took a sip of tea and nodded at the girl to do likewise. Miss Purdie lifted her cup hesitantly. "What speed?"

"I got up to a hundred and fifty words a minute before I had to leave, miss. I mean, madam. They said I should sit for the two hundred but I couldn't because ... well, anyway, I would've had to have gone away to sit it so ... but it didn't matter because my mother ... and then I left school and went to work at North Mill."

"And what about your typing? What it good too?"

"It was all right I think. Average, probably."

"Anything would be faster than me! Do you think you could type on this machine? I believe it's in full working order."

Miss Purdie peered at the typewriter, then pushed the carriage return. The mechanism gave a bright ting. "I think so."

"Excellent. You see, why I asked for you is that the medical superintendent, Dr Lockhart – my husband – well, he's asked me to prepare some pieces for a magazine he's thinking of starting for the asylum. I've talked to a few people and I've a number of ideas but it's difficult for me to speak to people and take notes at the same time. And I'm afraid that I'm not proficient with a typewriter. So I'm looking for someone to assist me. I thought you'd be ideal." Miss Purdie opened her mouth slightly and sat back in her chair. "What do you think?"

Isabella's former pupil looked puzzled. "But I work in the laundry for Miss Wilson..."

"I know. But I'm just talking about an hour here and there. I'm sure Miss Wilson would be pleased to release you ... if the medical superintendent requested it."

"Well, I suppose I—"

The front door opened. Angus came into the hall, calling for Isabella.

"Excuse me for just a moment. Why don't you try out the typewriter while I speak to my husband?"

She got up from the table and went back into the drawing room.

"Ah, there you are."

She kissed him on the cheek. "How was the Chairman's visit?"

"It couldn't have been better. Everything's arranged for the Americans coming."

"That's excellent." Isabella sat on the settee next to Tipper.

"Yes. They'll be studying every aspect of our operations and methods and they'll have free access to all areas of the asylum and every privilege. The medical director of the State Asylum in Massachusetts will be coming, as well as a member of the Illinois State Board of Charities, a—"

"Very prestigious."

"—Miss Worthington. Yes."

Isabella's stomach fluttered. "A *Miss* Worthington?"

"Yes indeed."

"My goodness. How exciting." Isabella rubbed her hands together. "Can you imagine, Angus?"

She looked out the drawing room window at the neat garden. Ever since reading about the Grand Tour as a child she'd fantasised about visiting Italy, but imagine sailing across the Atlantic Ocean to the other side of the world. She was very much looking forward to meeting this Miss Worthington and hearing all about her journey.

"Of course we must host a dinner for them one evening at the house," Angus said.

"Of course."

"Perhaps with Doctors Dorsie and Forbes."

"That would only be appropriate."

"Do you think that will be acceptable to …?" He nodded in the direction of the kitchen.

"I'm sure Mrs Drummond will be delighted to assist. It all sounds absolutely wonderful."

"Yes, I have to confess that I'm looking forward to it very much." Angus pulled at his lapels. "I believe they intend to report their experiences at the annual meeting of the American Medico-Psychological Association later in the year. Its proceedings are published, so Cappelmuir could become internationally renowned."

"How exciting."

"And that's not all."

"Oh?"

"No. I took the opportunity, while I had the Chairman's ear, of mentioning to him the matter of the carriage. I told him the horses have become unfit and that the veterinary surgeon has deemed them useless for further carriage work."

"Surely they're not as bad as that?"

"One of them's been completely off work for the past three months and the other's only been sporadically fit. I also told the Chairman that the carriage is old and in need of considerable repair."

"What did he say to that?"

"Nothing. I put my proposal to him before he had a chance to respond."

"What proposal?"

"Well …" Angus took Isabella's hand in his. "… I suggested that instead of the Board providing new horses and incurring the expense of repairing the carriage, I would purchase a motor car as my own property—"

"Purchase? A motor car?" Isabella was flabbergasted. It wasn't like Angus to be so daring.

"Yes, provided that an annual allowance of a hundred and fifty pounds was made to me towards its upkeep. It would take the place of a carriage and pair of horses, which, of course, I'm entitled to under my employment agreement. As well as bearing the cost of the motor car, I would bear the costs of maintenance and petrol. The driver's wages and livery would be paid by the Board, as at present, and the Board would defray the cost of licence duty and insurance."

"And what did the Chairman say to that?"

"He said he could see there was value in my proposition and that he'd consider it further before deciding whether to recommend it to the Board. Wouldn't it be wonderful? I could take you for a drive in the country and we could go up the coast and maybe take a yachting cruise. I've heard there's an excursion from one of them to the top of Ben Nevis."

Drives in the country? A yachting cruise? Excursions up

mountains? What had come over him? "But can we afford a motor car, Angus?"

"I wouldn't be suggesting it if we couldn't."

"Goodness me." It did sound rather excellent. And what would everyone back home make of Izzy Muir gadding about in a motor car?

The typewriter started to clack from across the hall.

"What's that?" Angus said.

"Oh, it's just—"

Mrs Drummond came into the room. "Dr Lockhart, sir? Mr Johnstone's just brought over this note from Matron Campbell and asked me to give it to you straight away."

Angus unfolded the piece of paper. "Well. This day just gets more and more interesting. I'll have to leave you for the moment, my dear. We may just have identified our mystery Irish patient."

JESSIE

It was Mary's idea to go to town for Jessie's first Sunday off. They'd attend church, get tea and a scone at the Temperance Hall and then take a stroll. Much better than listening to Reverend Fulton drone on at the asylum chapel, and good for them to get some fresh air after being cooped up in Cappelmuir for a fortnight.

When they arrived at the church, groups of people were milling around outside. Jessie paused and scanned their faces, hand to her forehead, ready to cover her eyes if need be. But the likelihood of her father being in the vicinity was low, for the nearby alehouse wasn't open. And even if he'd managed to get to church after a night's drinking, he would've staggered to St Columba's at the other end of town. Nevertheless, she wanted to be sure.

"Come on then." Mary pulled her arm. "Let's go in."

Logie Kirk was much bigger than St Columba's. It had three sets of pews rather than two, as well as a gallery upstairs that was already filling up. There were oak panels depicting biblical scenes along the walls of the nave and three stained-glass windows in the apse. There'd be plenty to look at during the service.

Mary stopped halfway along the right-hand aisle and leaned against a pew.

"Are you all right?" Jessie asked.

Mary wobbled along to the end of the pew and Jessie sidled in beside her.

"I'm fine. Just a bit hot." Mary flopped down, undid the buttons of her jacket and wafted her blouse. Then she took out her handkerchief and wiped the sweat from her upper lip. "That's better."

"That's what you get for missing breakfast."

Mary tutted. "It gives me indigestion. But I'll be ready for something after this."

"Well, if your stomach starts rumbling, you're not with me!"

Jessie sat down and lifted a Bible from the back of the pew in front. She opened it at a bookmarked page.

Whoever walks in integrity walks securely, but he who makes his way crooked will be found out.

She looked up at the stained-glass windows – was she walking in integrity by not revealing what Matilda had told her? Or had she made her way crooked? She flipped to another page.

Pray for us, for we are sure that we have a clear conscience, desiring to act honourably in all things.

She closed the Bible quickly and returned it to its rightful place.

Mary elbowed her and pointed to the front of the church. "There's Duncan. Third pew."

Jessie located a smartly dressed young man with neatly combed brown hair. "Goodness, I hardly recognised him. What's he doing here?"

"Same as us. Getting into the real world for a few hours."

"Reverend Fulton must be bad if everyone from Cappelmuir comes here on their day off."

"Don't get too carried away. The minister here's on the dull side too. But at least it's something different."

"And a change is as good as a rest." At least that's what Jessie's mother used to say.

The organist began to play and the minister came out of the vestry. Jessie looked at the board to check what the first hymn was. 'Praise My Soul The King of Heaven'. One of her mother's favourites. She would've loved hearing the full congregation singing in this church. St Columba's was so small that you could make out the individual voices. And Jessie's mother's had been one of the sweetest.

The minister wasn't as tedious as Mary had suggested he'd be and his sermon about the evils of excess was well-received, if the nodding in the congregation was anything to go by.

When Jessie stood for the benediction, Mary remained seated. Jessie dunted her on the shoulder and she woke with a start.

"How could you have slept through it?" Jessie said, as they left the pew. "What if he saw you?"

"He'd forgive me. He's a man of God."

Just when they'd shuffled their way to the vestibule, Mary paused. "I've left my hankie in the pew. You go on. I'll just be a minute." She started back, pushing against the flow of people.

Jessie waited outside on the little grass strip that separated the church from the pavement, admiring the ladies and gentlemen in their fine costumes. She touched her tweed skirt; the best that could be said for it was that it was clean. Which was more than could be said for her left shoe, which was streaked with mud. She bent over and tried to wipe it off with her finger.

"Here. Try this." Duncan flapped a blue-checked handkerchief at her.

She took it from him and wiped the dirt off. "That's better. My mother always told me that the state of someone's shoes tells you a lot about them." She glanced at Duncan's brown brogues, which had a dusty line around the stitching. "But she was talking about girls, of course. I mean, men, with the sort of work they do, it's not always easy to ..." She gave Duncan back his handkerchief. "Thanks. I'm just waiting for Mary. She won't be long. We're going to the hall for tea and a scone. Are you going too?"

Duncan shrugged.

"What did you think of the service? I thought it was all right. I haven't been here before. I used to go to St Columba's. This is like a cathedral compared to it. Have you been here before?"

Duncan nodded and Jessie shifted from foot to foot. How could he bear the silences? Although her father and brothers talked constantly – and mostly rubbish at that – at least she knew where she stood with them.

She glanced over to the church. How could it take Mary so long to retrieve a hankie?

"I was thinking about your horses," she felt the need to continue. "You're probably right just to speak to them and not to the patients. You probably get more sense from the horses. They say some strange things, the patients, don't they? All sorts of things. You don't know if it's the truth or lies. Or a bit of both. Mind, I don't suppose you have to deal with many patients at the stables, do you? It must be nice that, just having to deal with the horses. And your superiors, of course. Who gives you orders? Is it the steward? I know he's in charge of the gardeners and the tailor and the baker and the printer. Is he in charge of the stables too? It's Miss Wilson who's in charge of the laundry. She's all right actually, if you stick by the rules and do what you're told. Yes. Hmm." Jessie tapped her foot. "Yes, the patients ... so ... if a patient told you something, would you report it to a nurse or an attendant? Or ... what if a patient told you something important, then asked you not to tell the nurse or an attendant ..." *Stop blabbering!* "...what would you do? Or ... what would you do if—?"

"Nothing."

She stared at Duncan, slightly discombobulated that he'd finally spoken. "What?"

"Nothing. I'd not do anything."

"But it says in the rules we've to report anything significant a patient does. And—"

"I don't hear anything, I don't see anything, I don't say anything. That way I don't get into any trouble. I just do my job and keep my head down. Do the same and you'll be all right." He turned and walked away.

That, Jessie supposed, was that. Duncan might not say much, but when he did speak, it was worth listening to.

Mary appeared, waving her handkerchief. "Got it." She looked across the road. "What on earth's going on there?"

As Jessie turned to look, the slurred expletives of two men dragging a third along the pavement were reaching the ears of the churchgoers. She froze momentarily, as the tut-tutting grew louder. Then she dodged behind Mary so her brothers wouldn't see her.

"For goodness sake," Mary said, "look at the state of him. I wouldn't like to be his poor wife. I'd be battering down the doors of Cappelmuir either to take me in or put him in. Wouldn't you? Jessie? Jessie! Are you not coming for tea? Where are you going?"

She didn't know where she was going, only that it was in the other direction from her family.

KATHERINE

THE DOORMAN STOOD ASIDE to let Katherine into the theatre. As she crossed the foyer, the click of her heels on the white marble floor echoed up to the painted gold ceiling. She swished past the pay boxes at the bottom of the grand staircase and waited in front of one of the fluted marble pillars, watching people head down to the stalls and up to the circle.

"Dr Forbes!"

Dr Cowan was at the main doors, a hand in the air. Katherine gave a little wave back and watched his top hat as it came towards her through the crowd. When he emerged from the throng, it was with a lady in a mauve gown on his arm.

"Good evening, Dr Forbes. You look exquisite. I trust you've not been waiting long?"

Katherine smiled at the compliment. It was over six months since she'd worn her apricot chiffon dress, at a dinner party given by her brother and his wife. That was also the last time she'd been away from Cappelmuir for anything other than business. It was lovely to be out and about, and wearing something other than a drab skirt and matching jacket.

"Thank you. No, I've only just arrived."

"Excellent." Dr Cowan took off his hat and smoothed down

his hair. As ever, in black swallow-tail coat and white waistcoat, he was immaculate. "Let me introduce my sister, also Dr Cowan."

She had the same brown eyes as her brother and her nose had the same turned-up tip.

"It's a pleasure to meet you, Dr Cowan."

"And you, Dr Forbes. Please, call me Agatha."

"And I'm Katherine."

"Agatha's just started as a resident at the Royal Sick Children's Hospital. She's one of only four," Dr Cowan said.

"How impressive."

"Of course the position is what they call 'honorary'," Agatha said, "but I'm blessed that my brother and others in my family are willing to support me during my stint. Were it not for their generosity, I wouldn't be able to avail myself of the opportunity to work with such distinguished surgeons and physicians."

"Indeed, no." Oh that Katherine might have the good fortune to be offered such a prestigious position as well as the means to take it up. "And after you've completed your residency, what are your plans, Agatha?"

"I'll be marrying and—"

"Marrying?" How could Agatha be intending to give up her excellent professional prospects?

"Yes. And then my husband and I will be travelling to India, where he's joining a mission."

"How intrepid."

"Not really. But it means I'll be able to marry and still work. There's a hospital at the mission and I'm to be the doctor in charge."

"Really? Goodness." Katherine swallowed her envy. "That's wonderful."

The theatre bell rang and Dr Cowan put his hat back on. "Shall we go upstairs, ladies?"

The Cowans's box was level with the circle. Katherine sat to the left of Agatha, who was in the middle chair. In the stalls below, hundreds of people settled into their tip-up armchairs. The new theatre was one of the largest in the country but Katherine hadn't realised it was quite so cavernous.

Dr Cowan leaned forward. "Is the view all right for you, Dr Forbes?"

"Thank you, yes. It's magnificent. I won't be needing my opera glasses!"

He sat back again and crossed his legs. Then he ran a finger along the sharp crease in his trousers and bent his ankle to look at his shoe. Even in the subdued lighting of the box, it was gleaming.

Everything about Dr Cowan was effortless. When Katherine had been seasick during the crossing to Holland, he'd kept her company out on deck, seemingly immune to the cutting wind and drenching spray. While she, damp and bedraggled, was bent over the railing, praying to Neptune for some relief, he remained resolutely unruffled. She hoped they kept an adequate supply of smelling salts at the Royal Mental Hospital to revive every lady he walked by from their swoon. How envious they'd be of Katherine if they could see her now.

The orchestral part of the programme featured pieces by Dvorak, Tchaikovsky and Debussy. Katherine closed her eyes as a languid flute introduced 'Prelude a l'apres midi d'un faune', the purity of its sound far removed from the crackly rendition played on the asylum's phonograph a few months before at a ladies' social.

Top of the bill was Madam Nellie Melba, whose performance of 'Pale et Blonde' brought everyone to their feet. As Katherine clapped, Dr Cowan shouted "Encore!" and Agatha shook her head in delight.

After the curtain came down for the interval, the applause took some time to die away, only gradually being replaced by a crescendo of murmuring.

"Isn't she marvellous?" Agatha said. "Have you ever heard a voice like that?"

"Never," Katherine said.

"The nearest I've come to it was Madam Bertha Moore on her annual visit to the hospital," Dr Cowan said. "Her rendition of 'Whistle Daughter Whistle' brought the house down similarly."

Katherine laughed, brushing his arm with her fingertips.

Agatha reached behind her chair for her shawl. "Would you both excuse me? I'm just going to get some air."

"Of course." Katherine surveyed the stalls. Almost half the audience had disappeared to the saloon.

"I hope you're enjoying the programme." Dr Cowan slid across to the middle chair.

"Very much. I must thank you and Agatha again for your kind invitation."

"It's our pleasure."

Katherine clasped her hands together on her lap. "She's quite a lady, your sister."

"She is."

"And her husband-to-be sounds like an exceptional man."

"Mr Dockley – Alistair – is indeed a fine fellow, who's found a way for my sister to achieve her ambitions. I'm sure you'd be most impressed by him. In fact," Dr Cowan said, moving his chair closer to Katherine's, "you should meet him. Yes! Why don't you come and meet him? We could all take a little excursion. The three of us were planning to take the steamer on Loch Lomond soon. Why don't you come with us? They provide a substantial lunch on the way up and a comfortable tea on the way down. The scenery's delightful."

"Well, I—"

"I'm sure Alistair would be delighted to meet you and tell you all about the mission."

"I'd certainly find that interesting …"

"There you are then."

Katherine bit the inside of her lip as she pondered asking the question that was on her mind. "Tell me, Dr Cowan …" In for a penny, in for a pound. "… would you ever consider … such a career move?"

He looked across to the boxes on the other side of the theatre, then turned his seat to face Katherine's. "If there was someone who had captured my heart the way my sister has captured Alistair's, then yes. I think I would." He put his hand on Katherine's. "And if I were lucky enough to secure the hand of such a woman, I would go to the ends of the earth to make her happy."

Katherine touched her pearl necklace and glanced up to the gods. "Such a woman would be very fortunate indeed."

HELEN

Helen stepped into the corridor. There was no sign of Biddy yet, but it shouldn't be long. Dr Forbes wanted to see her as soon as she was escorted back from the laundry.

She returned to the day room and sat beside Nurse Haggarty on the window seat. "How's it going with the petition?"

"Quite well. Most of the nurses have said they'll sign as long as everyone else does."

"That sounds promising."

"Well …" Nurse Haggarty looked across to the other side of the room. "Sorry, I'm just keeping an eye on Clara."

Clara Brodie was swaying back and forth on the couch, holding the brim of her hat. With its silk and braid frame trimmed with full drapes of navy chiffon and sprays of green foliage, it was almost twice the size of her head. A milliner by trade, Clara had a liking for the dramatic; however, as a slightly built woman under five feet and only seven stone, her exaltations tended more towards the comic.

"She's started muttering to herself. If her hat comes off, I'll need to go to her."

"Of course," Helen said. "I take it her menses haven't returned yet?"

"No. But Dr Lockhart still believes that when they do, her mania will be cured."

"We shall see."

"Indeed. So yes, most of the nurses have said they'll sign the petition as long as everyone else does."

"That's good."

"Not really. There's bound to be someone who won't sign."

"You never know. You might—"

"*You*, for example."

"Me? Why me?"

"Why you? Because you're part of the establishment, doing the Red Book and all that."

Helen folded her arms. "I'm not the only nurse studying for the diploma."

"No, but you're the most conscientious and the one least likely to rock the boat."

"I see." Helen looked down to hide her smile. There were worse things to be called than 'the most conscientious'.

"But if *you* were prepared to make a stand," Nurse Haggarty said, "then they'd know there was something to make a stand about. Then we'd get all their signatures. I'm sure."

"Really?"

"Yes. And you did say you wanted to help."

"Yes, but it doesn't necessarily follow that just because …" Helen looked out the window. Mr Kennedy was sitting on a bench smoking a cigarette while his patients, on their hands and knees, weeded the grass verges along the path. As Mr Allan crawled by, Mr Kennedy stuck out a foot and pushed him over. Then he got up from the bench, flicked his cigarette onto the grass and indicated to Mr Allan to pick it up. The way Mr Kennedy held his head, chin jutting out, sneering, was infuriating.

Helen turned to Nurse Haggarty. "So what do you want me to do?"

"Seriously?"

"Yes."

"Well, if you were to sign it and ... uh-oh." Clara was taking her hat off. "I'll need to go over."

Clara stamped her feet on the floor and tugged her thick black hair. "This food is unfit even for the pigs!" She glared at the plate of scones on the table. "Are you trying to poison me?"

"Don't let the baker hear you say that. He'd be most offended," Nurse Haggarty said.

"Well, it won't work. They tried it in California and it didn't work there. No matter what they tried, they couldn't kill me."

"And very pleased we are about that. Now, how about you and I take a stroll in the garden, Clara?"

"I'm going back there to shoot those damnable people. They maltreated me and persecuted me and locked me away in a padded room. But I showed them. I learned to speak seven languages in ten months. I'm still fluent in four. And I had a score of proposals while I was there."

"That doesn't surprise me one bit." Nurse Haggarty took Clara's hand and gently pulled her up. Then she lifted the hat from the couch and plonked it back on Clara's head. "Come on."

"Did you know my father sent me to California from Santiago, Nurse Haggarty?"

"I did know that, Clara, yes."

"He let them take me to hospital, then he sent me back here. My own father. My brother tried to stop him but he couldn't. My dear mother, may she rest in peace, would've been horrified by his cruelty. They said she had a growth in her bowel but I know that he poisoned her. Just like you're trying to poison me."

"Best leave the scones for the moment, then," Nurse

Haggarty said, expertly manoeuvring her patient from the day room.

She was a good nurse, her expertise coming from years of experience. It was a pity she was so against the development of her profession, for she'd be an ideal candidate for the diploma. In fact, the model nurse described in the Red Book could have been based on Nurse Haggarty. Perhaps, while she was flattering Helen into taking a stand, she might be persuaded of the benefits of further study.

"Nurse Elliot?"

Miss Anderson from the laundry was standing in the doorway with Biddy.

"Where's Miss Purdie?" Helen said.

"Doing a job for Mrs Lockhart up at the house."

"What? She's not long started, hasn't she? I wouldn't have thought Miss Wilson would let her anywhere near Dr and Mrs Lockhart's washing."

"No. Well, anyway." Miss Anderson put her hands on her hips and arched her back. "So not only have I had my own work to do, I've had to supervise Miss Biddy here."

"Which I trust was uneventful?" Helen said, glancing at her patient.

"Yes, thankfully."

"Good. Well, thank you for accompanying her back here, Miss Anderson. Now, Biddy, come with me to the Admissions Room. Dr Forbes wants to see you."

The doctor was at the desk, studying the pages of one of the case books. Biddy sat on the cane chair, while Helen stood to the side.

"I have some news. The local police have contacted the medical superintendent to say that someone's been in touch about you and claims you may be known to him."

Biddy looked momentarily alarmed. "What?"

"Yes, he—"

Then she sniggered. "Is it the Duke of Connaught?"

"No, it's not the Duke of Connaught. It's a gentleman from Ireland who—"

"Ah." Biddy sighed. "The Emerald Isle."

"—believes you may be his wife who disappeared some weeks ago without explanation. The gentleman is a Mr Ryan and he currently resides in Belfast. The woman he's described is of similar look, stature and age to yourself and is called Eileen. Walsh was her maiden name."

"Pff."

Dr Forbes moved her chair closer to Biddy's. "Is that you? Are you Eileen Ryan? Eileen Walsh?"

Biddy stared at her for a few seconds and then giggled.

"This is no laughing matter. Mr Ryan is planning on travelling to Cappelmuir. You might like to know that a husband's allowed to take his wife home unless there's a medical reason for not doing so. So if you are Mrs Ryan, you may be leaving here very soon. If you're not Mrs Ryan, you mustn't inflict a wasted, not to say, unnecessarily distressing, journey on this man. He's sick with worry about what might have happened to his wife. Well?"

Dr Forbes glared at her patient and Biddy looked at the floor.

Helen knelt and took her hand. "Please be truthful with us. Even if you don't reveal your true identity, please be honest about Mr Ryan. You can't have him travel in such circumstances if—"

"I'm not Eileen Ryan." Biddy put her palm to her chest. "I swear."

Helen glanced at Dr Forbes, then stood up. "Do you want me to tell Matron Campbell, Doctor?"

"No, I'll do it, thank you, Nurse Elliot."

"And I'm not Biddy, either. I'm Matilda."

A look passed between Helen and Dr Forbes. The one that indicated a breakthrough.

"Well, welcome to Cappelmuir, Matilda. Do you have a surname?"

"Yes. But I can't say what it is. They can't know I'm here. They'll kill me."

"Who'll kill you? People in Ireland?"

"I can't say anything else. They might be watching. I can't stay in this room any longer."

Dr Forbes shot Helen another look. Of the questioning kind.

"First I've heard of it, Doctor."

"All right. Well, let's leave it there for the moment. We'll talk again soon, Matilda. But there's no one at Cappelmuir who's out to get you. And I can assure you that nobody's watching you except the doctors and nurses. And only because we're trying to help you. Now, I'll take you back to the ward on my way to see Matron Campbell."

Once the door was closed, Helen flopped onto the cane chair. So Biddy was actually Matilda. Assuming she was telling the truth, that was. She'd certainly looked and sounded sincere in the moment. Though it could be she was suffering from a delusion of impending calamity. Helen would consult the Red Book later.

She'd also perhaps suggest to Dr Forbes that it might be best if they were to send poor Mr Ryan Matilda's admission photograph – just to be on the safe side.

ISABELLA

Angus read each typed page before placing it face down in one of two piles. Isabella presumed one of the piles represented the pieces he favoured and the other those he wished to discuss in more detail. It was difficult to tell, though, for the expression on his face – neither approving nor disapproving – had remained the same since he'd started his review of her work. The line of his lower lip hinted at a smile, yet his upper one seemed on the verge of a frown. His left eye, open wide, might suggest pleasant surprise, while the narrowness of his right, contempt. And although every so often he would 'hmm', the tone and pitch of each utterance so differed that it was impossible to construe any meaning.

Tipper spread himself out on the settee. Isabella tickled his flank and he gave a satisfied snort. At least she knew where she stood with him; he didn't judge her, and his expectations extended only to receiving affection and treats. If only dogs ran the country, it would be in a much better state. She gave a little giggle.

Angus looked up. "What?"

"Nothing, dear. I was just thinking about something Tipper did earlier."

He went back to his reading.

"It was so … amusing."

She topped up her cup of tea, then gingerly placed the pot back on the side table. It wouldn't do to disturb Angus a second time. While it was gratifying he was taking her articles seriously, she hadn't anticipated he'd treat them as if they were submissions to one of his medical journals.

By the time he'd finished reading the final piece, Isabella's cup was empty again. She placed it on the saucer and held her breath.

"Well," he said, taking the topmost sheet from the larger pile. "This is an excellent account of the gentlemen's At Home. In fact, all the accounts of the entertainments are excellent. And this section …" He lifted the next page. "… 'Merrie Moments'. This is splendid. Where did you get all these riddles and jokes?"

"Mostly from the patients. And did you notice there's one from your mystery Irish patient?"

"Which one?"

Isabella pointed to a limerick at the bottom of the page.

"Oh, that one. Well, at least it's not indecent or offensive. Which reminds me, we may have made a step forward in identifying her."

"Oh?"

"Yes. Dr Forbes managed to get out of her that she's not the missing Mrs Ryan and that her name is Matilda. Mind you, she also said that people are trying to kill her, so I'm not sure I'd put too much stock in what she says. She might come up with another tale the next time she's threatened with a visit from a relative. However, in any case, I have another lead to pursue."

"Really?"

"Yes." He turned the page over. "Ah, now. This poem – 'The Leghorn That Doesn't Love The Ladies'. I'm not quite sure about it."

"A Mr Smith presented it to me. He was most charming."

"Yes. He tends to be." Angus scanned the verses. "Although I suppose it doesn't contain anything offensive or immoral …"

"Not at all," Isabella said. "And it does apparently reflect an incident where the kitchen maids were chasing a cockerel round the yard."

"Hmm." Angus stroked his chin.

"And you did say you wanted to encourage contributions from the patients, dear."

He peered over the page at Isabella. "I think you'll find I said the *other institution* encouraged such contributions."

"Don't be pernickety, Angus."

He put the piece of paper on the larger pile. "Oh, very well. I suppose at worst it's harmless nonsense."

Isabella smiled. Mr Smith was going to be pleased to see his words in print.

"And this is an excellent portrayal of Mr Gillies. It's caught his very essence. He'll be delighted with it, I'm sure."

"Thank you." Isabella sat forward. "I thought it might be nice if we could include photographs of those we feature."

"We could probably stretch to that," Angus said, continuing to read. "Just make sure the photographs aren't like the ones we take of the patients, otherwise we'll be in trouble with Mrs Gillies."

Isabella laughed with Angus. "Of course."

"Now, let's see. Yes, this is a very good summary of Dr Forbes's study visit to Holland. It shows Cappelmuir in a very positive light. And the proposals for celebrating the King's coronation, good. People will be eager to hear what we have planned. And the news section, everyone will enjoy that." He ran his finger down the page. "So Miss Milne from the kitchen is going to settle in her own property in the state of Montana? I didn't know she had connections across the ocean."

"You're so busy treating the patients, you're only informed

of things that are important to the immediate welfare of the staff."

"Yes, the news section is excellent. However..." He lifted the top sheet from the other pile. "... there are a couple of things I don't think suitable."

"And what are they?"

"Yes. Take this one in the 'Answers to Queries' section. About the chap 'Deceived' who wants his photograph back from the lady because of her inconstancy. And you say – 'We would be pleased to have the opinion of both sexes on the matter.' Really, Isabella?" He frowned.

"Yes. You see, the patient was most upset as he felt the lady had encouraged him to believe she favoured his suit. But he now suspects there's another to whom she's transferred her affections."

"Even if that's true – which of course it may not be – you must understand that 'Deceived' may well be suffering from delusions or a perversion of the emotions which mean he experiences unreasonable jealousy and hate. So even if it is true, it's not the sort of debate I want to promote in the asylum. I'm trying to encourage harmony, not incite a war between the sexes, my dear." Angus laughed and put the page aside. "And this one." He lifted the next sheet and waved it at Isabella. "We can't have this. I really can't imagine why you thought the forthcoming census would be a matter of interest or amusement to our patients."

"Why on earth wouldn't it be?" Isabella said. "It's a national event, like the coronation, and—"

"Hardly."

"—it's surely a good thing to keep patients apprised of current events? Some patients may be discharged soon and they'll need to know that the census is happening and what the requirements are."

"It's not a current event most of them need worry about."

"But all the article is noting is that the census is taking

place. That patients will be counted as part of the asylum's return."

"Yes, but it's—"

"And that everyone in a household must be counted and recorded," she added quickly.

"It's not really an event at all. It's just an exercise. A statistical exercise."

"But one which seeks a deal of information about people." Isabella clenched her jaw. "*Women*. But, as I say, all my piece does is mention the census will be taking place so I don't see why—"

"Isabella, I've said no."

"But it's harmless, Angus. Anodyne."

"In which case, its omission will be no loss."

"But people have a right to know." Isabella threw her hands up. "It's not as if anyone here can refuse to provide information since it's provided on their behalf. And it's not as if they can absent themselves from being counted if they feel it's a crime against liberty or—"

"*A crime against liberty?*" Angus laughed at her. "What on earth are you talking about?"

"I mean … they can't object to the information being recorded about them when—"

"Isabella!"

Tipper jumped down and skulked under the table.

Angus lowered his voice. "I've told you, no."

Isabella perched on the edge of the settee. "But your female patients should at least know what information is being collected about them even if they're not allowed to vote on any proposals that might come as a result of your so-called 'statistical exercise'."

"Isabella! It's not going in and that's that." Angus stood up and ripped the article in half, then half again. "This is my asylum and anything that goes in the magazine must be acceptable to me. That's my final word on the matter." He dropped the torn pieces onto the floor. "Good God, you'll be writing for *The Vote* next." He picked up his briefcase. "And another thing. I don't want that laundry maid here again or doing any more typing."

"What?"

"Yes. In future, I'll instruct the house secretary to provide you with any assistance you might need."

Isabella clenched her fists. "Why?"

"It's not fitting, a laundry maid working with you in this house on this matter."

"Miss Purdie's an excellent typist." She folded her arms. "In fact, she made some very good suggestions about some of the articles."

"She's a laundry maid. She works in the laundry." Angus put the acceptable articles into his briefcase. "Thank you for your hard work. I'll take these to the house secretary so he can make arrangements with the printer. Then I've a meeting with the Inspector of the Poor. He's most concerned about having to report to the Board that he still hasn't identified a person or parish to bill for the costs of our mystery Irish patient. Which is all the more reason to find out who she is. But I've told him to fear not. Inspector Lockhart's on the case." He chuckled. "Anyway … I've a lot of paperwork to do, so you should just carry on with dinner. I'll get something at the asylum."

Isabella remained rigid until the front door clicked shut. Then she bent over and collected the pieces of her census article.

Tipper emerged from under the table and licked her hand. She stroked his head and sighed. It was true – if dogs ran the country, it would be in a much better state.

JESSIE

JESSIE FINISHED off her milk pudding in just a few spoonfuls, then dropped a piece of bread into her apron pocket and got up from the long table. There were still fifteen minutes until the afternoon shift started so there was time to check on Mary. She'd said first thing that she wasn't hungry – but she might be peckish by now. Hopefully too, after a few extra hours' sleep, she'd be recovered from her sore stomach and able to return to work.

In her absence, Jessie had been given additional duties to ensure the regular loads were processed according to the usual timetable. While she'd enjoyed the extra responsibilities, it had certainly been a more tiring morning than usual. If Mary didn't return soon, it'd be Jessie who'd need more time in bed of a morning.

When she entered their room, the curtains were still drawn. She picked up a sour smell as she went to open them. "How are you feeling now?"

Mary put her hands over her eyes when the sunlight streamed through the windows.

"I brought you something to eat. Are you hungry?"

Mary groaned and turned to face the wall.

"What's wrong? Are you feeling worse?" There was a streaky liquid on the floorboards. "What's this? Have you spilled something?"

Jessie stepped over the pool and shook Mary's shoulder. As she sat on the bed, her weight pulled the blanket down, exposing red-stained sheets. "What on earth …?"

Jessie lifted the sheets and put her hand to her mouth. There were large clots of blood on the bedclothes. She rolled Mary over – her white face was smeared with tears and snot.

"What is it? What's wrong?"

Mary writhed on the bed and her nightdress rolled up, revealing brown streaks on her legs.

"What's happened?"

She rocked back and forth. "I didn't know, I didn't know."

"Didn't know what, Mary?"

She burst into tears and threw herself against Jessie, clinging on so tightly that the dampness of her hair seeped through Jessie's clothes. "I swear, I didn't know."

"What didn't you know?"

"I didn't know!" Mary wailed.

Jessie's breathing quickened. "Tell me!"

She glanced around the room in search of an answer. *Jane Eyre* and *The Channings* were on the floor next to the chest of drawers and the top drawer was open a few inches. She went to get up and Mary grabbed her arm.

"No! Don't!" she pleaded.

Jessie shoved her back.

Mary put her head in her hands and wept. "I didn't know."

Jessie went to the chest and pulled the drawer open another few inches – all she could see was some white linen. She opened it further. There was something solid wrapped in one of Mary's petticoats. It was about a foot and half long and a little under a foot wide, weighing about the same as a five-pound sack of laundry. Mary slipped from her bed onto the floor, sobbing.

Jessie unwrapped one end of the package and gasped. She glanced away, then folded the petticoat back over the face of the newborn child. She took a deep breath and unravelled the other end until five tiny yellowish toes appeared. "Oh my Lord."

"I swear I didn't know."

Jessie covered the limb and put the shrouded corpse back into the drawer. "What have you done, Mary?"

Her friend pulled her knees to her chest and hid her face.

"Right. We need to get help," Jessie said, on the verge of panicking.

"No!"

"But we can't just leave it. What are you going to do with it?"

"No! No one can know."

"What happened to it? Did you—?"

"No!" Mary began to slap herself about the head.

Jessie grabbed her fists. "What happened then?"

"I didn't know what was happening. I had these pains and then ..." Mary said through sobs, "... it just came out! I was just standing there. And it came out! Dropped onto the floor. It was already dead. I didn't kill it!" Mary shook her head violently. "I didn't do anything to it. I don't know how it happened."

Jessie let go of Mary and sat down beside her. "You must know how it happened."

"No."

"But there must have been a man who ... you know..."

Mary rubbed her eyes and wiped the tears from her cheeks. "He said it would be all right. That nothing would happen. He said he would make sure of it."

"Who did? Who told you that?"

"It must've been him." Mary wiped her nose with the back of her hand. "I didn't want to. I wouldn't! But I couldn't stop him. He made me."

Jessie felt sick. "Who made you?"

"That's why I left. Even though he always gave me extra time off afterwards. I didn't like it."

"The bank manager? The family where you worked? Did he ... force himself on you? The bank manager?"

When Mary's face crumpled, Jessie cradled her. "Shush, shush." She stroked her friend's hair. "We need to get help."

"No!"

"Yes. For your health. And also to deal with ..." Jessie glanced up at the top drawer. "... the situation."

"You can't. I'll go to prison. They'll say I killed it!"

"What else can you do? You can't keep it in a drawer forever! What are you going to do with it? You can't bury it in the grounds. Someone'll see you. They'll find it. And then what? They won't believe you didn't kill it if you cover it up. We need to get help. How are you going to get rid of it, Mary? How?"

"But I'll lose my job! No one else'll employ me once they know what's happened. I'll end up at the poorhouse." Mary dug her nails into Jessie's arms. "You can't tell anyone. Please! I'm begging you."

"But you're not well. Look at you. You've been bleeding. Who knows what it's done to you? If it was dead when it came out, you might have a disease or something."

"No, I can't, I ..." Mary thought for a moment. "But what if ..." She clapped her hands in excitement. "Yes! I know! I know what we can do! What if we hide it somewhere? We can hide it somewhere and tell Miss Wilson I'm sick and that I need to go away. And then we can take it and get rid of it somewhere! And then once—"

"Where, Mary? Where would you hide it?" Jessie said, throwing her hands in the air in frustration.

"I don't know ... somewhere! And then—"

"Stop, Mary! You're not thinking straight. Where would you take it? Where would you go? No. I'm going to get help."

"But I—"

"We can't deal with this on our own." Jessie stood up. "I'm going for help."

"No! Don't!" Mary lunged at her. "Jessie! Please!" But her arms just swished the air. Then she dropped onto her hands and knees and spewed on the floor.

Jessie skirted around the puddle of sick and helped her up. "Come on, you need to lie down."

She guided her wretched friend back to bed and waited until her eyes closed.

Then Jessie tiptoed from the room and made for the main building as quickly as decorum would allow.

KATHERINE

EVEN BEFORE SHE opened the door, Katherine knew Miss Purdie was telling the truth, for the stench of the secretions and excretions of childbirth was unmistakeable. She paused, then turned to her two companions.

"You stay out here and watch for anyone coming," she said to Miss Purdie, who was pacing on the spot. "And you," she said to Nurse Elliot, who was wringing her hands, "come with me."

Katherine turned the doorknob and side-stepped the patch of sick on the floor as she went over to the bed. A tangy whiff of blood came from the sheets, which were stained different shades of brown, red and pink. There was a shiny mix of birth membranes and expelled placenta on the floor.

Katherine lifted Miss Anderson's wrist to take her pulse. The girl jolted awake.

"It's all right. I'm going to help you."

"No!" Miss Anderson snatched her hand away.

"You're going to be fine but you need to rest. I'm going to prepare something to help you sleep."

Miss Anderson shook her head and pulled the sopping sheet over her.

"Could you sit with her, Nurse Elliot? While I ..." Katherine gave a little nod towards the chest of drawers as she got up.

"Certainly, Dr Forbes."

If the laundry maid's description was anything to go by, the baby was full-term. Katherine stared at the top drawer for a moment, then pulled it open. In the few seconds it took to lift out the swaddled corpse and place it on top of the chest, Katherine judged that the child weighed around five pounds.

She scanned the tiny parcel while considering her options. It was clear what she must do, as a medical professional. She must report a potential crime to the Procurator Fiscal for him to investigate and determine the next steps.

The newborn would undergo a post-mortem to ascertain whether it had been born alive or dead. Its scalp would be cut open to check for fractures, and blood and brain matter in the skull cavity; its lungs would be examined to determine whether they filled the chest, indicating that a breath had been taken; then they, along with the heart, would be cut into pieces and placed in water to see if they floated.

If the child was deemed to have been born alive, consideration would be given as to whether it had been murdered or had died accidentally. Whether murder or culpable homicide was the final charge, Miss Anderson would be tried, with every detail of the hearing printed in the newspapers. Opinions would be offered on matters such as 'wicked recklessness', 'intent to kill', 'negligence', 'omission' and 'diminished responsibility', not to mention the girl's character and background.

The best outcome that could be hoped for was that it could be established the child had been stillborn, in which case Miss Anderson would face a charge of concealment of pregnancy for having failed to seek assistance during the birth. Although a sentence of up to two years was possible, she would probably receive a lesser one – if the court believed she'd been wronged.

"Nurse Elliot, could I have a word with you over here?"

"Yes, Dr Forbes?"

Katherine lowered her voice. "If you want to leave, it's all right. All I ask is that you never speak of this to anyone. That you treat it as if it never happened."

"What do you mean?"

"If what Miss Purdie's reported is true, and I've no reason to doubt what she's said, then what's under this petticoat isn't Miss Anderson's fault. She's been wronged by a man while she's still a child herself. And still not wise in the ways of the world. She's naive and didn't know what his behaviour could lead to. She's suffering not just from childbirth but from shock. I can't imagine the fear she must've felt when the baby started to come. And then to deliver a stillborn must have been terrifying. So I think perhaps she's been through enough."

Katherine glanced at the bed as Miss Anderson turned over.

"You're an excellent nurse and have excellent prospects. I've no doubt you'll pass your diploma and excel in your career. So, I say again, if you want to have nothing to do with this, I'll understand. Just swear that you won't mention anything you've seen to anyone."

"But why would I want to go, Dr Forbes?"

"Because, Nurse Elliot, I intend to treat this unfortunate event as a stillbirth and to remove the body to my laboratory, where it can be collected by the undertaker, who's coming later to get Mrs Buchan, who died this morning. I'm not required to register a stillborn as a death and I'm sure the undertaker will inter it immediately on my say-so. I also consider that Miss Purdie could reasonably be assumed to have been called on by Miss Anderson for assistance in the birth. After all, was it not Miss Purdie who alerted you to the situation? In which case, there's been no attempt at concealment. I'll diagnose Miss Anderson with a gynaecological condition and recommend she have some time away to recuperate."

Nurse Elliot looked at Miss Anderson and tapped her foot on the floor.

"As I said, I'll completely understand if you want nothing to do with this."

"I think, Dr Forbes, that the scenario you've set out is … entirely plausible. Now, what do you need me to do?"

"Thank you." Katherine looked at the tiny package on top of the chest of drawers. "Take it to my laboratory and put it on the workbench in the research room. Wait until I come. If anyone asks, tell them you're delivering some clinical material for me and that I've instructed you to wait with it. On your way out, ask Miss Purdie to come in and clean up while I deal with Miss Anderson. Once she's done that, she must go back to work and tell Miss Wilson I've examined Miss Anderson and instructed that she's to remain in bed and isn't to be disturbed. And that I'll update Miss Wilson on her condition in due course. All right?"

Nurse Elliot nodded earnestly.

Katherine took a deep breath, then lifted the baby from the top of the chest of drawers. "Ready?"

Nurse Elliot held out her arms.

HELEN

IT SAID in the Red Book that understanding of the consequences of actions was impaired in many forms of insanity.

If someone had told Helen in the morning that by the afternoon she'd be conspiring with a physician to conceal the birth and death of an infant, contrary to the law of the land and to the rules of the asylum, she'd have said that that someone was labouring under a delusion. Yet, here she was, heading to the laboratory, clutching the bundle to her chest and lowering her head as yet another person seemed to eye her with suspicion. Was this what it was to be a patient? Like Clara, seeing threats in every corner?

Helen broke into a trot when she reached the short track that led to the black door of Dr Forbes's laboratory. Ignoring the 'Private, No Entry' sign, she tightened her grip on the bundle and pushed the handle with her elbow.

"Hello, Nurse Elliot. What are you doing here?"

"Oh!" She jumped at the sight of Mr Smith facing her in the corridor, then bumped the door shut with her hip. "What a fright you gave me."

"Sorry. I heard someone on the path and thought it was Dr

Forbes coming back. I need to talk to her about the guinea pigs. We have another order."

"Excellent. Yes. Dr Forbes is just coming. She, um …" Helen checked that the bundle was still tightly wrapped in the petticoat. "… asked me to bring over this clinical material for her so that she can … you know, with her experiments and research and the like."

"Indeed I do know. I'm her assistant. Did you know that I breed the guinea pigs for her now?"

"Yes, yes. That's excellent. Very good. Now if you'll—"

"She takes their blood and livers and uses them for her experiments. First she wipes their necks, then she cuts their throats so that the blood drips into a funnel. Then she slices them open, takes their livers and chops them up like mince. She puts the bits in a jar with some alcohol. She lets me shake the jars sometimes. They need shaken twice a day for four days. Then the mixture's run through a strainer. Do you want me to show you the jars, Nurse Elliot?" Mr Smith looked into the room to his left.

"No. Thank you. Perhaps another time. Is that the research room in there?"

"Yes. That's where it all happens."

"Right then. I'll just go and put this … Dr Forbes's *clinical material* on the workbench."

"It looks heavy. Can I carry it for you, Nurse Elliot?" Mr Smith reached out to take the package.

Helen lurched back. "No!" She attempted a smile. "No. It's quite all right, thank you, Mr Smith. Dr Forbes gave me strict instructions. Thank you for your offer of assistance, though. Now, perhaps you should go back to your guinea pigs and make sure all's well with them."

Mr Smith laughed. "You're quite right, Nurse Elliot. If I leave the little blighters alone too long, they might get up to all sorts."

"So I believe, yes. See you at teatime, Mr Smith."

Once he'd disappeared down the corridor, Helen went into the research room. She put the bundle at one end of the workbench, then sat on the stool at the other.

She rolled her head to release the tension in her neck and breathed deeply. The day's events had been truly astonishing from the moment Miss Purdie had appeared unexpectedly in the day room with an anxious look on her face.

Helen immediately thought there must be a problem with Matilda; that perhaps her recent progress had been derailed by the business with Mr Ryan. Pray to God she hadn't decided to brandish her dolly at Miss Wilson.

Miss Purdie spoke so quickly and incoherently that Helen thought the girl must be having some kind of manic episode. Or perhaps had ingested a cleaning substance that had caused hallucinations and delirium. How else to account for her strange disjointed story about a dead baby in a drawer and a bank manager? Gradually, however, as Miss Purdie repeated the story, the pieces came together into an awful tale.

Just as the laundry maid had looked to her superior for guidance, so had Helen. It was only right. She was obliged by her terms of employment to report anything improper to the physicians or other office-bearers.

She couldn't approach Dr Lockhart directly, of course, and she was in enough trouble with Matron Campbell over the dining room incident as it was. As for the dour Dr Dorsie, in all the time she'd been at Cappelmuir she'd hardly shared two words with him. So Dr Forbes it had to be, who in any case was the best choice. She'd been to university, so knew a bit of the world, and was an excellent physician. Sympathetic to boot. It would be Dr Forbes's responsibility to deal with the matter and Helen's to obey her orders. The dead baby wrapped in a petticoat a few feet away was testament to how the system worked.

Helen went over to the bundle. That the baby was dead when she and Dr Forbes had arrived at the scene was indisputable; the cause of death, however, was not. It wouldn't be the first time a panicked girl had killed her newborn in terror and desperation. Miss Anderson might even have convinced herself that the child would be better off dead than living a stigmatised life which would likely include a journey to the orphanage then the poorhouse. Helen had seen many babies during her time in both places. Sickly and scrawny, more of them perished than lived.

She took a deep breath. Then she tugged the petticoat so that it fell open.

The little boy had a shock of downy ginger hair. The skin on his face was peeling and blue veins showed underneath. His eyelids were puffy and his nose flattened. There were greasy white smears all over his body but it was perfectly formed, with no injuries or bruises. She touched the baby's arm with her pinkie. It was cool as marble.

As she lifted the petticoat to cover the corpse again, a floorboard creaked behind her. Matilda was in the doorway, staring at her, open-mouthed.

"What are you doing here?" Helen said sharply. "You're meant to be …"

Matilda folded her arms.

"This isn't what you think."

Matilda smiled. "It seems we both have secrets, Nurse Elliot."

ISABELLA

ONCE THE CARRIAGE taking Angus to town had passed by the house, Isabella stepped away from the front-room window and went over to the little display table. On one side of the aspidistra was her picture postcard album; on the other, the Lockhart family Bible Angus had inherited on the death of his mother a year before his marriage. As an only child, he had also inherited the entire Lockhart estate, including the family home in the city, which was rented out while he occupied the position of medical superintendent at Cappelmuir.

With no parents or other living relatives, there'd been no one to disapprove of his match with Isabella. She often wondered if his parents would have been content with him taking her as his wife. Would they simply have been satisfied he'd finally married? Or would they have tried to persuade him to hold out for someone more on his level?

Isabella's parents couldn't have been more delighted that their daughter was marrying up. And she had been flattered by the quiet attention of a wealthier, older man; a doctor, no less, whose compassion towards his patients and his progressive thinking about asylums so impressed her. And remained impressive. Under his charge, ward doors were no longer locked and the use of restraint was forbidden. The small group of matrons had status and power, and his introduction of female nurses to the male wards had ended up being a revelation, despite being frowned upon at first. Indeed, the initiatives her husband had pioneered were increasingly being applied in other asylums. He was becoming quite the leader in his professional sphere. In the domestic one, however, his attitudes increasingly seemed those of a past generation.

When Isabella had considered standing for the School Board, he'd suggested she wait a few years and concentrate instead on managing the household and preparing to have a family. And while he'd never told her that he disapproved of her association with the suffragists, he certainly hadn't encouraged it.

She opened the album, which memorialised summer holidays and day excursions she'd enjoyed over the years with family and friends. There were the postcards of steamers and the destinations they'd taken her to: Arran, Dunoon, Rothesay, Ayr. There was the photograph of her and Effie the day they'd taken the train to Edinburgh. They'd visited the Scott Monument, then had a fine lunch, followed by a walk through Princes Street Gardens. And when the rain had started, they'd sheltered in a hotel where they were royally entertained by a fiddler. It had been a lovely day, the last trip away Isabella had had since her marriage.

She closed the album and glanced out the window again. Dr Forbes was coming up the path. Why was she visiting now? She must know Angus had just left to go to a meeting of the Board.

Isabella went to the front door and opened it before Dr Forbes had a chance to chap the knocker.

"Dr Forbes, good day. Dr Lockhart isn't here. He's just left for—"

"Yes, I know. It's actually you I've come to see, Mrs Lockhart."

"Me?"

"Yes. I wonder if I might ask for some advice?"

Why would a doctor be seeking the advice of a medical superintendent's wife? "*My* advice?"

"Yes. Well, assistance really."

Even one who'd once been a teacher. "Would you like to come in?"

Dr Forbes peered into the hall, where Mrs Drummond was skulking. "It may be better if we remain here."

"Certainly." Isabella closed the door and stepped onto the path. "What can I help you with?"

"There's a member of staff in the laundry, a young girl, who is … unwell … and who would benefit from some time away from the asylum to … aid her recovery."

"Not Miss Purdie, I trust?"

Dr Forbes's eyes darted back and forth. "You know Miss Purdie?"

"Yes. She was a pupil at Park School when I was there. I had reason to engage her recently in some work on the asylum magazine. Although she'll have no further role in that, I'm afraid. Anyway, yes, I know her. She's a bright girl."

"I'm sure she is. Although I really only know her by sight. But from all accounts she's a good worker, who's also empathetic with the patients. But no, it's not Miss Purdie. It's another girl, who unfortunately has no family in the immediate area. So as such, I wondered whether … you mentioned to me, Mrs Lockhart, that you're an acquaintance of Mrs Huntly-Sykes."

"Yes. Did you decide to consult her son on your legal matter?"

"I did, as it happens. And I must thank you for the recommendation. I've engaged him to represent me. At first I wasn't sure of his experience, but he had some most interesting insights which persuaded me of his expertise."

"Good. So I trust matters on that front are progressing satisfactorily now?"

"That I've heard nothing from Mr Huntly-Sykes since our meeting, I take as a positive sign. He believes the case against me to be egregious and expects that it won't see the light of day in court."

"That's encouraging. Let's hope he's right."

"Yes. And as it happens, I had occasion to meet his mother in the tea room across from her son's place of business."

"You went to the Suffrage Centre?" Isabella hadn't taken Dr Forbes for a supporter of the cause.

"Yes, I had some time before my train and I had a bit of a thirst and, well, the tea room is most conveniently situated. As it happened, Mrs Huntly-Sykes was in attendance and we happened to get chatting and she happened to mention that she and her husband have established a number of initiatives—"

"With ambitious plans for more."

"So I believe. I wondered, therefore, whether you might ask Mrs Huntly-Sykes if she knows of an establishment or household which might offer the opportunity for this girl to … shall we say, *recuperate* for a while. I'd speak to her myself, only I really can't ask for any more time off and I'd rather not put the details in a letter."

"But if the girl's unwell," Isabella said, "wouldn't she be better remaining here? This is a hospital, after all."

"Her situation, Mrs Lockhart is – how shall I put it? – somewhat delicate."

"Ah." Isabella looked through the glass panel of the front door to ensure Mrs Drummond wasn't there. "And I'm taking it, since you're visiting me and not my husband, that the medical superintendent has no knowledge of the girl's … condition … and that you intend that he won't have?"

Dr Forbes tugged the collar of her blouse, then looked Isabella in the eye. "Please believe me, Mrs Lockhart. I have no intention of deceiving the medical superintendent or of misleading him about any matter. However, there are some things that, for the good of the asylum, he needn't know about. I know I'm asking a lot of you, and obviously I'll understand if you feel uncomfortable with my request, or indeed with what I've already told you. In which case I'll leave and only ask that you consider my visit didn't take place. However, if you're able to offer some information about a place of respite for the girl, or enquire of Mrs Huntly-Sykes, then I assure you I'll ask nothing more of you."

JESSIE

JESSIE HELD Mary's arm tightly as they waited on the platform. Dr Forbes had said to make sure and put her on the train and wait until it left the station. Someone would meet Mary at the other end and would 'take matters from there'. Jessie didn't know what *taking matters from there* meant but it had to be better for her friend than lying in bed weeping.

Dr Forbes had also said she'd 'sort out' Jessie's absence from the laundry. And so, after lunch, Jessie didn't return to work, but instead travelled to town. Dr Forbes had paid for the tickets and had even given Jessie a few extra pennies in case she wanted to get a drink in a tea room once Mary was dispatched to the city.

Jessie wasn't going to waste the pennies on a drink, though; she was going to put them in her cloth bag. She kept it under her mattress now rather than tucking it under her clothes in the chest of drawers. The less she had to open a drawer, the better.

She didn't think Dr Forbes would mind if she saved the money rather than spend it on tea, because when she'd cleaned the room while Dr Forbes tended to Mary, she'd said what a good friend Jessie was and how lucky Mary was to have her.

And once Jessie had finished washing away all the bodily fluids and scrubbing the stains off the floorboards, Dr Forbes had thanked her very much and told her to go back to work and tell Miss Wilson that Mary was unwell and had to stay in bed.

"If she asks, tell her it's doctor's orders."

And Jessie was just fine with that. She didn't want to speak of the matter ever again. She just wanted to do her job and keep her head down. She would see nothing, hear nothing and say nothing. Just like Duncan.

The train for the city approached and Jessie guided Mary nearer the edge of the platform. Her friend shuffled a few paces, head down, shoulders slumped.

A third-class carriage came to a halt directly in front of them.

"Right, come on. It's here. On you get." Jessie manoeuvred Mary up the steps, then sat her in the compartment. "When you get there, a lady will meet you. At the newspaper kiosk. Remember?"

Mary leaned against the window and stared into the distance.

"Well anyway, there aren't any other stops so even if you don't get up, the conductor will put you off."

There was a whistle from the platform.

"I have to get off now. All right?"

Mary didn't respond.

"But I'll see you soon." Jessie tried to sound chirpy. "It'll be no time till you're back at work, right as rain."

She made it back onto the platform just before the guard closed the carriage door. Then she watched the train pull off along the curved track away from town.

There was a little wooden bridge to the opposite platform where her return train would soon be arriving. Jessie stopped halfway across it to survey the townscape. The spire of Logie Kirk was poking above the shop roofs of Bell Street and, beyond that, the top of North Mill's red-brick chimney was visible.

She scanned to the left, pausing to stare at the cemetery. The high slopes lined with tall statues and large headstones were where wealthy merchants had their family vaults; the grassy low ground was where everyone else was buried, some of the graves marked only by stones. Jessie's mother was in the low ground, against the boundary wall in the last plot on the right. Her grave was marked by a circle of white pebbles and a clutch of brown gravel. No one had ever said as much, but Jessie knew the gravel had been placed there in memory of her sister, who, like Mary's child, had been born dead.

Perhaps her parents and brothers had never mentioned it because they thought Jessie was too young to remember the night her mother had woken the house with her screams. Or maybe they imagined she'd slept through the anguish. But Jessie was awake the whole time.

She remembered the strain on her father's face when he left the house at first light carrying a small bundle wrapped in a sack. She remembered that on his return he prepared breakfast, the first time she'd ever seen him do so. She remembered her mother resting in bed for the day. And most of all, she remembered nothing being said and nothing being explained.

She hadn't visited the grave in ages as it upset her father. The thought of it now, probably overgrown and the pebbles perhaps washed away by the rain, made her well up.

It wasn't right. Although her family might not be able to afford a headstone, that didn't mean the plot shouldn't be kept tidy. She shouldn't have neglected it for fear of upsetting her father. But it didn't matter what he thought anymore.

She looked across to the platform. She ought to continue over the bridge and wait for the train back to Cappelmuir; it'd be arriving any minute.

She leaned on the railings and swayed to and fro. She could always say that the city train had been delayed, causing her to miss the intended return connection. Surely Dr Forbes wouldn't mind and would able to 'sort it out' again with Miss Wilson?

Jessie set out on the short walk to the cemetery.

~

At the entrance gates she looked through the bars towards its furthest corner. Someone was kneeling on the grass at her mother's grave. She peered at the figure. A man. In light trousers and a dark jacket. Wearing a cap.

Jessie pushed the squeaky gate gingerly with her shoulder and squeezed through when the gap allowed. Then she tiptoed along the path that ran parallel to the boundary wall.

The closer she got to him, the greater her disbelief that it could be her father. Yet the man's build and gait resembled his. But how could it be her father? He'd be at work. And if it wasn't him … her brothers should be at work too. In any case, the man was too slight to be either of those two hulks.

She stopped at the end of the path and lurked behind a grey headstone. The man started to mutter. Jessie backed against the granite. Though she couldn't make out the words, she recognised his voice. There was no doubt they were the ramblings of her father.

What was he doing at the grave if it upset him? He didn't appear to be drunk – or, if he was, he wasn't displaying his usual recalcitrance. Jessie peeked around the stone. What should she do? If she retraced her steps, he might notice her; if she remained where she was, he might meet her on his way out. She squatted down, then looked around the headstone again. He had his back to her now. She took cover again, jiggling on the spot, until footsteps on the gravel made her dash back the way she'd come.

She flung open the gates and glanced over her shoulder. He was trotting after her.

He called her name, a hand in the air. Then he started to cough.

She set off again, faster. With his rheumatics and his bad chest, he wouldn't be able to keep up with her, let alone catch her.

Even as his calls became more distant, she carried on running. All the way back to the station. Then all the way from the Cappelmuir siding until she reached the safety of the asylum.

KATHERINE

KATHERINE TUCKED the letter from Charles Huntly-Sykes back into her jacket pocket. His update on her situation was benign, if unchanged: *discussions are continuing with the plaintiff's representatives and it is hoped that court proceedings can be avoided.* Would her solicitor be so confident if he knew of her conduct over Miss Anderson?

Katherine snorted. She wasn't being sued over *that* conduct. No, she was continuing to perform her duties with impunity, with everything and everyone seeming just as they normally did. Except Nurse Elliot, who, whenever their paths crossed, glanced uneasily at Katherine. A secret often made people anxious around others who were in on it.

The laundry maid, Miss Purdie, though, whether through youth, ignorance or survival instinct, was behaving impeccably, having carried out all Katherine's instructions in exemplary fashion. As for Mrs Lockhart, she must have remained silent on the matter (as far as she understood it), since the medical superintendent was presenting as he usually did. Katherine hadn't been summoned or consulted by him since the incident – until now.

As she waited for him in the Admissions Room, she opened

the thick book of case notes and flicked through it until she came to the pages for Mr Smith, the subject of the imminent clinical review. The first two entries were in her and Dr Dorsie's hands: *very depressed, threatens to commit suicide; depressed, speaks in the most hopeless fashion about his health.* The last four entries, one for each of the previous months, were in her colleague's hand alone: *much improved, works with outside squad; works in laboratory, dancing and says he feels brighter; brighter, cheerful, eager to work; appears bright and in good spirits.*

On paper there was no reason to query Mr Smith's recovery or to delay his discharge. And yet.

Katherine tapped her top lip with her index finger.

If it was asylum life that had tempered Mr Smith's insanity, would a life outside see its return?

Dr Lockhart breezed in, holding a sheet of cream paper. "Good day, Dr Forbes. I'm sorry to keep you waiting but I had to deal with a matter regarding Mr Douglas."

"Ah, yes. Has he managed not to tear his latest set of clothes to shreds?" Katherine said, recalling the patient's behaviour on his recent admission.

"Ha!" Dr Lockhart pulled over the cane chair and sat beside her at the desk. "He has. But it appears that things in respect of our Mr Douglas aren't as they seem. This morning I received this." He waved the letter at her. "It's from the Inspector of the Poor of his home parish. The Inspector has accepted liability for him, which means we'll receive payment. However, the Inspector has also stated that our so-called 'patient' has been in the hands of the police three times in the last twelve months and each time seems to have feigned insanity, tearing his clothes and threatening suicide."

"Well, well."

"The Inspector says: *He is a most troublesome pauper and always pretends to be insane when he gets into trouble – at all events, that is the conclusion one must come to as he always seems to recover so soon after being admitted.*"

"He certainly gave a very good impression of insanity."

"Indeed. The Inspector also asks that, if we intend to detain Mr Douglas long, he should be transferred to his own district asylum rather than have his parish continue to pay for maintenance here."

"Their financial gain will be our loss."

"Quite so. If we could only find out the mystery Irish woman's home parish, we could sort that one out too. But I've drawn a blank with the latest lead. Though I'm told there may be another line of enquiry." Dr Lockhart flicked through the case notes and tucked the letter in at Mr Douglas's entry. "But it's not Mr Douglas we're here to discuss, it's Mr Smith." He turned back to the entry he'd marked with his finger. "But before we get on to him … how is *your* case coming along?"

"My case?" Katherine said warily.

"Yes. I trust the recommended solicitor's doing a good job of making it go away?"

"Oh, *that* case." Katherine hesitated. While the recommended solicitor was doing a good job, he wasn't Dr Lockhart's recommended solicitor. "Yes, well, he, um …" Although he had been recommended by another Lockhart. "Yes, absolutely, sir! In fact, I've just heard from him that discussions are continuing and that he still hopes to avoid court proceedings."

"That's excellent news. Didn't I tell you? That's what mostly happens." He gave a little clap of self-satisfaction. "Yes. You see, Dr Forbes, most of these fellows are just opportunists who're in it for the money. And when the reality of the thing is pointed out to them, of how much a court defeat will cost them, they usually withdraw … if not with their tails between their legs, then at least quietly. Of course that's because most of them are rational people. Unlike my Mr Noakes, who is neither rational nor quiet, and instead is someone who will never accept the lawful verdict." Dr Lockhart chortled. "Actually, I received his annual diatribe just the other day. I'll say this for him, he's persistent. And consistent. And he's got a long memory."

"His 'annual diatribe', sir?"

"Oh, yes. He's written me the same letter every year since the trial, repeating his original allegations and saying he'll see me back in court."

"Goodness me." The prospect of having a complaint hanging over her like that for years, even if nothing came of it formally, struck Katherine at best as unappealing. "And do you reply to him, sir?"

"Not anymore." Dr Lockhart took his pipe out of his jacket pocket and lit it. "I did the first few times he wrote. You know, trying to reason with him and persuade him that it was over and that he should put it behind him." He sucked on his pipe and blew the smoke in the air. "But then the lawyers – well, you know what they're like – said they should send a letter on my behalf hinting at libel and defamation and such like. But as I explained to them, it was a waste of their time and my money because Noakes will never see reason. So now when his annual epistle arrives, I read it then throw it in the fire."

Dr Lockhart flicked his wrist with a flourish. Katherine didn't understand how he could be so blasé.

He put his pipe down next to the case book. "Now … to our Mr Smith."

"Yes." Katherine grimaced as the smoke infiltrated her nostrils. "Of course."

"Dr Dorsie's of the opinion that he's now recovered, so he's recommending discharge. I've reviewed his case …" Dr Lockhart tapped the page. "… and concur. However, given you're very familiar with him through his work in the laboratory, I'd also like to hear your thoughts."

"Thank you, sir." Katherine studied the photograph of Mr Smith pasted on the page. He no longer had the gaunt and haunted look he did on admission. "Well, he's certainly much better than when we first saw him."

"Yes."

"And in reviewing my original comments ..." She pointed to her entry. "... there's no doubt that he's much improved. Recovered, even."

Dr Lockhart folded his arms. "Precisely."

"Although ... he's still prone on occasion to grandiosity and—"

"If that alone were a sign of insanity, Cappelmuir would be bursting at the seams with members of the parish council. Ha!"

"Yes. Very good, sir! But also—"

"Yes?"

"It's just that ..." Katherine got up and went to the other side of the desk. "He undoubtedly settled very well into a routine here and has been very hard-working. I've certainly appreciated his assistance in the laboratory. And of course, his involvement in the social life of the asylum has been most valuable. I do wonder, though, whether ..."

Dr Lockhart lifted his pipe to his mouth then put it back down without smoking it. "Yes?"

"... whether Mr Smith will be able to, as it were, withstand the strains of the outside world."

"We're an asylum for the certifiably insane." The medical superintendent stood up. "My view, like Dr Dorsie's, is that Mr Smith is no longer certifiable. Do you dispute our diagnosis?"

"Well, I ... no, but ..." Katherine scanned the notes again.

"While you're considering your response, Dr Forbes, let me inform you of another matter. An item of good news which should interest you. The American Psychiatric Association wish to host a symposium in the city during their visit. The topics to be discussed will be varied but they've invited me to contribute a lecture on the employment of nurses in male wards. I thought given your experience in Meerenburg ..."

Katherine looked up from the case book. "Yes?"

"... you might wish to accompany me."

"Accompany you?"

"Yes. I'll present, of course. But there may be some detailed points to which you might be able to add some ... artistic verisimilitude. The event's to be widely advertised and I don't doubt there will be a great many esteemed practitioners in attendance. It'll be very good for the reputation of Cappelmuir. I'm sure if you were to accompany me, your attendance wouldn't go unnoticed."

"I see." Apparently having a lawsuit hanging over one's head didn't present a bar to possible career progression.

"So, Dr Forbes?" Dr Lockhart hitched up the sleeves of his jacket. The engraved gold cufflinks on his white shirt glinted. "Are we in agreement that arrangements for Mr Smith's discharge should proceed?"

Katherine momentarily drummed her fingers on the desk. Then she closed the case notes. "Yes sir, we are."

HELEN

When Nurse Haggarty suggested hiring bicycles from the Asylum Ladies' Club for a trip to town, Helen was reluctant. What if her state of mind caused her to swerve into a ditch or steer into a hole?

Every night she was falling into broken sleep seeing the soft hair of Miss Anderson's dead baby. In the early hours she was waking to visions of the child being buried alive. And in the morning she was jolted into consciousness at her colleagues' footsteps in the corridor, imagining them to belong to Dr Lockhart and the local police sergeant, who must finally be coming to apprehend her.

The days were little better. Every time she turned round, Matilda or Mr Smith seemed to be there, smiling as if to say *we know what you did*. And although Matilda hadn't said anything yet, it couldn't be long before she blurted out something to somebody about what she'd seen in the laboratory.

Dr Forbes said not to worry. That, if it came to it, anything Matilda might say could be dismissed as the ravings of a mad woman. Which was all very well. But what about Miss Purdie? What if she decided to expose them? Or what if, distraught and guilty, she felt compelled to confess her own part in the exercise?

If there'd been a patient in the same frame of mind as Helen, she would've known what to diagnose, for she'd scoured her Red Book for the explanation: *Imperative ideas: morbid suggestions and ideas imperiously demanding notice, the patient being painfully conscious of their domination over his wish and will.* And she might have been reassured about the patient's prognosis, having learned that *there was no intellectual disturbance in most cases beyond the unbidden thought or idea which haunts the mind and which cannot be dispelled. The great majority of persons suffering from imperative ideas and obsessions are not insane, as they are fully capable of looking after themselves.*

Applying the same objective assessment to her own predicament, however, was quite a different matter.

So, unable to think of a legitimate reason to decline Nurse Haggarty's proposal, Helen found herself sitting on a black Raleigh bicycle, concentrating fiercely on the click of its chain every time she pushed down on the pedals.

Long after she'd lost count of the rotations, they finally arrived at the park and dismounted at the bandstand.

"This is us." Nurse Haggarty leaned her bicycle against the railings and looked at her watch. "Nurse Millar's cousin should be here any moment."

Helen put her bicycle next to Nurse Haggarty's and went up the steps to be out of the light drizzle that had just started.

There were lots of people out and about enjoying a Sunday afternoon stroll: parents holding their young children's hands to keep them from falling off the low walls that bordered the grassed areas; elderly couples sauntering slowly along the winding pathways; youngsters playing tig on the lawns. Happy pictures of family life. Experiences Helen had never had.

There'd been a time when she thought she might. When she

thought her mother had found a nice man, a good man, to care for them. But he turned out to be worse than the father Helen had never known. So she and her mother had to flee again.

A girl of around seven fell down on the lawn. Her father sprinted straight over and lifted her into his arms. Consoling her, he gently stroked her hair. Helen sighed, then pinched her cheek firmly in punishment for her unworthy resentment of the apparent good fortune of others.

Nurse Haggarty joined her on the bandstand and pointed at a dark-haired young woman approaching on foot. "This looks like her."

The young woman raised the brim of her hat to glance at them.

"Nurse Millar?"

She came up the steps. "Yes."

"I'm Nurse Haggarty and this is Nurse Elliot."

"Is my cousin not with you?"

"No, she had another matter to deal with, I believe," Nurse Haggarty said. "Thank you for agreeing to meet us. We've been following events at Mount Hope very keenly and any advice you might be able to offer would be most welcome."

Nurse Millar tutted. "She'll be with that Mr Kennedy again, no doubt." Helen and Nurse Haggarty looked at each other. "I've told her no good'll come of it. One of our attendants served with him in Africa. Don't believe anything you hear about him being a hero. A bully and a coward more like."

Helen could have told her that. "Oh?"

"Yes. And if she thinks she's going to end up married to him and living in one of the cottages at Cappelmuir, she's got another think coming. The sooner she sees he's no good, the better."

"Is that right?"

"Not that she listens to anything I've got to say."

"Well, she listened to what you had to say about the

petition at Mount Hope," Nurse Haggarty said. "In fact, were it not for her, we wouldn't be doing what we're doing now."

"And what are you doing? Do you have a petition?"

"We have. Signed by all the nurses. Nurse Elliot was instrumental in persuading everyone to sign up."

"Oh, I wouldn't say that." Helen sighed. The moment to find out more about Mr Kennedy had passed.

"And what about the attendants?" Nurse Millar said. "Do they support the action?"

"The petition's just on behalf of the nurses."

"I thought as much. The men are hardly going to support it when they're trying to stop us working in their wards. The Asylum Workers' Union has said that having nurses in male wards is a conspiracy to secure cheap labour. The attendants at Mount Hope would work a hundred hours a week if it meant they could get rid of us from their wards. Anyway … what are you going to do with your petition?"

"We're considering submitting it very soon," Nurse Haggarty said.

"Well, you might want to think long and hard about it. Some of our senior nurses have been dismissed on the back of ours."

Helen gave a start. "What?"

"Yes. Our medical superintendent decided they were the ringleaders. They weren't, although they did sign the petition. They told him that, but he said it didn't matter either way because as seniors it was their place to put down any insubordination."

Nurse Haggarty snorted. "That's outrageous."

"He told them if they apologised, and came out against the petition, he would keep them on. They refused and he dismissed them. With no consideration of where they'd go or what they'd do. The ringleaders are still there, of course. And now they're saying that the rest of the nurses should resign in protest."

"Resign?" Helen's breath caught the back of her throat. She didn't like the way things were heading.

"They reckon it might force the medical superintendent to reconsider. He won't be able to run the place without us," Nurse Millar said.

"And if he won't reconsider?"

"Then at least we've resigned and not been dismissed. We'll be able to get a job at another asylum that way. Unlike the seniors. But we're hoping it won't come to that. The ringleaders have been in touch with the Trades' Council to see if they can get the seniors reinstated. It's going to send a deputation to the next meeting of the parish council to put their case. They're going to say the medical superintendent's a tyrant." Nurse Millar threw her head back and laughed. "And that it's scandalous nurses are being asked to work all these hours when the Inspector of the Poor only works thirty-six himself!"

"Good for them," Nurse Haggarty said, with an admiration Helen didn't share.

She couldn't afford to leave her job, whether through dismissal or resignation. Moreover, she didn't *want* to leave her job, even if she did have to work eighty-four, or ninety-one, hours a week. She wanted to get her diploma to secure a better job so she'd never end up back at the poorhouse. So that she'd never have to rely on any man to look after her. So that she wouldn't be trapped between choosing a life of poverty or a life of shame.

Nurse Haggarty and Nurse Millar could never have known hardship or indignity if they were willing to be so reckless with their livelihoods. Helen should never have signed the petition. She'd let her guard down and now things were getting out of control.

"It's the principle," Nurse Millar said. "Isn't it?"

Helen went over to the railing and stared at the people in the park.

Cappelmuir was the nearest thing to family she had and she wasn't going to risk losing it.

Principles were all well and good – until you had nothing to eat and nowhere to live.

ISABELLA

WHEN ISABELLA and Effie entered the meeting room at the Suffrage Centre, Mrs Huntly-Sykes got up from her seat at the head of the long table.

"Mrs Lockhart! Come! Sit by me."

Isabella glanced at Effie and gave the tiniest staccato shake of her head. She had no desire to be seated near the windows, even if they were a floor above street level.

She took a deep breath. Maybe it was a mistake coming to the meeting, after all. Maybe Angus was right. Maybe it was too soon for her to be resuming her former activities.

"Thank you but we'll be fine just here."

She pulled out a chair at the opposite end of the table from Mrs Huntly-Sykes and nodded to Effie to take the place next to her.

"It's lovely to see you back anyway, dear!" Mrs Huntly-Sykes chirped, before retaking her seat and shuffling through her paperwork.

Isabella made her best effort to smile back, then took her gloves off finger by finger while she tried to settle herself.

Effie nudged her. "Are you all right?"

"I'm fine. It's just if we sat up there, everyone would be

looking at us." Isabella laid her gloves across her lap. "And they'd notice if we nodded off while she's speaking."

"Ha!"

Isabella untied the ribbon of her beaded floral trinket bag to prevent Effie noticing that she was on the verge of tears. She rummaged around in it for nothing in particular, then sniffed, faked a cough and pulled out a handkerchief.

"Dear me. There's something tickling my throat." She coughed into the handkerchief, then covered her face with it. "Gosh, it's making my eyes water." She sniffed again. "Ah, that's better."

Effie chuckled. "It'll be all that dirt and grime in the street. Robert's mother was suffering with it last week. She was going to complain to the Corporation. You're obviously used to more refined air now. Cappelmuir's made you feeble."

Isabella pretended to chortle. "That must be it. Yes." She dropped the handkerchief back into her bag, then gave a jolt when the gavel was banged on the table.

"Ladies, ladies. I call the meeting to order." Silence gradually descended and Mrs Huntly-Sykes continued. "Thank you all for coming. I don't intend to say much, other than remind you of some matters concerning the League's plans to avoid the census. There's another splendid article this week in our magazine by Mr Housman. It makes some very useful points about the bureaucratic detail of the Act – or, as he so eloquently puts it, the 'red tape stewing in its own juice' – which will help us make sure that any action we take as passive resisters won't fall foul of the legislation. And, more importantly, won't result in any of us receiving a five-pound fine."

There were some murmurs around the table.

"In particular, for those of you who may be absenting yourselves from your homes, make sure you leave in good time on the Sunday and don't return until after noon on the Monday. Otherwise a census return is required. And if you fail to give it, you may be fined. Please consider holding house parties or simply putting up those coming from other areas. We also need volunteers at the Centre throughout the night, when we intend to provide entertainment and games for those present. Finally, if anyone can lend a hand with the correspondence ..." Mrs Huntly-Sykes lifted her pile of papers. "... I will be forever in your debt."

"You could do that," Effie whispered to Isabella.

"I've no doubt that between us we can make a significant contribution to our cause. Thank you all again. And remember ladies, raise your eyes to a wider morrow. And 'No...'?" Mrs Huntly-Sykes raised her hands as if conducting a choir.

"No Votes for Women – No Census!" came the chant in response.

"Precisely!" she said, applauding the room. "And here's to more red tape stewing in its own juice!"

As the ladies dispersed into small discussion groups, Isabella winced at the screeches of the chairs scraping across the wooden floor.

"So what d'you think?" Effie said. "I know it's difficult for you with Angus, but you could help with the correspondence and such like."

Isabella pouted. "It's not quite as daring as what you'll be doing."

"No, but every little helps."

"Or as daring as what everyone else here will be doing." She stared up at the high windows. "Although ..."

"Although what?"

"Well." Isabella turned her chair to face Effie's. "It may not happen, but there's a chance Angus might decide to stay in the city during the census. There's a delegation visiting from the American Psychiatric Association. After they've spent a few days at Cappelmuir, they're hosting a symposium and a dinner. They've asked Angus to attend and then accompany them to another asylum whose methods they're also studying. He's been considering lodging in the city to avoid travelling back and forth. The asylum horses aren't really fit for that many journeys over such a short period. And while the Board's agreed we can get a motor car, Angus isn't—"

"A *motor car?*"

"Yes. Angus isn't sure when he'll take delivery of it. So I've—"

"How exciting! Think where you might go!

"—been wondering whether … well …" Isabella glanced around at the other ladies.

"What?" Effie's eyes opened wide. "You're not going to disobey Angus and put up evaders?"

"Technically it wouldn't be disobeying him if he hasn't explicitly forbidden it. And he can't forbid it if he doesn't know about it. And he won't know about it if I don't tell him about it."

"You mean you'd keep it a secret from him?"

"Oh, I don't know." Isabella shrugged. "Perhaps." She stood up. "Anyway, the opportunity might not present itself. He might decide just to make the journey each day. You know what he's like about being away from Cappelmuir. I'm probably just daydreaming. In any case, even if he did stay away, it'd be impossible to have people in the house. Someone would notice. In fact, no end of people would notice. I'd need to get rid of Mrs Drummond somehow …"

Effie giggled. "You might make it permanent."

"I could probably bribe Mr and Mrs Gillies and—"

"Oh, he'd be all right. He thinks you're the bee's knees!"

"True."

"And if you threw in a bottle of sherry for Mrs Gillies, well, that would be her taken care of. Or," Effie said, wagging a finger in the air, "you could bypass the gates entirely and have your visitors come through the fields and climb over the wall. Now that would be daring!"

"Don't be ridiculous." Isabella laughed. "No. It's impossible, no matter the circumstances."

"Nothing's impossible, my dear, if you set your mind to it."

Isabella turned towards the voice. "Mrs Huntly-Sykes. How are you?"

"More to the point, my dear, how are *you*?"

"Oh …" Isabella cleared her throat. "… I'm quite all right."

"Well, you look wonderful."

"That's very kind of you."

"Not at all. And will you both be assisting with the census activities?"

"As much as I'm able," Effie said.

"Excellent. And you, Mrs Lockhart?"

"If you need help with any correspondence, I'd be more than happy to oblige."

"Thank you. There's much to do and these things don't just organise themselves. Efficient administration is a much-overlooked art."

"And I might be able to do more," Isabella quickly added, "depending on what happens."

"Well, any additional assistance will be gratefully received. Now, if you'll excuse me, I must mingle." Mrs Huntly-Sykes turned to go and then paused. "Oh, Mrs Lockhart – I'd be obliged if you could relay to Dr Forbes that the young lady for whom she was seeking a place of respite is doing very well."

Isabella felt her heart give an extra thump. "Oh, yes." She glanced around. She'd rather not discuss Cappelmuir's secret scandals in a public place. "Thank you. I'll tell her. Now Effie we really must get on. I've—"

"Yes. She's in the household of two spinster sisters whose kindness knows no bounds. They'll ensure she recovers from her … illness."

Isabella felt a flush rise from her chest to her neck. "Good. Thank you for your assistance in the matter." She looked to the other end of the room as her face burned. "Oh, is that Mrs

Inglis trying to catch your eye? Yes, I think it is. We'd better not keep you!"

Mrs Huntly-Sykes glanced over, then bustled away.

Once she was out of earshot, Effie leaned in. "What was that about?"

"There are some things, Effie, you're best not knowing about."

A baby conceived by unmarried staff at Cappelmuir being one of them.

JESSIE

"Is it nearly dinner time?"

"No." Jessie totted up the number of times Clara Brodie had asked her that since the beginning of the shift – eleven. "I'll tell you when it's time. Just keep stirring the clothes round, nice and smooth and slow. And try not to splash. Don't worry, you won't miss your dinner. It's Tuesday, so it's potato soup and bread, then rhubarb tart."

"The pigs wouldn't eat that slop."

"Just stir."

It was only Clara's second day at the laundry but already Jessie had concluded she wasn't suited to it. She lacked the physical strength required and wasn't motivated to learn technique. And she must be sweltering in that big fancy hat she insisted on wearing. Nurse Haggarty said that if she ever took it off, she was to be led promptly outside and a nurse summoned.

"Anyway, I'd be happy to miss that pig swill. In fact, it's better if I do." Clara stopped stirring and leaned on the dolly. Then she glanced around the wash room before turning back to Jessie. "They're trying to poison me, you know? My father's ordered them to do it. He tried to do it to me just like he did to my mother – may she rest in peace – but he didn't manage it. So he sent me here for them to try."

Jessie hesitated. Nurse Elliot had told her that patients with insane beliefs weren't to be laughed at. Nor was anything to be made of their delusions. Equally, there was no purpose in trying to point out their faulty reasoning because they were – what was it now? Yes – 'inaccessible to argument: their conviction of truth was evidence of truth'.

Mary would've known what to say. She would've given Clara a sympathetic smile and a quick retort that would neither rile nor encourage. Jessie missed her presence in the laundry, her company in the dormitory. Although not a friend of long standing, she was more than a colleague. Jessie felt as close to her as she once had to her old schoolmate, Lilian, who she'd seen for the last time the day her father took her out of school. Lilian would still be at the high school, doing the classes Jessie had planned to do – had her mother dying not put paid to it.

She put her hand to her mouth, ashamed. It wasn't her mother who'd turned to drink and encouraged her brothers to do the same. It wasn't her mother who'd made Jessie the woman of the house. And it wasn't her mother who'd made Jessie renege on her family duties.

Yet neither had her father given her mother the consumption. Nor caused her to shiver and shake, and wither away until all that was left of her was phlegm-filled lungs. 'I hope your father goes before me because he won't be able to cope.' That's what her mother joked in healthier times. 'Women marry for security, men for health.'

Matilda, at the next copper to Clara, spoke out. "D'you not think if they were trying to poison you they'd've succeeded by now? After all, how long have you been here?"

Jessie stepped between the two unpredictable women. "Just carry on with your work, Matilda. It's almost dinner time."

Clara hauled her dolly around indignantly. "I know I'm right."

"If you say so." Matilda looked at Jessie, then raised her eyebrows.

Clara's tally of enquiries had reached fifteen by the time the dinner break did arrive. Thankfully Nurse Haggarty came promptly to collect her.

Jessie admired the patience of Nurse Haggarty, Nurse Elliot and most of the other nurses. They never seemed irked by the tiresome behaviour of some of their charges and they always seemed able to produce a calm smile in the face of repeated provocation. It wouldn't suit Jessie, being a nurse. She was glad she didn't have to spend her day curbing her urges to silence the emotional and scold the quarrelsome.

When she took Matilda outside to wait for Nurse Elliot, Mr Johnstone, the hall porter, was coming up the laundry path.

"Ah, Miss Purdie. The very person." He reached into his satchel and pulled out a small white envelope. "This is for you."

"For me?"

"Unless you know any other Miss Purdies who reside here?"

She took the envelope and looked at the jagged writing: *Miss Jessie Purdie, Staff, Cappelmuir Asylum.* "No."

"Right then. Good day to you, miss."

Jessie stared at her name. She'd never seen it written in someone else's hand on an envelope before.

"That from your young man, is it?" Matilda said.

Jessie's cheeks burned. Not only had she never received a letter, she'd never had a young man.

"No."

"Who's it from then?"

"I don't know, do I?" She tucked it into her apron pocket. "Anyway – letters are private."

"You know ... I need to send a letter. Could you get me some paper? Then send it for me?"

Jessie knew the regulation answer. "Anything you give to me, I have to give to Nurse Elliot then she has to give to Dr Forbes. Then she'll read it and decide whether or not it's to be sent."

"Oh." Matilda pursed her lips.

"And anyway, I heard Matron Campbell tell Miss Wilson that most patients' letters aren't posted because they're full of nonsense and lies."

"But I wouldn't be telling any lies or saying anything bad about the asylum. I swear. So you wouldn't have to give it to anyone else. I just need to write a few lines. You could take it and post it."

Jessie laughed. "Oh, I've to pay for the stamp as well, have I? You've some cheek."

"You know I don't have any money."

"Out of the question. It's more than my job's worth."

Matilda kicked a pebble. "Don't you want to know who I want to write to?"

"No. I already know more about you than I want to. So I'm going to forget you ever mentioned it and just get on with my work."

When Nurse Elliot came to collect her, Matilda didn't say her usual cheery goodbye.

Once they'd set off for the main building, Jessie took the letter out of the envelope. Her heart felt like it might burst through her chest.

Dear Jessie

It's not right without you. We're sorry how we've been. But it's hard since your mother. It'll be different if you come home.

Your loving father and brothers

She scrunched up the scrap of paper. If she believed that,
she was as deluded as Clara Brodie.

KATHERINE

WHEN KATHERINE STEPPED off the train at Balloch pier there was still a smirr in the air.

"Why don't you go below deck, ladies?" Dr Cowan suggested. "Alistair and I will go aloft for a few moments to admire the scenery before joining you."

Agatha looked at the grey sky. "Excellent idea." She linked arms with Katherine and led her to the gangplank of the *Prince George*, where a uniformed crewman saluted them. As Agatha stepped forward, she scuffed her boot on some iron cleats and tripped into the arms of the purser who was welcoming passengers on board.

She steadied herself. "This doesn't bode well for our voyage to India if I can't navigate a loch steamer."

They followed the purser to their table in the saloon, where Katherine eagerly studied the luncheon menu. The journey from Cappelmuir to the city and then on to Balloch had been hungry work. "How long will it take you to get to India, Agatha?" she said, perusing the selection of dishes.

"A month on the liner to Bombay, then several days by train to the Himalayas."

"Goodness, that is a long journey."

"Well, not the Himalayas themselves, the foothills. First Darjeeling and then Kalimpong. I think I'm going to be drinking rather a lot of tea."

"I doubt you'll have any time for tea. Your brother told me about the work you'll be doing and I fear you'll have even less time off than an asylum doctor."

"Yes, it'll be hard work, I'm sure, but rewarding. There's a twenty-five-bed hospital and a small dispensary. I hope to establish a children's clinic and train local women in nursing. Perhaps, too, the boys can be trained as compounders for the pharmacy. And Alistair will be preaching and teaching, of course. A new school will be opening near the hospital thanks to the kind sponsorship of many from our local parishes. That'll mean more children – girls, especially – will get the chance of an education. Great strides are already being made. Just the other week a lace handkerchief made by one of the village girls trained by the mission was gifted to Queen Mary by a marchioness who'd bought it at a charity auction. The local girls make exquisite pieces. In fact, I'm hoping I might be able to learn some new craft skills myself during our tenure."

"It all sounds very exciting."

"Well … the missions are always looking for committed professionals. I'm sure someone with your skills and experience would be highly sought after."

"Oh, I couldn't possibly."

"Why not? If I can do it, you can do it."

"Well, for one thing, you'll have your husband to accompany you."

"You know," Agatha said, "my brother is very fond of you. You featured prominently in his reports of the visit to Holland."

"Yes, our party was very tight-knit," Katherine said quickly. "We spent a great deal of time together each day on visits and at lectures. All of us, I mean. The group."

"Oh?" Agatha took off her velvet stole and summoned the

purser with the slightest twitch. "From the way he talks I imagined you were his only companion."

There was a smear on the table. Katherine rubbed it, unable to think of anything to say that wouldn't betray her affection for Dr Cowan. Thankfully, the rumble of engines signalled that the boat was about to set sail and Agatha's attention was diverted to the scenery.

Clouds were clearing from the tops of the lush slopes surrounding the southern end of the loch and sunlight was spreading gradually across the saloon. The edge of a rainbow emerged and Katherine pressed her forehead to the window to watch it extend into an arc.

"Go outside and see it before it disappears," Agatha said. "I'm sure my brother would be delighted to have your company." She winked, then looked out the window again.

Katherine climbed to the upper deck and angled her hat to shield her eyes from the sun. Down on the pier the photographer who'd been taking snaps of the day-trippers was rummaging in his bag and the merchant who'd been selling toffee was dismantling his stall.

Dr Cowan and his brother-in-law-to-be were standing near the prow, looking back at the steam rising from the red funnel. When the vessel began to drift from its moorings, Dr Cowan came forward and offered her his arm. "Dr Forbes. It's turning into a lovely day. Although by the time we reach Ardlui we may have witnessed several weather fronts."

"It wouldn't be Scotland otherwise."

She nodded a 'hello' to Mr Dockley, who stepped back from a nook in the railings. "Dr Forbes. Please take my place here. It's a safe spot should we encounter any waves."

Katherine looked at the calm water of the bay. "Waves?"

"Oh, you'll be surprised how exposed it is away from the shelter of land," Mr Dockley said.

"Oh, dear. I'm afraid I'm not a very good sailor, as Dr Cowan can attest to."

Mr Dockley smiled. "I heard! Now if you'll excuse me, I think I'll join Agatha inside."

Katherine took his place in the nook and leaned against the railings. The gently rolling hills might be mere mounds compared to Agatha's Himalayas, but the glens and villages of the Lomond foothills were surely as picturesque as anywhere in the world.

There was a shout from the pier. When Katherine and Dr Cowan glanced down, the photographer took their picture.

"D'you think we'll be appearing on a tourist postcard?" Dr Cowan said.

"Oh, I hope not! I trust he was taking the boat and not us."

He edged closer to Katherine and the sleeve of his jacket touched the sleeve of her coat. "It's a bit different to the last time we were together on the deck of a ship."

"Thankfully, yes. I wasn't quite at my best on that occasion."

"Nonsense. You're at your best on every occasion."

"That's not true in the least – but thank you. However, I'm sure I'll have my sea legs today. It's hardly the North Sea."

"Be assured, Dr Forbes, that should you suffer in the same way you did in the North Sea, I'll be here to assist." Dr Cowan gave a little bow. "Although … perhaps a longer sea voyage would inure you to *mal de mer*. I've no doubt my sister and her fiancé will be accomplished mariners by the time they reach the subcontinent."

Katherine laughed. "I fear I'd need an even longer journey than that before my stomach would settle."

"Ha! Not at all! Not at all."

When the engine started to chug, they sat on one of the white metal benches fixed to the deck. An osprey soared against the sky and a skein of geese swept across the horizon. Katherine ought to recommend her father take a trip on the loch; he was a keen birdwatcher.

"Tell me, what do your parents think of your sister's plans, Dr Cowan?"

"My mother's appalled, but proud. My father's simply happy Agatha will be supporting her husband's career."

"I see." Katherine wondered what her own parents might think were she to do the same as Dr Cowan's daring sister.

"You know, there remain opportunities where Agatha and Alistair are going in India."

Would they view it as a betrayal of their faith and conviction?

"I might consider it myself ... "

Or would they recognise it as an opportunity which afforded their daughter a choice that most women could never aspire to?

" ... only they tend to prefer married men."

"I'm sure." Katherine looked up to try and locate the source of a high-pitched bird call.

"Would you ever consider it, Dr Forbes?"

Her heart thumped. What was he asking her? She looked past him towards the shore. "Consider what, Dr Cowan?"

"A period overseas would be very good for your professional development. And the experience would doubtless stand you in good stead in future years, when perhaps there might be more openings for women physicians here at home."

"That could well be true." A buzzard disappeared into the trees along the shoreline. "Are *you* genuinely considering it? Going to India?"

"I might ..."

"Surely you have better prospects here?"

Dr Cowan stood up and looked across the loch. "... if I were married."

Katherine swallowed. "Well ..."

Was he going to propose? What would she say if he did?

She was trapped on board a steamer – there was nowhere to run.

"… if you do decide to go to India …" She gave an unconvincing laugh. "… just be sure to find a wife who shares your capacity for resisting seasickness."

She tapped her toe on the deck as she squirmed

"Oh, look! Over there!" Dr Cowan pointed to a speck directly above their heads. "D'you think that's an eagle?"

Katherine let out the breath she'd been holding. The moment was gone.

HELEN

Between dodging Nurse Haggarty, settling a spat between Matilda and Clara, then listening to Miss Wilson witter on about her hope that the Laundry Committee might agree to her request for a new foul-linen washing machine, Helen was frazzled. She hadn't been able to concentrate on her Red Book for days, and if she didn't start applying herself again, the success she'd been hoping for in the exams would elude her.

Only a few weeks ago she'd been thoroughly familiar with all the required aspects of anatomy, physiology and first aid. But now she was struggling to recall any of it. Perhaps she should take her annual week's leave and spend the time away from the asylum re-familiarising herself with the curriculum. Though where would she go, with no family to stay with and no money to pay for a respectable lodging house?

She dawdled along a wide corridor in the men's wing, easily navigating the chairs, side tables and potted ferns without having to look up. It was said you could go for a mile without leaving the asylum building; if that were true, Helen must have walked further than from John o' Groats to Land's End and back since she'd been at Cappelmuir.

She stopped in the main hallway that separated the two

wings, and off which the administrative corridor branched. The unassuming door to the left of the corridor led to an outside courtyard, the location of the Asylum Shop. She glanced along both corridors in case Matron Campbell was on the prowl. Then, when she was certain there was no one to see her, she slipped out.

"Good morning, Nurse Elliot," Mrs Rae said from behind the shop's wood-panelled counter. "You must've heard that I've just stocked up." She pointed to the shelves behind her. "I've got ginger wine, biscuits, tinned salmon. Some lovely smelling toilet soap. Pretty notepaper. Jam and sugar. What are you after today?"

Helen looked at the sweet jars on the top shelf for her favourite treat, which thankfully was also in stock. "Just my usual quarter of striped balls please, Mrs Rae."

The shopkeeper climbed a small set of steps, lifted the jar down and carefully shook some sweets into the brass bowl of the balance scales.

"Don't bother, you're more accurate than they are," Helen said when Mrs Rae picked up a weight. She put some money on the counter.

"Likewise I don't need to check that. You always give the exact amount."

A shout came from outside as Mrs Rae poured the sweets into a paper bag. "I don't know what's going on but it's been a good ten minutes they've been at it now."

"And no one's sounded a whistle for assistance?"

"No." She put the payment in the till. "It'll be the men up to their high jinks again, I expect."

"Possibly."

"You know what they're like." Mrs Rae handed over the bag.

"Yes, quite. But there's no harm in taking a look. Just to check."

Helen left the shop and waited for a moment outside, head

tilted towards the courtyard's high wall. There was a dull thud from the other side, then some moaning. She stood on her tiptoes but couldn't see into the orchard.

"The more you struggle, Mr Allan, the longer we'll need to stay like this."

That voice – she'd recognise it anywhere.

There was another thud. A cry of pain. Then his sneering laugh.

Helen tensed. If she called out to ask if everything was all right, Mr Kennedy would have the chance to deny any wrongdoing. She could just imagine his snide tone: *How could Nurse Elliot know what was going on when she didn't see anything? Mr Allan and I were merely joshing.* And what was it Nurse Millar's cousin had said? He was a bully and a coward. The only way Dr Lockhart would believe her was if she caught him red-handed.

She rushed back the way she'd come, then sprinted the length of the building to where she could access the rear grounds.

As she approached the orchard, she slowed to catch her breath, then zig-zagged from tree to tree, following the trail of increasingly loud cries.

She saw him before he saw her. Mr Kennedy was on top of Mr Allan, one knee on his neck, the other on his abdomen.

He slapped Mr Allan's face ferociously. "Are you ready to stop struggling now?"

A twig snapped under Helen's foot. Mr Kennedy spun round and leapt up, leaving his injured patient limp on the ground.

"Nurse Elliot! What are you doing here? I didn't whistle." He pulled Mr Allan to his feet and put his arm around him for support. "We're quite well here. Aren't we, Mr Allan?" The patient's head lolled. "I'm afraid he struck me and then tried to flee. When I found him he was most belligerent and wouldn't come as requested. His fists started flying, and in the absence of any of my fellow attendants I put him down … as the rules entitle me to do. With as little force as possible."

"Why didn't you use your whistle?" Helen said. "I'm sure someone could've come to help. And you wouldn't've had to hold Mr Allan down for so long."

Mr Kennedy pushed some hair from his forehead. "It was just a minute or two."

"I think not. I've just come from the shop. Mrs Rae told me she'd been hearing cries for at least ten minutes. In any case, by whatever measure, you're well outwith what the Red Book and the rules say."

Mr Kennedy let Mr Allan fall to the ground, then moved closer to Helen. "Don't you quote the Red Book at me. I'm more than aware of the rules. I don't need any lectures from a poorhouse girl."

Helen rocked back. "What?" How did he know about her past? She'd told no one.

"Yes, that's right. I know all about you and your sob story."

There was a pulsing in her temple. "I don't know what you think you know," she spluttered, "but—"

"Save your breath. I know all about your charwoman mother. Dr Scott recognised you."

She felt a thump in her chest. "What?"

"Yes. He was here a few months ago advising Dr Dorsie on a patient and he spotted you in the wards. Said how well you'd done and how he'd come across you as a girl when your mother was dusting and polishing at the subscription library. Said he'd felt sorry for you. Told us how your feeble mother couldn't keep your father and how she ended up on the street and then the poorhouse. How she had you sent to the orphanage and—"

"Don't you dare talk about—"

"Oh, be quiet, woman. Are you saying it's not true? If it hadn't been for Dr Scott taking pity on you and giving your mother a job after she couldn't hold on to another man –

though at least she was married to this one – you'd be in the gutter. Are you going to deny it?"

Helen felt her legs go weak, then start to shake.

"No. So, as I was saying, I don't need any lectures from a poorhouse girl. From the daughter of a street—"

"I …" she croaked.

Mr Allan began to whimper.

Rage allowed Helen to find her voice. "I know what you were doing! I heard it and I saw it!" she shouted.

Mr Kennedy lunged forward. "I'd strongly advise, Nurse Elliot, that you go back to your ward and carry on with your duties. Given you're such a stickler for the rules, I'm sure you're aware that you shouldn't be here. Matron Campbell doesn't like her nurses to be where they shouldn't be."

Helen stood her ground. "I think in the circumstances, Matron Campbell would—"

"But don't worry." Mr Kennedy smiled then stepped back. "I won't let on to her."

He hauled Mr Allan to his feet and propped him up. There was blood trickling from the poor man's nose and mouth.

"Nor will I share what Dr Scott told me. Not yet anyway. Instead, though, I might tell Matron Campbell and Dr Lockhart that their conscientious Nurse Elliot is actually leading a revolt of the nurses. And not only that, but she's also been rabble-rousing to gain signatures for a petition against the medical superintendent! How do you like the sound of that, poorhouse girl?"

Helen's heart was beating so fast she thought she might faint. Nurse Millar must have let slip what was planned.

"Precisely, Nurse Elliot."

And her despicable paramour would have no compunction in revealing – and embellishing – Helen's recent activities. He had her.

"So do you agree, Nurse Elliot, that everything's quite all right?"

Helen opened her mouth but couldn't speak.

"I'll take that as a 'yes'. Excellent. I'm going to take Mr Allan back to the ward now so he can rest and think about his behaviour. The medical superintendent takes a very dim view of patients who assault attendants. I doubt he'll be allowed to attend the ladies' At Home tonight. But I'll be there." He winked at her. "Perhaps we could take a turn on the dance floor … given our … understanding."

Mr Kennedy turned and headed slowly from the orchard, his victim slumped against him.

Helen wanted with all her heart to pick up the large stone at her feet and throw it at the senior attendant. But all she could do was sink to the ground and weep.

ISABELLA

ISABELLA SLID the printed copy of the magazine out of the envelope.

"Oh my word!"

There it was, at the top of the front page in large black print. *The Passing Hour*. Angus had approved her suggestion for the title.

She scanned the list of contents, her heart beating faster and faster. Except for Angus's editorial, every prose piece was hers: the proposals for the King's coronation, Dr Forbes's visit to Holland, the review of entertainments, the inspection by the commissioners, Cappelmuir Characters – all of them were there. Even Mr Smith's poem.

She put the magazine on the dining room table and gazed at it. The printer had done a wonderful job. Each article was separated by an elegant line, each section headed up in capital letters and every photograph reproduced to the highest quality. Mr and Mrs Gillies would be overjoyed with his picture.

Angus had decided that copies would be distributed to coincide with the visit of the delegation from the American Psychiatric Association. 'We must take advantage of every opportunity to show Cappelmuir in the best possible light.' He was right, of course, but that didn't make Isabella any less impatient to see everyone's reaction to the magazine (and to her contributions).

She rocked back and forth on the spot, admiring the crisp cream paper on which the magazine was printed and the impressive photograph of the asylum that took up almost two thirds of the cover. Had Angus asked her advice, she'd have suggested a photograph of patients or staff. But maybe he was right about that too. After all, the building had been in existence longer than any patient had resided in it and would doubtless still be standing when all the current patients were gone.

She put the magazine back in the envelope to avoid the risk of marks or creases, then went to the sideboard. The Royal typewriter was still there – the house secretary must have forgotten to send someone for it. Miss Purdie's typing had been excellent and some of the credit for the magazine's production must surely go to her as well.

Isabella consulted the wall clock. If she were to take a walk through the grounds now, she might happen upon Miss Purdie going for dinner. And if she did, perhaps she could show her the first edition of *The Passing Hour* in advance of its distribution, in thanks for her labours. The girl might appreciate that; just as Isabella might appreciate having someone compliment her own efforts.

Miss Purdie was towards the rear of the line of girls trooping out at the end of the morning shift. Isabella did a little shuffle so she'd be at just the right spot when she intersected it.

"Good afternoon," she said when she got alongside her quarry.

Miss Purdie stepped out of the procession. "Mrs Lockhart, madam."

Isabella waited until the last of the laundry maids had gone by. "Might I have a word?"

The girl glanced round at her colleagues disappearing into the servants' dining room. "With me?"

"It won't take a moment. I've something I'd like to show you." Isabella took the magazine from the envelope and held it up. "It's not been distributed yet so please don't mention that you've seen it. But I thought given all the work you did you'd like a sneak preview." She opened the magazine and pointed to an article. "There's the King's coronation." She turned the page. "And there's Dr Forbes's visit to Holland."

Miss Purdie was wide-eyed. "I typed these from your handwritten pages!"

"You did! Isn't it splendid to see them in print?" Isabella turned to another page.

"That's Mr Gillies! Oh – doesn't he look smart?"

Miss Purdie's enthusiasm was gratifying. "Yes, very distinguished!" And infectious. "Maybe *you* could be the subject for a Cappelmuir Character in future!"

The girl took a step back. "Oh, no, I don't think so, madam. I don't want anyone to know I'm … I mean, no one wants to know about a laundry maid, do they?"

"Why ever not?" Isabella put the magazine back in the envelope. "The place couldn't run without all you girls. You do excellent work. And the work you did on the magazine was excellent too. So thank you."

"Thank you, madam."

"So good in fact that I wonder whether you might be willing to do a bit more typing for me?"

"For the next issue of the magazine?"

"No, something else. I'm writing a few pieces about the census for a group of ladies."

"The census?"

"Yes. D'you know what it is?"

Miss Purdie frowned as if slightly put out by the question. "Yes."

"Of course. Well, there are some people who don't think women should take part in it because we don't have the vote."

"What's the census got to do with the vote?"

"In and of itself, nothing. But the information from the census will be used to inform how taxes are spent. And although some women have to pay taxes, they've no say in how they're spent. The government wants to count women yet won't give them the vote." Miss Purdie looked at Isabella quizzically. "You see ... if the government thinks women count for nothing, then why should women allow themselves to be counted?"

Miss Purdie thought for a moment. "And will these pieces be printed in a magazine too?"

"No, they'll probably just be circulated to the ladies I mentioned."

"Oh."

"But there are quite a lot of them. And of course, you never know where these things might end up."

"Well, I ..."

"It might give you something to do while your dormitory companion's away."

Miss Purdie jerked her head. "You know about Miss Anderson?"

"Yes. I helped find a place for her to stay during her recovery."

"Oh." The girl looked down.

"Is everything all right?"

"Yes. It's just that ... I was wondering ... do you know what happened to ..." Miss Purdie stood closer to Isabella and lowered her voice. "... the baby?"

"The baby?" Isabella feigned a sneeze to disguise the

involuntary start her body had given. "Please excuse me." She reached into her coat pocket for a handkerchief.

Miss Purdie glanced to her left then right. "You know … its body."

"Its …?" Isabella blew her nose. "… body?" Small wonder Dr Forbes hadn't wanted to explain the detail of Miss Anderson's indisposition. A baby most certainly was a delicate situation. And one born to an unmarried laundry maid would do little for the reputation of the asylum. While Isabella suspected that something of the kind was the cause of Miss Anderson's discreet departure, she hadn't for a moment considered that any baby might be a dead one. It was going from bad to worse. And she was complicit in it. However unknowingly.

"It's just that … one of my friends from school once told me that a woman her cousin knew had a baby born dead. And that instead of burying it the doctor took it away and … cut it up. So when Nurse Elliot took Miss Anderson's away for Dr Forbes … You don't think Dr Forbes would cut up a dead baby, do you, madam?"

"Em …" Any speculation that Dr Forbes might use the cadaver of an infant for medical research would surely bring Miss Purdie to tears. "No, I'm sure that—"

"I had a baby sister who died. I wouldn't have liked that for her."

Isabella squeezed the girl's arm. "Dr Forbes would make appropriate arrangements. Of course she would. It would have been very …"

"Do you really think so?"

"Yes. Dignified. Very dignified. Now …" Isabella was anxious to change the subject as much for her own good as for Miss Purdie's. "… if you're interested in helping me out again, I could have Mr Gillies bring the typewriter to your room?"

Miss Purdie shrugged. "Why not?"

"Excellent. Now … if you'll excuse me … I'd better not

keep you any longer. On you go now." Isabella gave the girl a little shove, then hightailed it away as quickly as she properly could.

～

She walked until she could go no further, never once looking back. At the asylum boundary wall, she sat on a stile and pulled some weeds.

What on earth was going on? What had Dr Forbes involved her in?

Whatever it was, it was certainly something Angus ought to know about.

But with the visit of the Americans looming, the last thing he'd want was any kind of scandal. That wouldn't show Cappelmuir in the best possible light. Far from it.

Isabella got up and started to plod back to the house.

Tipper jumped up and down to greet her at the garden gate. She lifted the latch, then bent over and stroked him until his enthusiasm for it waned. Then she took a deep breath and gave a firm nod, her mind finally made up.

Just as it wasn't time to confess to her census activities, it wasn't time to inform Angus that an illegitimate child, most likely fathered by another of the asylum's workers, had been born – apparently dead – to one of the laundry maids, with the whole thing being covered up by trusted staff, aided and abetted by his wife.

JESSIE

ALTHOUGH IT WAS her day off, Jessie was content to stay within the confines of Cappelmuir. She didn't want to risk going into town and bumping into any of her family.

In any case, without Mary to chum her, it would be more of a chore than a trip out. Plus, if the darkening sky was anything to go by, rain was coming.

She flopped onto her bed and dangled her feet over the edge of the mattress, imagining Mary in a fancy house on a posh city terrace, being waited on by some kindly old lady's maid. That would surely nudge her friend out of the dwam she'd been in in the days following the baby.

A knock on the door nudged Jessie out of her own dwam. She shuffled off the bed.

"Who is it?"

"It's Mr Gillies. I've something for you."

She got up and smoothed down her skirt. "Come in."

"I can't. My hands are full."

Jessie opened the door and stepped aside to let him in when she saw he was carrying a wooden crate.

"Mrs Lockhart asked me to bring you this."

Jessie peered in at the typewriter.

"Where would you like me to put it?"

"On Mary's … on the other bed."

"Right you are. There are some papers underneath. Mrs Lockhart says you'll know what they are."

"Yes, I do. Thank you."

"Not taking a turn out today?"

"No. I thought I'd just stay in. As you can see, I've some typing to do."

Mr Gillies rubbed his hands together. "Maybe you should think about getting a job as a typist rather than doing it on your day off."

"Yes, maybe." Jessie glanced at the door.

"Oh, right. I'll be off, then. Mrs Gillies will have my dinner ready." He paused. "By the way … I take it your father's not been trying to get in to see you again?"

Jessie felt her heart miss a beat. "My father?"

"I certainly haven't seen him hanging around. Mind, he'll probably be too ashamed to show his face again for a while yet."

"What do you mean? When was he here?"

"Oh, a few weeks ago now. Not long after you started. Came rolling up to the gates shouting and bawling. I told him in no uncertain terms he wouldn't be getting in unless he behaved himself. I've seen plenty like him in my time. And in front of Mrs Lockhart too." Mr Gillies shook his head. "But after our little – how might I put it? – *chat*, he made himself scarce."

A blush of shame spread over Jessie's face. "I'm sorry."

"It's not your fault, miss. None of us can choose our family."

"No." She looked down. "Thank you."

"You're welcome, miss. Anything for Mrs Lockhart. Good day to you now."

Jessie fell back against the door. If her father had tried to visit her once, he'd likely try again. He might even stay sober long enough to persuade Mr Gillies to let him in next time, for when he wasn't drunk he could be quite agreeable.

He must have been agreeable at some time, otherwise her mother wouldn't have married him. And it wasn't as if he could offer her more than any other young man, so there must have been some reason she chose him above any other suitors.

He hadn't been agreeable since her mother's death, though – only disagreeable and loutish. And now he was pursuing her to the asylum. Was she safe nowhere?

She went over to the crate and lifted the typewriter out, then removed the sheets of paper covered in Mrs Lockhart's now familiar hand. When she'd first done the typing for the magazine, there'd been a few letters Jessie hadn't been able to decipher, but now she could read the writing easily enough.

She flicked through the papers, pausing to read some words and phrases here and there – *evaders, boycott, head of family, jumble sale, passive, Housman*. She lingered over some lines about uneducated and ignorant men having the franchise while educated and intelligent women didn't.

Did that mean her father could vote but doctors and teachers like Dr Forbes and Mrs Lockhart couldn't? That certainly didn't seem right. Yet how was not being counted in the census going to change anything? All Jessie knew was that while her name would've been listed below her father's, mother's and brothers' the last time the census information had been collected, it wouldn't be this time round.

She looked out the window at the clearing sky, then dropped the papers back into the crate and put her shawl around her shoulders. Mr Gillies was right – she shouldn't spend her day off typing in her room.

She went along the lane towards the stables. On Sundays there was a calm about the place and the click of her boots on the cobbles was the only sound. Even the horses, whose neighing and snorting usually echoed from the yard, seemed to be having a day of rest.

She turned down the passage in search of Duncan. Perhaps he'd like to take a walk in the grounds with her.

He was sitting, head bowed, on a low stool by the stable door, turning his cap in his hands.

"Duncan? What is it?"

He shook his head and thumbed towards the stables.

"What?"

Jessie stepped forward, peered inside, then promptly turned away.

The two horses lying in the hay were dead.

"What's happened?"

Duncan pinched his nose. "They weren't good in the night. The vet came this morning and injected them. The knacker's coming to get them this afternoon." He thrust his cap on and pulled it over his eyes. "You don't want to know what he'll do to them."

When Jessie put her hand on his shoulder, he got up and started to pace. "And they're not replacing them. Dr Lockhart's getting a motor car."

She looked at her feet. She hadn't mentioned to Duncan that she'd overheard the Lockharts talking about that very thing when she'd first been called up to the house. It wasn't her place to. "I'm sorry."

"They've said I can train to drive the motor car and be a mechanic."

"Well, that's good. You've still got a job then."

"But I couldn't do that. If I can't work with the horses, then I can't work here at all." He turned away and wiped his nose with the back of his hand.

"But surely if they're offering you another job, you should take it? You'd be a chauffeur! And you'd learn all about motor cars and how they work! You could maybe get a better job. You know, driving!"

Duncan shook his head. "I need to work with horses. And if I can't do that here, then it'll need to be somewhere else."

"But where would you go?"

He shrugged. "Don't know yet. But I'll find somewhere. There's always someplace. A bad place with horses is better than a good place without them."

"But you can't just leave and—"

"I can't stay where there are no horses." He slumped back down on the stool. "It'll be fine. Haven't you ever been somewhere you just can't stay?"

"You know I have."

"Well then."

It was starting to drizzle. Jessie put her hands on her hips and looked at the sky. Duncan could count himself lucky that if he couldn't stay, then at least he had someplace to go.

KATHERINE

Katherine knew precisely how many deaths there'd been at Cappelmuir in the previous twelve months, because Dr Lockhart had insisted that his assistant medical officers be drilled in the numbers so they could respond promptly should the American visitors enquire.

There'd been forty-eight: twenty-four men and twenty-four women. Organic brain disease and other cerebral conditions had been the cause in fourteen cases; general paralysis had accounted for ten; heart disease nine; cancer, eight. There were three patients who'd died from exhaustion due to acute mental disease, two from phthisis and one each from epilepsy and alcoholism. Most of the deaths had been expected, a few not.

Katherine looked at the body lying on the slab in front of her – this death certainly had not.

From all accounts, Mr Allan had appeared hale and hearty the previous morning but had retired to bed early complaining of feeling unwell. The night attendant reported that he'd been alive at lights-out, but come the wake-up call he couldn't be roused. He'd been pronounced dead by Dr Dorsie at ten past seven.

Katherine glanced at her colleague, who was standing a

couple of feet away from the post-mortem table, ready to verify her observations and record their opinions on the cause of death. Of all the post-mortems carried out in the past year, Katherine had performed the majority, her colleague preferring – despite being first assistant medical officer – to adopt a secondary role, as he did in most things.

How Dr Dorsie had ended up in medicine was a mystery. He seemed singularly unsuited to it, lacking any enthusiasm for patient interaction and being prone to squeamishness. Even though they'd worked together for a few years now, Katherine knew little about him. Their paths crossed only while on duty and he spoke only when clinical purposes required it. With his premature baldness, his pointed features and a look of permanent alarm, he presented as older than his years. The only time he showed a semblance of enjoyment was when he played the violin at asylum concerts. Were it not for his white coat, he might easily be taken for a patient.

"Bruising," she noted, measuring the blue and purple marks on Mr Allan's neck. "Pre-mortem?"

Dr Dorsie leaned forward. "I concur."

Katherine made an incision in one of the bruises. "Extravasated blood present." She stepped back from the body to better consider the marks. "They don't look like strangulation. Perhaps pressure from an elbow or knee."

"Hmm."

She opened the head and skull to examine the membranes. "Healthy."

"Hmm."

There were no skull fractures either.

She removed the meninges and rotated Mr Allan's brain in her hands. "Healthy."

"Hmm."

"Ah now," she said, exploring the trachea. "Pharyngeal bruising consistent with that observed on external examination."

When Dr Dorsie didn't mutter his agreement, Katherine looked up. He was staring at the corpse, perhaps speculating, as was she, that Mr Allan's death might have been neither natural nor accidental.

She made an incision from chin to pubis, then opened the chest and abdomen to expose the internal organs. "Did Mr Allan ever tell you his joke about his diet of eggs? I think he told everyone he met." She chuckled. "He said he was on a special diet of eggs and that he ate them shell and all because eggshell was good for his insides as it helped scrape off the hairs that were in the pudding."

"Hmm."

Katherine sighed. Poor Mr Allan. Many's the time she'd admired his accomplished accordion-playing. She'd miss his silly tales and even his occasional barbed remarks which sometimes prompted a sharp retort from fellow patients. But she couldn't imagine him doing anything so heinous as to provoke a violent assault, if violent assault there had been. She'd performed enough post-mortems to know that nothing ought to be assumed or dismissed until every part of the procedure was concluded.

She worked through the internal examination, declaring organ after organ healthy, with no signs of disease. Could it be that the bruising on the neck was incidental?

"Oh dear. What have we here?" There was damage deep in the intestines and to one of the kidneys. Those parts of the body weren't easily reached from the outside and the injuries they'd sustained couldn't have been self-inflicted or the result of an accident; they could only have been caused by extreme violence.

She put her tools on the table and turned to Dr Dorsie. "Cause of death: shock and haemorrhage from internal injuries which were the result of direct violence."

"I concur." He wrote down their conclusion then handed her the report.

Katherine wiped her hands on her apron and signed her name next to his.

"Leave it with me. I'll finish up and let Dr Lockhart know. You can get back to your rounds if you want."

Dr Dorsie grunted an acknowledgement and left.

Katherine took off her apron and put the report in the pocket of her white coat. She would tidy Mr Allan up shortly, but first she had to preserve the damaged body parts. She went through the adjoining door to the laboratory to fetch some jars and alcohol, just as Mr Smith was passing in the corridor.

"Good day, Dr Forbes."

"Oh hello, Mr Smith." She went to the sink to wash her hands. "I'm afraid I'm a bit busy at the moment."

"I'm just going to check on the guinea pigs, if that's all right? Remember we've another order going out tomorrow."

"Oh, of course." She let the water flow over her fingers, wondering how best to break it to Dr Lockhart that a suspicious death had occurred on his watch.

"Dr Forbes?"

"Hmm?" That wouldn't do the asylum's cherished reputation any good.

"Who's going to help with the guinea pigs if I'm discharged? I've been worrying about it."

"Oh. Well, I hadn't really thought about it."

Mr Smith's face fell.

"But whoever it is," she added quickly, "I'm sure they won't be as expert as you. But don't worry. I'll make sure they're properly cared for."

"I'm being boarded out, you know?"

"Yes, I know. And isn't the gentleman a railway worker? Perhaps he'll be able to help you get a job. Then you can earn some money and maybe find a young lady to court and—"

"Dr Forbes. D'you not just think I should stay here and look after the guinea pigs and things for you?"

"You don't need to be here anymore, Mr Smith. You need to

go out there and live your life." Katherine lifted a couple of jars from the shelf. "Now, if you'll excuse me, I really must get on with what I'm doing."

Mr Smith clasped his hands together. "Could I at least come and visit the guinea pigs? I wouldn't be a bother."

"Well, I ..." It wasn't uncommon for patients to worry about their discharge. In that, he was behaving quite normally.

"Please, Dr Forbes."

"Yes, of course. Why not? I don't think that would be a problem."

What was a problem, however, was that she was likely to be making an appearance in court sooner than anticipated. Only not as the defendant in a case of professional misconduct, but as an expert witness in a case of murder.

HELEN

HELEN WAS glad when Matilda announced that she had 'no desire whatsoever' to attend the marionette show of *Dick Whittington and his Cat* in the main hall. It meant they could stay in the relative quiet of the Blue Room.

Aside from Helen and her patient, the only others who remained behind were the habitual dozers, elderly women whose daily routine extended only to being moved between the ward, the dining hall and the day room. They were arranged evenly around the room, each slumped in an easy chair, while Matilda was in the nook by the window, staring out at the grounds.

Helen got out of her upright chair and rubbed the small of her back. It had been aching for days and it didn't matter whether she sat or stood, there was no respite. She stretched her neck and shoulders, then went over to the two-seater couch near the door and flopped down. She closed her eyes and let her head fall back, hoping the deep tiredness she felt meant sleep would come easily later on and that she wouldn't spend yet another night tortured by bleak images. Bleak images, not only of a dead baby, but of Mr Allan now too.

There was speculation his sudden demise was down to his

heart. But surely it couldn't be coincidence it had occurred less than a day after the awful assault by Mr Kennedy? Something wasn't right and it made Helen feel sick.

"Nurse Elliot?"

When she opened her eyes, Matilda was standing in front of her.

"I wanted to ask you something."

Helen sat up. "Yes? What?"

Matilda bounced onto the couch next to her. "This is comfortable."

"What is it, Matilda?"

"Well ..." Matilda grinned like a child. "... I'd like you to do something for me."

"You'd like *me* to do something for *you*?" Helen spluttered.

Matilda folded her arms and nodded.

Helen folded her arms too. "Go on then."

"I need you to get me a pen and some paper so I can write a letter."

"You *need* me to?"

"Yes. And then I need you to post it, without showing it to Dr Forbes or anyone else. I know that patients' private correspondence is read and isn't sent if it's deemed inappropriate but—"

"Oh you do, do you?"

"—my letter won't be inappropriate. It won't criticise the asylum or anyone in it. And it won't say anything that isn't true. It'll just be a message."

Helen sat forward. "Who do you want to write to? And what message do you want to give them?"

"That doesn't concern you."

"Oh, I think it does concern me if—"

"All you have to do is get me the materials, then send the letter."

"—you're asking me to—"

"I'm not *asking* ..."

"What? Now just hold on a minute! You can't tell me what to do."

Matilda tilted her head. "No?"

"Eh, no."

"Maybe not. But you'll do it nonetheless."

Helen leaned back. "I think not."

"You will. Otherwise I'm sure the medical superintendent would be very interested to learn that you concealed a dead child from him."

Helen grabbed Matilda's wrist. "What did you say?"

"I'm sure that whatever you were doing was for the best. Really, I am." Matilda pulled her arm away. "But as to what others might think? Well ..." She shrugged. "I mean, they might not see it that way. Dr Lockhart might not see it that way."

"Dr Lockhart's well aware of the circumstances," Helen said flatly.

"Well then, let's go and find him to discuss the matter."

When Matilda sprang to her feet, Helen held her back, panicked. "Wait!" She tried to gather herself. "You should know that Dr Lockhart's very close to finding out who you are. If I were you, I wouldn't want to do anything to draw attention to myself."

Matilda laughed. "And pigs might fly!" She beckoned Helen. "Come on then."

Helen clasped her hands together. If Matilda were to make wild claims about a dead baby to Dr Lockhart, would he believe her? Surely he'd take a nurse's word over a patient's? And Dr Forbes would certainly deny it, too, if he were to enquire of her. But there was something unsettling about Matilda. It was almost as if she were on the cusp between sanity and madness. "If I send your letter, you'll say nothing about the child?"

"Nothing. I swear."

Helen pressed the nail of one thumb under the other until it hurt. Helping Matilda send a letter was a small misdemeanour compared to others she'd committed of late. But she was certain of one thing – if she did this for Matilda, it would be her last misdemeanour. Her days of fighting others' battles were over.

"All right. I'll do it."

Matilda sat down next to her. "Thank you."

"Tell me – what would you have done if you hadn't seen me with the baby? How were you going to get your letter sent then?"

"I'd've found someone else. If you look carefully enough, there's plenty going on that people don't want others knowing about. Everyone's got secrets here."

Helen shifted in her seat. The more Matilda said, the less insane she seemed.

"So who are you writing to? And what's the message?"

Matilda was silent.

"You might as well tell me. After all, I'll be able to read it for myself if I'm sending."

"I suppose that's true."

Helen did a double take in response to Matilda's Scottish accent. "What did you say?"

"I said I suppose that's true," she said in the same lilt.

"*What?* Are you …?"

Matilda smiled. "My granny was Irish. That's why my Irish accent's so good."

"So you're not Irish?"

"No."

"Where are you from then?"

"Here."

"Here?"

"Well, not exactly here. The other side of the country. But this country, not Ireland."

"But I don't understand. What about the ticket from Belfast and the clipping from the Irish newspaper? They were writing about you in the papers here too. An Irish woman who'd been hauled out of the river."

"I found it down the side of a seat in the railway station waiting room. The ticket was inside. That's what gave me the idea."

"The idea?" Helen stared at Matilda – she was no more insane than she was a relative of the Duke of Connaught. "No wonder no one's come to get you. There's nothing wrong with you. Is there?"

"No."

"You know exactly what's going on. All that nonsense about being a lady was just made up, wasn't it?"

"Yes."

"But why? Why did you come here? Someone must be missing you."

"I needed to get away for a time. Somewhere he wouldn't think to look."

"He?"

"My husband. Although in name only. He's cruel and unfaithful and he's emigrating to America. I told him I wouldn't go and he said he'd drag me there if he had to. I haven't got fifty pounds for a divorce. I'll never have fifty pounds in my lifetime! And I wouldn't want the scandal anyway. So I ran away. Somewhere he can't find me. Somewhere I can stay till he's gone."

"And then?"

"I have a friend – a man – who's kind and loving. Who treats me well. Once my husband's gone, we're going to move away and start a life together. Somewhere we aren't known. It's him I need to write to. To tell him to come and get me the day my husband sails from Liverpool. My friend will present himself as my husband and have me discharged into his care."

Helen shook her head at the cunning and ingeniously executed plan. "And you're sure your husband will leave for America without you?"

"Oh yes, I'm sure. To him I'll just be another item of lost property. At first he'll search and search. But after looking in all the usual places he'll give up, thinking he can just as easily get another one. And hopefully, one better than the one he's lost."

"You're very brave. I wish I was as brave as that."

"It's not bravery, Nurse Elliot – just survival."

Helen looked away. She knew all about survival. And something told her she was about to have the fight of her life.

ISABELLA

ISABELLA SNEAKED a smile at Mrs Drummond, who, although hovering in the hall a discreet distance away, was close enough to check that the two maids drafted in to assist with the dinner party were doing everything as instructed. Mrs Drummond gave the briefest of glances in return, which told Isabella that despite her complaints that the event would be 'a lot to manage in a small house like this', she took some pride in seeing it go well. The American guests seemed to have enjoyed both food and company, and even Dr Dorsie, as unprepossessing and reserved a man as Isabella had ever known, had managed a few words of polite conversation as befitting the occasion.

After the maids removed the dessert dishes, Angus rose from the table.

"Ladies and gentlemen, if you please." He tapped his wine glass with a silver teaspoon. "I'd like to say a few words to formally welcome you, Dr Norman, and you, Miss Worthington, to Cappelmuir. I'm delighted you've chosen to include us in your tour of Scottish asylums and trust you'll find your stay both informative and productive. Please come and go as you please, either on your own or in the company of

Dr Dorsie, Dr Forbes or myself. I know you've already toured some of the wards, but you're free to visit any part of the asylum at any time as part of your observations. We're very proud of this establishment and we want you to see every aspect of its operation. Dr Norman, you have all the privileges of an assistant physician."

Dr Norman nodded. "Thank you, I appreciate that. And if Dr Forbes doesn't mind, I'd be interested in accompanying her on her rounds." When he smiled at Katherine Forbes, his dimples deepened.

"Certainly. Of course," Angus said. "And Miss Worthington, I've asked Matron Campbell to assist you with anything you may need. She's particularly knowledgeable about matters which I know are of interest to you and your State Board. And, of course, my wife will also accompany you wherever you might wish to go."

Miss Worthington touched her pearl necklace. "That's most kind of you, Dr Lockhart. And you, Mrs Lockhart. Thank you."

Dr Forbes frowned when the men looked admiringly at the young American lady, who couldn't yet be thirty. As a single woman who'd travelled to another country in the service of others, there was much more to commend Miss Worthington than just her undoubted beauty.

"Excellent. Well," Angus said, raising his glass, "here's to you both and to a successful visit."

He smiled as the toast was repeated around the table. It was the first time Isabella had seen him relax since the news of Mr Allan's suspicious death. It seemed the unfortunate business hadn't cast too much of a pall over the visit which meant so much to her husband.

Dr Norman pushed back his chair and got to his feet. Although he must be in his sixties, he was still a handsome man. He had a full head of greying hair, a neatly shaped moustache and a glint in his blue eyes. He was taller than

Angus and held himself with the confidence of a man who'd achieved success in life.

"Doctors, Mrs Lockhart. On behalf of Miss Worthington and myself, as well as everyone associated with the APA, the State Asylum of Massachusetts and the Illinois State Board of Charities, I thank you very much for the warm welcome and excellent hospitality we've received. Already we've seen some most interesting practices. Indeed in the men's infirmary ward just this afternoon, a nurse struck a match for a patient who was confined to bed and the old man smiled at her as if she were an angel. I also observed a muscular young man who was having a mild manic episode being gently held in bed by four comely nurses. His expression wasn't fear or rage. No! He was grinning. And I couldn't escape the impression that his desire to get out of bed might not be so great as his desire to be held there."

Dr Norman laughed, then glanced at Dr Forbes, who gave him a polite – if pained – smile.

"Dr Lockhart," he continued, "it seems to me already that you're building a reputation for this asylum of which any hospital physician would be proud. Even in the short time we've had to observe it, I believe this asylum is more dominated by women than any other hospital for the insane I've seen. The benefits of that are evident and we very much look forward to learning more about how you've accomplished it. And not only that, increasingly you have another string to your bow as an amateur sleuth, tracking down mystery patients and sending them back where they belong!"

Angus tapped the side of his nose with his forefinger as if he were Sherlock Holmes and everyone except Isabella laughed.

"Anyway," Dr Norman said, "thank you again for your welcome and hospitality." He raised his glass. "To Cappelmuir."

"Cappelmuir."

Isabella tapped the table and looked over to Miss Worthington and then Dr Forbes. "Ladies, shall we retire and allow the gentlemen to smoke?"

"That would be lovely," Miss Worthington said. Angus was first to help her from the table.

While Mrs Drummond showed the young lady where to attend to her toilette, Isabella and Dr Forbes settled in the drawing room.

"That went well I think, Mrs Lockhart."

"Yes. Angus was worried, what with everything going on, so I'm sure he'll be very relieved. Already they seem impressed by what they've seen."

"As they should be."

"I'll ask Mrs Drummond to bring us coffee. I imagine that's what Miss Worthington would prefer. And perhaps something to drink. Would you take a glass of something?"

"Thank you, yes."

Isabella stroked Tipper's belly when he rolled onto his back next to her on the settee. "Dr Forbes, before Miss Worthington joins us again, I wonder if I might ask you something?"

"Certainly."

"It's about Miss Anderson."

Dr Forbes glanced over to the door. "Oh?"

"Yes. I trust she's still doing well where she's been placed?"

"I've no reason to believe otherwise."

"Good …" Isabella scratched Tipper's ears. "… good. Now, I know you told me you hadn't any intention of deceiving Angus or of misleading him in any way …"

"Of course not."

"… and that for the good of the asylum, he needn't know about the circumstances surrounding Miss Anderson's departure …"

"Yes."

"And I know that I agreed to assist in finding her a place of respite, taking on trust what you'd said. However ..." Isabella hesitated as Dr Forbes held her eye. "... well, I happened to be taking a stroll when I crossed paths with Miss Purdie. We exchanged a few words – she's been assisting with the typing for the magazine – and she asked if I knew what had happened to ..." Isabella looked out into the hall to check that Mrs Drummond and Miss Worthington were still occupied elsewhere. "... the *baby*." She sat forward. "And its *body*."

Dr Forbes shifted in her chair. "Ah."

"Yes. Miss Purdie was very concerned that it should have a decent burial and not be disposed of in a way that ... in another way."

"I can assure you, Mrs Lockhart, I attended to matters with as much decorum as I could."

"Of course, yes. That's what I told Miss Purdie." Isabella tickled Tipper under his chin. "But Dr Forbes ... are you entirely confident that what's been done is ... well, correct and lawful? If it ever comes out that—"

"Mrs Lockhart." Dr Forbes held up her hand as if taking an oath. "You have my word that any reasonable person considering my actions would deem them to have been correct in the circumstances."

"That doesn't quite answer my question."

Dr Forbes looked down. "No."

Isabella's mouth was dry. What was she to think? And did she really want to know the truth?

Dr Forbes looked up and clasped her hands together. "Mrs Lockhart, can you trust me?"

"Well ... I ..." Mrs Drummond appeared at the door with Miss Worthington. "Ah, Miss Worthington!" Isabella said, a bit more enthusiastically than she'd intended. "Please come in and make yourself comfortable. You must tell us about your work on the State Board. I've an interest in charitable endeavours myself, so I'm most keen to learn from your experience."

Miss Worthington turned away as she went to sit down, which gave Isabella just enough time to mouth 'yes' to Dr Forbes.

JESSIE

"THEY'RE COMING!" Miss Wilson called, marching into the wash room and scanning the floor again to make sure there were no stray pools of water. "Remember, I want everything shipshape and Bristol fashion. These are very important visitors and they must gain a good impression. Keep your heads down and perform your tasks diligently and quietly. Only speak if you're spoken to and keep your answers short and to the point. Don't stare. I expect you all to be on your best behaviour."

"That means you too," Jessie said to Matilda. "If you misbehave, it reflects on me."

"I want everything shipshape and Bristol fashion," she replied, expertly mimicking the head laundress.

"Wheesht!" Jessie elbowed her charge. "She'll hear you!"

"Ach, but I'm just a poor Irish lunatic who doesn't know whether she's comin' or goin'."

"Well, just be one who keeps her mouth shut. Now wheesht."

Jessie lowered her head when the dignitaries came into the wash room but raised her eyes so she could catch a glimpse of them. Miss Wilson said they were from America, that one was 'a very eminent physician' and the other 'a renowned philanthropist'. Jessie wasn't sure exactly what a renowned philanthropist was, but she thought it maybe had something to do with charity and the like. That must be the tall lady in the blue costume who was standing between Matron Campbell and Mrs Lockhart. She was much younger than Jessie imagined a renowned philanthropist would be – prettier, too. Her thick hair, piled in a swirling pompadour, was different shades of gold and yellow and her smile put even Mrs Lockhart's in the shade.

As the ladies approached, Matron Campbell was in full flow. Jessie stared into her copper and lowered the dolly carefully so as not to cause any splashes.

"Dr Lockhart considers the wash house to be excellent physical occupation for our female patients. He believes being usefully engaged expends excess nervous energy and prevents unrest. Miss Wilson runs a very tight ship and we've seen great progress in all the patients who work under her."

"Thank you, Matron Campbell," Miss Wilson said, in an uncommonly sweet tone.

"And do you find that an ability to work is indicative of recovery?"

Jessie couldn't help glancing up at the American lady's strange accent. She'd never heard anything like it.

"Yes. Very much so," Matron Campbell said. "Take Matilda here …"

Jessie gripped the dolly. *Pray to God Matilda wouldn't do or say anything inappropriate.*

"Yes, when she first came to us, oh, what a state she was in. Weeping and wailing and refusing to engage in any activity whatsoever. We could hardly get a word out of her. But now, as you can see, she's productive and her mood and manner are much improved. Isn't that so, Matilda?"

Matilda stopped stirring. "Yes, Matron."

Jessie breathed out as the very important people merely smiled, then moved on.

"And it's all down to Miss Purdie here. She's been my saviour, so she has."

Jessie shot Matilda a look. What bit of 'keep your answers short and to the point' didn't she understand?

"Without her, I'd still be at the weepin' and wailin'."

The American lady turned back. "That's very interesting. So it's not just the attendants and nurses who assist the patients, it's other workers too."

"Oh yes, Miss Worthington," Matron Campbell interjected before Matilda could. "Here at Cappelmuir we pride ourselves – Dr Lockhart prides himself – on the fact that every staff member has a role to play in the recovery of our patients. Everyone's efforts are directed to that goal and to that goal alone, whether a laundry maid like Miss Purdie or the medical superintendent himself."

Jessie wanted to grin. Imagine having been mentioned in the same sentence as Dr Lockhart.

"And how do you feel about that? Miss Purdie, is it?" Miss Worthington said.

"Oh. Em …" Jessie let go her dolly and put her hands by her side. Mrs Lockhart gave her a little nod of encouragement. "Fine. I feel fine about it, madam, thank you."

"Very good. And who knows?" Miss Worthington said. "Perhaps you'll become a nurse one day. It sounds as if you've just the right temperament for it."

Miss Wilson doubtless wouldn't consider the statement worthy of a response, even one that was short and to the point. Nevertheless …

"Thank you, madam. You're very kind," Jessie said. Miss Worthington's smile ensured that Matron Campbell couldn't frown.

"Shall we continue?" the matron said, ushering Miss Worthington to the door. "The drying room's next."

As the group moved on, Miss Wilson explaining the system of separating the laundry to Miss Worthington, Mrs Lockhart lingered. Once the others had gone from the wash room, she stood in front of Matilda's copper.

"Tilda? Is it you?" she asked quietly.

Matilda's stirring became more vigorous.

"Tilda White?"

Matilda looked over to the door, then lowered her head again.

"What on earth are you doing here?" Mrs Lockhart said.

"Shush! You can't tell anyone!"

"But what are you …? Why are you …?"

"Please. I just need a bit more time," Matilda said, reverting to her Scottish accent. "Then I'll be gone."

"You're the so-called Irish woman from the river, aren't you? What on earth …?" Mrs Lockhart looked at Jessie. "Did you know about this?"

"Em …" However she replied, she'd probably end up in trouble. "Well … I …"

"She doesn't know anything," Matilda said. "She's got nothing to do with any of it. She's only ever been kind to me."

"Then what are you doing here, Tilda? Why are you pretending to be Irish? And insane? I take it she's not insane, Miss Purdie?"

"I don't think so, madam."

"I take it you're not insane, Tilda?"

"Of course not!"

"Does Matron Campbell know about this? She can't. She wouldn't permit anything like this."

"Izzy, please. Just leave it be," Matilda said. "I'm not doing any harm and I'll be gone soon. Very soon."

Jessie stared at Mrs Lockhart, who used to be Miss Muir and who now seemed to be Izzy. How did she and Matilda – Tilda – know each other?

"You can't just enter an asylum and pretend you're insane," Mrs Lockhart said. "D'you realise the trouble people are going to to try and find out who you are? One poor man from Ireland was on the verge of coming over to see if you were his missing wife. And do you realise how much it costs to keep you here for no good reason?"

"She had nowhere else to go, Miss Muir. I mean, Mrs Lockhart. They were going to kill her," Jessie said.

"Who was going to kill her? And I thought you didn't know anything about it?"

"I don't. I just …"

"That's all she knows," Matilda said. "Nothing else. I let something slip and I had to explain, otherwise she was going to report me. She's done nothing wrong. But please, Izzy. If I have to leave now, he'll find me and my life won't be worth living. It's not for much longer. Please. Remember what we used to say about being friends forever and keeping each other's secrets?"

"We were children then, Tilda. This is serious. You can't carry on with it. Surely your situation isn't so bad that you can't do something other than this?"

"It is! I can't! Please, Izzy. You can't tell them. He'll kill me!" Matilda put her head in her hands and sobbed.

Jessie leaned on her dolly as she kept an eye on the door. If Mrs Lockhart didn't move along, Matron Campbell would be back to look for her, demanding an explanation of what was going on. And if Mrs Lockhart revealed the secret, what might happen to Matilda?

"Mrs Lockhart?" Jessie stepped out from her copper, her legs trembling. Then she spoke in as firm a tone as she could muster: "Have you heard how Miss Anderson's getting on and any more about what happened to the—?"

"No!" Mrs Lockhart glanced at the door. "No," she said, lowering her voice.

"All right." Jessie went back behind her copper and started to pound the clothes again.

Whether Mrs Lockhart was furious or fearful, Jessie didn't

know – she didn't look up until her former teacher left the wash room.

Matilda put her arm round Jessie's shoulders. "Thank you."

"Never mind that, just get on with your work."

Jessie let her dolly fall away and held onto the rim of the copper as she swayed back a little. For once, a piece of her father's advice had stood her in good stead. 'People's secrets are like pennies – save them up and spend them wisely.'

It might be the one useful thing he'd taught her.

KATHERINE

KATHERINE PUT the sheet music on top of the piano, pulled out the stool and trilled a few notes on the upper octaves. The piano still maintained a decent tone despite frequent use by the inexpert. It certainly lived up to its name of 'The People's Piano', with many patients (musical or otherwise) trying their hand at a tune or two.

She ran her fingertips over the rosewood of the upper front board and traced around the candlestick holders. Then she took the topmost piece of music from the pile and placed it on the rack. She studied the treble notation, considering transposing the piece into a lower key. Dr Lockhart had struggled with the high F's and G's at last year's staff concert and it was doubtful that his range had improved twelve months on.

The hall doors opened. But it wasn't Dr Lockhart coming towards her, whistling, it was Mr Johnstone.

"Hello, Dr Forbes. Is this you getting in some practice before the concert?"

"Yes. I'm just waiting for the medical superintendent. We're having a quick rehearsal. You know how he likes to prepare."

"I do, yes. He's a fine singer. I always look forward to hearing him."

"Indeed." Katherine looked at the high G of 'Lark In The Clear Air', hoping that Dr Lockhart wouldn't sing that particular favourite of his. What with Mr Allan's suspicious death and keeping the American visitors distracted, he would surely have more on his mind than his repertoire at the concert. Maybe she should suggest some songs that were more … within his reach.

"It's such a pity, of course, we won't have the pleasure of hearing Mr Allan on the accordion anymore."

Katherine twitched. Was Mr Johnstone psychic as well as nosy? "Hmm, yes. He'll be sorely missed."

"Ah well." He put his satchel on top of the piano. "Dr Dorsie and I will just have to fill in with a few more fiddle tunes."

"And I'm sure the audience will be most appreciative."

"I'm sure they will. Anyway … I have something for you." He reached into his bag, then handed her a postcard. "Yes, you can do worse than a trip on Loch Lomond."

On the front of the card was a photograph of the *Prince George* at Balloch Pier, with two tiny figures standing on deck.

"Have you ever been, Dr Forbes?"

Katherine grinned. There they were in the picture, she and Dr Cowan, hiding in plain sight from Mr Johnstone.

"Yes. And very pleasant it was too."

"Ah, there's nowhere like it." Mr Johnstone tipped his hat. "Good day, Dr Forbes."

She looked again at the postcard, wondering whether or not their faces would be recognisable under a magnifying glass. She'd check later in the laboratory. She turned the card over and read the message on the other side – *Next stop Bombay? Yours, A.C.*

Next stop Bombay? *Bombay? Next stop?* Was Dr Andrew Cowan actually asking her to go to Bombay with him? Or was he suggesting she go alone? Surely not. Katherine had long admired his understated style but there was also such a thing as being too subtle.

Maybe he was waiting for her to give him a sign that she might be open to a proposal. Or perhaps he sensed her contradictory feelings and was allowing her space to choose her path. That way, whatever the outcome, his ambiguity might protect their dignity. She sometimes thought Dr Andrew Cowan could read her better than she could herself.

The hall doors opened again and this time Dr Lockhart came in. Katherine slipped the postcard into her jacket pocket.

"Good afternoon, sir. I have the music here," she called.

He continued towards her, head down. Katherine swallowed – could he somehow have found out about Miss Anderson? Had he had occasion to see the undertaker, who'd let something slip? Perhaps Mrs Lockhart hadn't been able to conceal the matter from him after all.

"Dr Forbes, I'm afraid there's some bad news." His downcast look suggested sorrow rather than anger. He pulled a chair over from the side of the piano and sat opposite her. "There's been a terrible accident."

"Whatever's happened?"

"One of the patients left the grounds this morning and went onto the railway line. I'm afraid he was killed by a passing train. And I'm sorry to have to tell you … it was Mr Smith."

"What?" She gasped. "No."

"I'm afraid so."

"Surely not. He was—"

Dr Lockhart patted Katherine's arm. "I know, my dear. He was doing so well, and as you know was soon to be discharged. There's no accounting for it."

She sat back and let her arms fall by her side. "No *accounting* for it?"

"Yes, unfortunately that's sometimes the way of things," he

continued, oblivious. "Even when patients aren't regarded as suicidal, sometimes they can have a sudden impulse of a suicidal nature. That seems to have been the case with Mr Smith. There were no signs."

Katherine closed her eyes. There were signs all right. He'd been standing in her laboratory asking for help and she'd ignored him.

"I'll have to communicate the facts to the General Board and the Procurator Fiscal. But I don't think there'll be any doubting the circumstances are as I've outlined. We all know that sudden impulses can get the better of the sanest of men. Ah well." Dr Lockhart stood up. "I think in the circumstances we should postpone our rehearsal. I've asked Dr Dorsie to deal with Mr Smith's remains and I've completed the formalities in the case notes and the Register of Deaths. So there's nothing for you to do, other than take a few minutes to compose yourself. I'll see you for rounds in an hour."

Katherine remained rigid as Dr Lockhart's footsteps became distant. When all she could hear was the ringing in her ears, she put her palms together and gazed upwards. She'd let Mr Smith down. Instead of tending to the needs of her patient, she'd tended to her own need to be seen at a symposium in eminent company.

Blessed is she whose transgressions are forgiven, whose sins are covered, she mouthed.

She wiped away the tear trickling down her cheek and slammed down the lid of the piano. Dr Lockhart had said there was no accounting for it. But he must have accounted for it in Mr Smith's case notes. Katherine had to know what he'd written.

She rushed along to the Admissions Room, where the book still lay open on the table at Mr Smith's record. And there it was, freshly-inked in Dr Lockhart's impressive hand, the final judgement on *Robert Smith (deceased)*.

In the morning appeared bright and in good spirits. Shortly after going to work in the garden, he left the grounds and went to the railway. He committed suicide by throwing himself in front of an express train. Death was instantaneous, the head being completely severed from the body.

HELEN

HELEN WAITED outside the supplies store while Mr Thomson unloaded the delivery of aerated water. Down the lane, at the entrance to the yard, a huddle of male attendants and their patients waited to catch a glimpse of Dr Lockhart's motor car.

Helen didn't know what all the fuss was about. It didn't have any windows and the roof looked as if it was only made of canvas. She'd heard the attendants say the engine was fifteen horsepower, but that was no good if you were soaking and windswept when you arrived at your destination.

"I'll just be sticking with these lads," Mr Thomson said when he emerged from the store, stroking each of his two horses. "They might be slower but I'll tell you this for nothing – they're a lot more reliable. Mark my words, they'll have no end of trouble with a motor car."

Helen followed Mr Thomson as he went to climb up on the cart. "Might I ask you something?"

He took the reins from the lad sitting up front. "Yes, m'dear?"

"I was wondering if you might do me a favour?" Helen took Matilda's letter from her apron pocket. "I forgot to post this. It's for my cousin. It's her birthday tomorrow. The asylum mail's already been collected and I'd hate for her card to be late. I wondered if you could drop it at the post office when you're back in town?"

"Of course." Mr Thomson reached down and took the letter from her. "It would be my pleasure, Nurse." He pushed the brim of his cap up. "And maybe when you next have a day off, you might like to join me for a stroll in the park."

"What?"

Helen stared at the cobbles as she felt her cheeks warm. She'd exchanged pleasantries with Mr Thomson before but she'd never had any inkling he might be interested in her in *that* way. He seemed a nice enough man. Polite, respectable. Respectful. But then so had the men her mother had known. No, she couldn't step out with him. She knew nothing about him.

"I'm there most Sundays after church," he said. "I'll keep an eye out for you." He flicked the reins for the horses to walk on. "Good day, Nurse."

"Oh, yes ... good day, Mr Thomson."

He raised his cap and looked back at her as the cart rumbled away.

Helen peered inside the supplies store to hide her blushes. Then she picked a bottle of aerated water from one of the crates and rolled it in her palm. The embossed letters on the green glass felt solid beneath her fingers. She couldn't step out with him, could she? After all, it might be pleasant to mix with people from outwith Cappelmuir for a change ... and she could always take Nurse Haggarty with her ... it would all be quite proper.

"Stop it," she muttered to herself. No, of course she couldn't.

In fact, instead, she should consider just moving on. If she passed her exams, she could secure a higher position in another asylum. Wasn't she always telling the other nurses about Miss Sim's success after passing the Red Book? There were asylums other than Cappelmuir. Other opportunities beyond its gates.

She reeled at her inconsistency of thought and returned the bottle to the crate. What was she thinking with all this nonsense? *Impaired judgement.* That's what the Red Book called it.

She shook her head. No. Cappelmuir was where she belonged. It put a roof over her head, food in her belly and gave her a few shillings to spend.

"What's all this? You slacking, Nurse Elliot?"

"No!" Helen spun round. "Oh, it's you."

"Ha! Did you think I was Matron Campbell?" Nurse Haggarty said.

"No, I was just—"

"I might as well be, the way you're avoiding me."

"I'm not avoiding you. I'm just busy with the Red Book and things. The exams are coming up soon."

"Never mind the exams – Nurse Millar's heard from her cousin that the Mount Hope nurses might be getting reinstated."

"Really? That's good."

"So maybe it's time for our petition to go in now."

"D'you think so?"

"Yes. I'm going to gather everyone together this evening. Will you come?"

"Yes," Helen said without hesitation, and despite herself. *Impaired judgement.*

"Excellent. Right, then. I'd better get on, otherwise Matron Campbell *will* be putting in an appearance."

"Indeed she will. You're riding your luck."

"Oh, but before I go, have you heard what they're saying about poor Mr Allan now?"

Helen gave a start. "No. What?"

"Well, apparently Mr Kennedy told Dr Lockhart that he saw Mr Smith arguing with him and that he had to break up some fisticuffs. Something over nothing it seems. But Mr Kennedy thinks Mr Smith might've hit Mr Allan a bit too hard and then killed himself as he couldn't live with the guilt of what he'd done."

"What? No. That can't be true. Mr Smith wouldn't—"

"Yes. Mr Kennedy thinks it must've been a freak punch from Mr Smith that caused Mr Allan's fatal injury."

"And does Dr Lockhart believe that?"

"Why wouldn't he?"

Helen shifted on the spot. "I don't know. I just wondered. It doesn't sound like Mr Smith at all."

"It would explain things, though, wouldn't it?"

"I suppose so."

"Yes. I was beginning to think there was some sort of curse on the men's ward. I mean, you know that some patients are going to die ... but you wouldn't have predicted those two."

Helen bit her lower lip. "No. Not those two."

"Anyway, I'd really better get on now. Matron Campbell will be sending out the search party."

Helen returned Nurse Haggarty's wave, then nipped past the store and ducked down the gap between it and the wooden tool shed to take refuge at the rear of the building. She leaned against the wall and stamped the ground in fury. To prevent his misdeeds being discovered was one thing, but for Mr Kennedy to implicate Mr Smith, who'd cheered everyone up with his ditties and doggerel, and twirled the ladies around the dance floor as if they were princesses ... it was too much.

And the last time she'd spoken to poor Mr Smith, so concerned was she with her deceit over Miss Anderson that she'd fobbed him off and dismissed the stories about his beloved guinea pigs. She owed it to him to protect his reputation. And she owed it to Mr Allan to try and right some of the wrongs committed against him.

She ran back the way she'd come and headed straight to the Administrative Wing.

"You can't go in there. Stop at once!" the house secretary shouted at her through the reception window.

Helen paused outside Dr Lockhart's office. If her insistence that she be allowed to see the medical superintendent as a matter of urgency breached a host of protocols and trampled on the authority of the matrons and assistant medical officers, so be it. What was the point of rules and regulations if the likes of Mr Kennedy could always evade them?

Dr Lockhart stormed into the corridor. "What is the meaning of this?"

"Sir, I must speak with you!"

He put his arm out to stop her proceeding into the office. "Any matters you wish to raise should be raised first with Matron Campbell. She'll decide whether or not they ought to be raised with one of the assistant medical officers, who in turn will decide if they should be raised with me. Now get back to your duties, Nurse."

"But I must speak with you. It's—"

"Nurse Elliot," he said, raising his voice. "This is most inappropriate."

"But it's about Mr Allan. I saw what happened! It wasn't Mr Smith."

Dr Lockhart's cheek twitched. "What?"

"I need to tell you what happened to Mr Allan, sir!" Helen shouted. Her judgement wasn't just impaired, it was destroyed.

Dr Lockhart indicated to the house secretary to retreat, then glared at Helen. "You – in."

There was no going back now.

He moved an ashtray containing a smoking pipe to the window sill, then slammed down the lid of his desk. "Well?"

Helen took a deep breath before rattling out the truth. "It was Mr Kennedy! He was kneeling on top of Mr Allan. On his neck and his body. He hit him. Mr Kennedy hit him! It was nothing to do with Mr Smith. They were in the orchard. Mr

Kennedy said Mr Allan had struck him and then run away and that when he caught up with him, Mr Allan punched him. I didn't see any of that. I don't think any of it happened. All I saw was Mr Allan flat out on the ground and Mr Kennedy on top, hitting him. Mr Allan was bleeding from his nose and his mouth."

A vein in Dr Lockhart's temple was throbbing. "You actually witnessed this?"

"Yes!" Helen gasped in frustration. "… sir."

He went over to the window and took a long draw on his pipe, slowly blowing smoke into the air. "Are you absolutely sure, Nurse Elliot? You're not perhaps still angry with Mr Kennedy for causing you to be fined for your carelessness?"

"What?" How could the medical superintendent think she'd concoct such a story simply to get back at someone? She folded her arms. "Of course I'm sure. And if you don't believe me, ask Mrs Rae in the shop. She heard it too. She said it had been going on for ten minutes."

"If all that's true, why didn't you report the matter immediately?"

Helen looked at the polished floor so he couldn't see her utter shame.

"Loyalty to colleagues mustn't override your duty to protect the patients," Dr Lockhart said. "While tale-bearing isn't encouraged, the cardinal object of the asylum is the protection of every patient, even at the expense of getting a fellow attendant into trouble. And where downright cruelty and brutishness are witnessed, they must be reported without further thought."

"I wasn't being loyal." That would have required her to have affection or respect for him.

"What then? Self-protection?"

"I …"

"Even on those grounds, you're absolved of any feelings on the matter where the welfare of a patient is at risk. Anyone silently witnessing alleged violence is responsible as an accomplice, no matter how much she might dislike what she's seen."

Tears pricked Helen's eyes. Mr Kennedy's threat to reveal her involvement with the petition was scant excuse now. Dr Lockhart was right. Had she not neglected her duty, Mr Allan might still be alive. Her conduct had been utterly reprehensible. She was utterly reprehensible.

"Nurse Elliot," Dr Lockhart said calmly. "Do you think the rules are there just for the sake of it?"

"No sir," she said quietly.

"And do you think that we, and the Medico-Psychological Association for that matter, would go to the trouble of drawing up rules unless compelled to do so by experience?"

"No sir."

"And do you think there's a reason why these rules must be blindly accepted and faithfully carried out?"

"Yes sir." Helen rocked from foot to foot.

"And that reason would be what?"

"For the proper care of patients, sir."

"And do you think you've demonstrated the proper care of the patient in this instance, Nurse Elliot?"

"No sir."

"There we have it." Dr Lockhart went over to his desk and opened the lid. "Be gone from here by the end of the week. You're dismissed."

ISABELLA

ISABELLA ASKED the coachman to let them off at the asylum gates so she could show Miss Worthington something of the gardens. He opened the door of Mrs Huntly-Sykes's plush Clarence carriage and helped them down, before doffing his top hat and waiting until Mr Gillies had seen them safely into Cappelmuir.

"It's a grand wagon that, Mrs Lockhart," Mr Gillies said. "Now is there anything else I can assist you with?"

"Thank you, Mr Gillies, but no. I'm going to the house and Miss Worthington is going to the wards. I'm sure we'll be quite safe."

"Of course, madam." He glanced back to his sentry box. "Em, Mrs Lockhart? I have a parcel for you." He nodded in the direction of the laundry. "From Miss Purdie."

"Ah yes, excellent." And just in time, for Mrs Huntly-Sykes had handed over more material to type up after the luncheon she'd organised in honour of Miss Worthington.

"Shall I bring it up to the house, madam?"

"Yes, thank you, Mr Gillies."

He gave a little bow. "Madam. Miss. Enjoy your stroll, ladies."

They set off along the path. Miss Worthington linked arms with Isabella.

"Thank you so much for today. It was an unexpected addition to my schedule but very worthwhile."

"I'm glad you found it useful," Isabella said. "But while it may have been unexpected to you, it wasn't surprising to me. I'd no doubt that when Mrs Huntly-Sykes discovered there was a woman in the APA party, she'd insist on meeting her. And when Mrs Huntly-Sykes insists on something, it happens."

"I'm sure it does. She's quite the force of nature. However, I learned a great deal about the charitable work she's doing for young women. I'm just sorry my schedule won't permit me to see some of it in practice or to hear more about her work on the vote. The women of Illinois could learn a lot from the campaigning you're doing here."

"It's probably best you weren't briefed on suffrage matters. I'm sure my husband wouldn't want your attention distracted from Cappelmuir."

"Surely a man as progressive as Dr Lockhart is supportive of the aims of the suffrage campaign? His employment of nurses shows his admiration for the contribution women can make."

"Miss Worthington, my husband values nurses not because of their skill and intellect but because of their nature and temperament, which he believes are well-suited to dealing with the insane. He believes that a woman has the same influence over an insane man as she does over one of sound mind. After all, chivalry and honour don't die in a man because he suffers from a derangement."

"But he's also employed Dr Forbes. And – I shouldn't say this – but she seems far superior to Dr Dorsie."

"Ah yes. But Angus views Dr Forbes's cold temperament, compared to that of other women, particularly suited to pathology. She'll never advance her career in the asylum system. Apparently it would be 'absurd' for a woman to be a medical superintendent. I'm told it would cause consternation in every asylum in the country! And possibly even a revolt!"

"And we couldn't have that."

"We most certainly could not."

They continued along the path, pausing every so often while Miss Worthington complimented the gardens or asked another pertinent question about the running of the asylum. Informed by the work she'd done on *The Passing Hour*, Isabella was able to answer every one of them. She hadn't realised she'd taken in quite so much in the process of writing her articles. But it was amazing what you could learn just by talking to people. Or rather, by listening to them.

When they reached the house, Miss Worthington sighed. "Here we are. Ah well. It's a pity you won't be joining us at tonight's dinner with the members of the District Board."

"Don't worry," Isabella said. "I believe Mrs Dixon has been drafted in as your chaperone and to keep you company. She's the only lady on the parish council. They'll be delighted to have finally found a use for her."

Miss Worthington laughed. "I know all about that. The only reason I'm on the State Charitable Board is so they can continue to benefit from my late father's fortune."

Isabella bade farewell to Miss Worthington with a kiss on the cheek. "At least you serve a purpose."

She settled down for the afternoon in the drawing room with Tipper and the new paperwork Mrs Huntly-Sykes had handed in. There was a write-up of the latest branch activities intended for submission to *The Vote*, a list of dos and don'ts for ladies who were going to be spending census night away from their homes, and a piece on child poverty, about which Miss Worthington and Mrs Huntly-Sykes had had an animated conversation over lunch. If they were ever to team up, they would make a formidable philanthropic duo.

Isabella scratched Tipper's back. "What would *we* do with a fortune if we had one? Give it away? Travel?" That's what she and Tilda White had daydreamed of when they were children, of being wealthy ladies who never had to lift a finger, grand ladies who travelled to exotic places and whose every whim was catered to. Of course she knew better now – whether you were rich or poor, it was purpose that mattered in life. And meaning.

Tipper stretched out his front paws and gave a satisfied snort. He didn't need much to be content, just a roof over his head, regular meals and some affection. Oh that people could be so simply fulfilled when they grew out of childish notions.

And what notions she and Tilda had had. Fantasies really. Of foreign lands and dashing men. Of exploration and adventure. They'd lost touch after leaving school, Isabella concentrating on becoming a teacher and Tilda heading to the city to try her luck where there were more opportunities (and more bachelors). The last Isabella heard was that Tilda had become engaged to an up-and-coming businessman. And if that was the case, what on earth was she doing masquerading as a lunatic?

Were there really people who wanted to kill her, or was she hiding out for some other reason? Whatever it was, her caper couldn't last. And although Isabella had kept her word and not mentioned anything to Angus, how long could she reasonably keep up the pretence? Yes, they'd sworn as girls to keep each other's secrets but this was something entirely different. If Angus ever found out Isabella knew anything about his mystery Irish patient, he would surely never trust her again. And rightly so. She was a liar by omission. First the census, then the dead baby, and now, of all things, Tilda White.

The front door opened and her husband appeared in the hall.

"What are you doing here?" Isabella said abruptly. "I thought you were showing Dr Norman and Miss Worthington the wards?"

Angus went over to the decanter on the table by the window and poured a brandy.

"Are you all right?"

He took a large swig. "That's better."

"What's happened?"

He perched on a chair, balancing his glass on the arm. "The senior attendant's been arrested and a report on him's been sent to the Procurator Fiscal."

Isabella set down her paperwork. "What on earth for?"

"Mr Allan." Angus tapped his glass. "It seems there wasn't a fight between him and Mr Smith but that his injuries were caused by Mr Kennedy."

"Mr Kennedy? Surely not. I wouldn't have thought him capable. He's always so charming."

"I thought so too and that Nurse Elliot must be making it up."

"Nurse Elliot? Why would Nurse Elliot make up such a thing?"

"I don't know. Spurned perhaps? Anyway, I spoke with Mrs Rae in the shop, who Nurse Elliot claimed knew something of the assault. And when she confirmed she'd also heard a commotion, I confronted Mr Kennedy."

"And did he confess?"

"Not at first. But when I told him there was more than one witness, he claimed Mr Allan was belligerent and ran off. He said Mr Allan struck him and that he had to defend himself from some strong blows. He said he restrained Mr Allan to protect himself and that there was no intent to cause injury."

"Oh my goodness. What'll happen to him?"

"He'll be detained in custody until his trial for murder."

"*Murder?* Oh, Angus. How awful."

"Well, more likely culpable homicide."

"And if he's found guilty?"

"That'll depend on the jury. There was a similar case at Mount Hope some years ago when two attendants maltreated a patient who later died from his injuries. They claimed provocation. They said the patient had taken a violent turn and lashed out at them. The jury took twenty-five minutes to reach a unanimous verdict of guilty under provocation and strongly recommended mercy for the accused. They were sentenced to three months in prison."

"Is that all?"

Angus lifted his glass and took another gulp of brandy. "Yes."

"Do you think Mr Kennedy will receive the same?"

"If the jury believes him. Although his version isn't how Nurse Elliot describes it. However, she waited until Mr Allan died before reporting the incident. The jury may not find anything she has to say credible."

"She must have had good reason not to report it," Isabella said. "I mean, she's an excellent nurse. Matron Campbell said so. You said so yourself. And I would certainly agree."

"I can think of no reason, let alone a good one, for not reporting the assault of a patient. Anyway, it's immaterial now." Angus finished his brandy.

"Why?"

"Because I've dismissed her."

"What? But where will she go?"

"That's not my concern."

"But Angus! This isn't just her place of work, it's her home. She'll need time to find alternative lodgings and—"

He banged his glass on the side table. "She's got until the end of the week. Now, I must go and get ready for tonight's dinner. I'm only grateful that our visitors have been well-occupied today and didn't witness Mr Kennedy being taken away." He paused in the middle of the room. "By the way, I met Mr Gillies earlier and told him just to take the typewriter he was bringing you back to the house secretary since you won't have any further need of it."

"*What?*"

Angus started to go from the room, then turned back. "Oh, and to burn any papers there might be in the box, as they wouldn't be anything important."

JESSIE

Miss Wilson said if there was space in the hall, the laundry maids could attend the staff concert as long as they 'conducted themselves properly'. Which as far as Jessie could fathom, meant not talking to anyone other than your colleagues, and even then only briefly. 'Keep yourselves to yourselves and do it quietly – I won't have the reputation of the laundry tarnished by any unbecoming behaviour.'

Although Jessie wasn't quite sure what Miss Wilson considered 'unbecoming behaviour', she nevertheless stood in silence at the back of the hall, eyes fixed on the stage, in case glancing at a patient or acknowledging one of the nurses fell into that category.

Mrs Lockhart and the American visitors were sitting in the front row, directly in Jessie's eyeline. Fortunately, that meant Miss Wilson couldn't accuse her of staring at them, even if that was exactly what she was doing. It was impossible not to. Even from behind, Miss Worthington, in her emerald gown, was compelling. Mrs Lockhart equally so in blue. The American doctor and Dr Lockhart looked handsome too, all done up in their tails.

Not only did the group look impeccable, they behaved

impeccably, enthusiastically applauding each act, irrespective of its merits. They roundly cheered Reverend Fulton after his monotonous recitation of 'Tam O'Shanter' and called for more screechy renditions from Mr Johnstone and Dr Dorsie when their violin set had come to a welcome end.

The best-received turn so far was Mr Gillies, whose performance of 'Come into the Garden, Maud' (dedicated to his 'good lady wife') brought a tear to the eyes of many. To Jessie, it brought back a sudden memory of when she was very young. Of her father kneeling on the ground, serenading her mother, imploring her to love him forever. Of her mother laughing and shooing him away. Then of her looking into his eyes and him springing to his feet to hug her. Of her parents' embrace ending, and her father punching her brothers' arms affectionately then lifting Jessie onto his knee to play Pat-a-cake.

Murmurs rippled through the audience. The medical superintendent and Dr Forbes were taking to the stage.

Dr Lockhart introduced his first song, 'The Lark in the Clear Air', then put his hands behind his back and looked upwards as he waited for Dr Forbes to play the introduction.

"Dear thoughts are in my mind,
And my soul soars enchanted ..."
Jessie winced as he fluffed a high note.
"As I hear the sweet lark sing
In the clear air of the day.
For a tender beaming smile
To ..."
When he went off-key, Dr Forbes flinched and played the piano louder. After what seemed like too many verses, the performance finally came to an end.

Dr Lockhart took his bow and Dr Forbes stood up to acknowledge the appreciation. While the audience cheered, the hall doors burst open and a grimy man strode down the aisle waving a cane in the air. He waited until the applause died down before turning to face the concertgoers.

"Where's my daughter?" he bawled, scanning the faces in the front row, pointing his cane at each person in turn. "Where is she?"

Jessie froze. If she stayed absolutely still, he might not notice her standing at the back with the other laundry maids.

Her father shuffled to the second row, then the third, shaking his head. He searched the fourth, then smashed the tip of his cane on the floor. "Where is Jessie Purdie?"

A few people turned to look at her. Jessie pulled her cap down over her brow. A lighthearted shout from the audience broke the silence: "She's behind you!"

As the audience tittered, Dr Lockhart and the American doctor got up and edged towards the intruder.

"Get away!" He brandished his cane like a sword.

They approached within a few feet of him.

"Get away!"

Dr Lockhart took a step back as the cane swished in front of his face, then he signalled to the attendants for assistance. Two crept from the back of the hall, another three from the flanks.

Jessie's father circled round and whirled his cane at the men, who ducked in between attempts to grab him. She glanced at the doors – could she make a run for it without him seeing her?

More attendants were lining up behind their colleagues. When her father spotted them, he swirled the cane faster. "Get away from me! I'll kill you! I'll kill you all!"

The nurses began to usher patients towards the back of the hall, creating a barrier between Jessie and the scrum. She stood on tiptoe to see what was happening.

Her father was surrounded, swaying and swooshing from one man to the next. When he made a faltering lunge at Dr Lockhart, one of the attendants rushed him to the ground.

Jessie couldn't help herself. She fought against the tide of patients and pushed Dr Lockhart and the American aside.

"Stop! Don't hurt him! I'm Jessie Purdie. He's my father!" She knelt beside him, rearing at the smell of alcohol and filth. "Please don't hurt him!" she cried. He continued to flail. "Daddy! Stop struggling. Please. I'm here."

He peered at her. His eyes were bloodshot, his face red and bloated.

"It's me! Jessie."

He screwed up his face. "You're not my Jessie. Away to hell!"

He lashed out with his fist, catching her chin with an uppercut. Jessie's teeth knocked together and she fell backwards, her head cracking on the hard floor.

The attendants piled back on top of him and he started to kick. Jessie rolled onto her hands and knees to crawl away from the ruckus. But before she was able to get away, the hard toe cap of her father's boot caught her flush in the face.

"Away to hell!"

The last thing Jessie heard him say before she passed out.

KATHERINE

KATHERINE WENT into one of the sick rooms off the ladies' ward and instructed the duty nurse to take her leave. She closed the door and consulted the chart hanging above Miss Purdie's bed. The patient had had a relatively undisturbed night, having woken only once in a state of mild confusion. Both her temperature and pulse were normal and she'd not suffered any fits or seizures.

Katherine gently shook her arm. "How are you feeling?"

Miss Purdie blinked. "Hmm?" She touched the purple bruise on her chin and grimaced.

"Don't worry. There isn't any lasting damage. Your head may be tender but there don't appear to be any fractures." Katherine took the girl's wrist and felt her pulse. Strong and steady. "You took a couple of knocks but you're going to be all right. We're just keeping you here until you get your sea legs."

Miss Purdie started to haul herself up in bed.

"Take it slowly," Katherine said, leaning over to arrange the pillows.

Miss Purdie sank back, then gave a start. "Where's my father?"

"You remember what happened then." Katherine straightened the sheets. "Your father's been admitted. He's—"

Miss Purdie sat forward. "He's been admitted? *Here*?"

"Yes. He's in the men's hospital ward. He—"

She threw off her sheet and swung her legs round. "I have to go."

Katherine blocked her way. "You can't go and see him at the moment, he's—"

"I don't want to *see* him. I have to leave!" She pushed Katherine aside and looked round the room. "Where are my clothes?"

"Miss Purdie …" Katherine took her arm and led her back to bed. "… listen to me."

"Why has he not been arrested?"

"Dr Lockhart thought it might be more appropriate to admit him. He's very ill, you know."

"I know," she said quietly.

"The nature of his illness provides grounds for admission. He's suffering from what we would call 'chronic alcoholic insanity'. As a result, I suspect, of years of intemperance. His confusion and aggression, why he didn't recognise you, that's because of the effects of alcohol on his brain. If he's to recover, he needs treatment. He could be here a while. You don't have to leave. You're quite safe. He's been given a sleeping draught. He'll need to rest for some time."

"Is Miss Wilson angry with me?"

"Miss Wilson? Why would she be angry with you?"

"She said we were to be on our best behaviour and not do anything to tarnish the reputation of the laundry."

"No, she's not angry with you. No one's angry with you. It wasn't your fault." Katherine smiled sympathetically. "All we're concerned about is that you haven't suffered any serious injury. And as far as I can see, you haven't. But I'll advise Miss Wilson that you should rest for today and that you shouldn't return to work until tomorrow."

"Thank you."

"Also, I wanted to tell you that ..." She lowered her voice. "... Miss Anderson's baby got a proper burial. And I understand Miss Anderson's recovering well too. You were a very good friend to her. And thank you for, well ..."

"It's all right. What you did ... what we all did ... it was right." Miss Purdie leaned back and closed her eyes.

"That's it. Just you rest. The nurse'll keep an eye on you now. I have rounds but I'll come back to check on you later."

Poor girl. She'd been as good as her word, keeping quiet about their shared secret. It was a pity she'd been dealt such an unfavourable hand in life. She was intelligent and hard-working, unlike some of the girls who came and went from the laundry. She deserved more.

As Katherine passed through the atrium on her way to the men's wing, her name was called. She kept on walking; she could do without hearing Mr Johnstone's opinions on matters today.

"Dr Forbes? There's a gentleman here to see you."

Katherine stopped. Surely Dr Cowan hadn't come to plead with her to leave for Bombay with him?

"It's a Mr ..." Mr Johnstone consulted the white calling card he was holding. "... Charles Huntly-Sykes ... Esquire."

"What?" Katherine froze. What had happened that required a personal visit from her solicitor? It could only be bad news.

"I've put him in the Visitors' Tea Room. After last night, Mr Gillies wasn't for letting him through the gates at all. But when he found out the gentleman was a solicitor and ..." Mr Johnstone eyeballed Katherine. "... an *acquaintance* of yours, he thought it would be safe enough. I take it you do know the ... gentleman?"

"Of course."

"I say 'gentleman', but he hardly looks old enough to be working, let alone to be a professional man."

"Yes, well, thank you for letting me know, Mr Johnstone," she said, setting off at a pace just short of a trot.

Except on Wednesdays and special occasions, the Visitors' Tea Room was devoid of activity. Katherine peered through the square glass panel in the door. Mr Huntly-Sykes was sitting at an empty table by the window. It was a dull day outside, and perhaps with the lights being off, he wouldn't notice her dread at what he might be about to say.

He got to his feet as soon as she entered. "Dr Forbes. Good to see you. How are you?"

Katherine shook his hand. "What are you doing here? What's happened?" she couldn't stop herself blurting out.

"Well, I was visiting a client in town so I thought I'd come and tell you in person rather than have you wait for a letter. It's good news."

"Oh? Tell me."

"The complainant's finally seen sense and the case against you has been dropped."

"Truly?"

"Truly."

"Oh, thank goodness." Katherine's legs suddenly felt weak. She pulled out a chair. "What changed his mind?"

Mr Huntly-Sykes sat down too. "Let's just say he was persuaded of the futility of his action by an appeal to his wallet. I understand he was shown an estimate of the fees he'd incur and that his solicitor didn't stint on the projections."

Katherine let out a long breath.

"Didn't I tell you the case was ill-founded, feeble and egregious?" Mr Huntly-Sykes folded his arms triumphantly. "I knew it."

"Yes, you did. I don't know what to say. Thank you. Thank you very much."

"All in a day's work, Dr Forbes."

"I'd offer you a cup of tea," she said, glancing around the empty room, "but it's only served on a Wednesday at visiting time."

"That's quite all right. Perhaps the next time you visit the city, I might join you for one at the Suffrage Centre."

"I'm sure your mother will be very impressed by the work you've done for my cause."

"Oh, your case wasn't a cause, Dr Forbes. It was a symptom. I leave my mother to deal with the causes."

When he laughed, Katherine laughed too.

"Yes. Though I wonder, Mr Huntly-Sykes – in your line of work, don't you sometimes get tired of just dealing with the symptoms of things? Don't you sometimes wonder if it might be more satisfying to deal with the causes?"

"Not at all," he said. "In any case, without causes there would be no symptoms. Unless you're suggesting that symptoms of causes should go untreated. If you get my drift. If that's what you're suggesting, might I respectfully suggest you're in the wrong line of work?"

"No, no. I was just speculating that if perhaps we did pay more attention to causes, then the occurrence of symptoms might be reduced."

"I'm sure that would be the case. But think of it this way, Dr Forbes – if all the causes were addressed, you and I would be out of a job."

Katherine studied the young man opposite – his looks might not be mature but his cynicism was.

HELEN

As a matter of routine, new nurses were assigned to the hospital wards to learn the basics of caring for patients with bodily diseases. Now Helen was back there seeing out her notice, consigned to the men's wards to give bed-baths and perform a never-ending sequence of cleaning rituals.

She pushed her mop into the corner of the room, then got onto her hands and knees and began rubbing the floor with a flannel. She swished it from side to side, staring at the skirting board and moving her head to the rhythm of two thoughts: *Where will I go? What will I do?*

Dr Lockhart might have given her a few days before she had to leave (and certainly she was glad of the pay), but all it was doing was giving her more time to fret about how she was going to manage.

Where will I go?

And while Dr Lockhart hadn't said as much, she assumed that neither he nor Matron Campbell would be providing her with a recommendation.

What will I do?

And without a recommendation, how would she get another position?

She wouldn't be able to take the exams now either. All that effort wasted. All that work to ensure she'd never end up at the poorhouse again. Or, like her mother, having to do favours for a gentleman to get a leg-up in life. Oh, Dr Scott had seemed nice at first, taking an interest in the raggedy child of the char woman who cleaned the subscription library and the offices of the professional men in the same city street. *What a clever girl, reading* Gray's Anatomy! *She could do well in nursing. I could show her the way and put in a word.*

Except, as Helen now knew, in this world you didn't get something for nothing. Everything was a contract. Thus Dr Scott did some favours for Helen's mother, she did some favours for him. And what had Helen now done? She'd dishonoured the woman who'd sacrificed her dignity for her. All her mother's shame and humiliation, it had all been for nothing.

Where will I go? What will I ...

Helen stopped rubbing the floor and sat on her hunkers. Maybe there was a way she might salvage something. Maybe in return for keeping her silence about Miss Anderson, she could get a letter of recommendation from Dr Forbes. Dr Lockhart need never know and Helen could go to another asylum far away, confident she'd be able to gain employment.

A surge of hope propelled her to her feet. But as she hung the flannel on the mop handle, despair rose again in the pit of her stomach. What was she thinking? How could she even contemplate threatening Dr Forbes for trying to do the right thing by a young girl? If only Helen had done the right thing when she'd first witnessed Mr Kennedy's behaviour towards Mr Allan, she might not be working her notice now.

So what if Mr Kennedy had told Dr Lockhart about her involvement with the petition? At least she could've left Cappelmuir with her head held high. As it was, she'd be as bad as Mr Kennedy if she tried to blackmail Dr Forbes, and would deserve no better than him. No – everything that had happened to her was of her own making and she'd just have to live with the consequences.

There was a draught from one of the open windows. Helen consulted the thermometer on the wall: fifty-eight degrees Fahrenheit, the lowest in the acceptable range. She scanned the beds to check whether any of the dozing patients seemed uncomfortable, then fetched a screen to put in front of the window, just in case. As she did so, she caught a whiff of excrement.

She started along the row of beds, sniffing the air to locate the source, then stopped at the third one along, where the smell was stronger. She went to the head of the bed and inhaled – there was no doubt who had soiled himself.

"Do you need a bed-pan, Mr Purdie?"

He was lying on his back, moaning. Helen lifted the sheet and almost retched. The mattress was covered in faeces and urine.

"It's all right. I'll get you sorted out."

He groaned, then rolled into his own filth before Helen could stop him.

"Oh dear Lord." A delirious patient couldn't take a bath, so Mr Purdie was going to have to be washed and dried in bed, and his soiled linen removed immediately from the ward.

She punched the mattress. *Endurance* and *cheerfulness; forbearance* and *absolute kindness; altruism* and *inexhaustible patience.* Those were the values the Red Book encouraged. If Helen had ever possessed such qualities, she didn't possess them now. It was maybe just as well she was leaving.

Mr Purdie whined. Perhaps she should just go from Cappelmuir right now and leave him to wallow. All staying on was doing was torturing her.

She felt a tap on her shoulder.

"Oh! Nurse Millar." This was all she needed, someone gloating. Or more likely, Nurse Millar would berate her for having reported Mr Kennedy and ruining any plans for matrimony she might've been harbouring. For he'd been arrested now and charged. And, irrespective of the verdict of the court, he'd never be back at Cappelmuir. That at least was something to be glad of.

"Do you need a hand?"

"What?"

Her colleague smiled. "Don't look so surprised."

Helen's eyes started to water. "I wasn't … I'm not … I …" She looked away. "I'm afraid Mr Purdie's soiled himself."

"Well, we'd better get him sorted out then, hadn't we? Do you want to do him or the bed?"

"Definitely the bed."

Once they'd positioned the waterproof sheet under Mr Purdie, Helen left Nurse Millar to sponge him down. She dropped the stinking bedding in a sack, tied it tightly then listed the items on a chit which she slipped under the string.

She took the bundle out to the courtyard for collection by the laundry maids. There were two other sacks in the far corner of the courtyard so she put her load beside them. Hopefully it wasn't Miss Purdie's turn to do ward rounds. It was enough that her father had been admitted as a habitual drunkard without her having to wash his fetid bedding as well.

What was worse – having a father like Mr Purdie or never knowing one at all? In all her years at the orphanage, Helen only ever dreamed about having a father who was loving and caring. A father who'd comfort and take care of her. One she could rely on and who'd be proud of her. But if her father was anything like Mr Purdie, she was well shot of him. She stamped her foot on the ground. She'd survived worse things than leaving Cappelmuir; she'd survive this too.

When Helen returned to the ward, Nurse Millar was tucking in the fresh sheet on top of Mr Purdie. He was lying on his side now, grunting. He looked twenty years older than his thirty-nine.

"Good job," Helen said. "I expect Dr Dorsie will be administering another draught on his next rounds."

"I imagine so."

"And thank you. I appreciate your help."

"You're welcome. I was coming to speak to you anyway."

"Oh?"

"Yes." Nurse Millar stepped back from the bed. "The nurses, we've been chatting. It's not right what's happened to you. Something has to be done."

Helen shrugged. "The medical superintendent's perfectly entitled to—"

"So we've decided we're going to add you to the petition."

"What?"

"And if Dr Lockhart doesn't keep you on, we're prepared to strike."

"You can't do that!"

"I mean, it's all very well for him swanning around and showing off to the Americans."

"No! You'll lose your jobs!"

"No we won't. I've been speaking to my cousin. She says the Mount Hope nurses are back at work. The Trades' Council got them reinstated. And they've sorted out their hours. So if they can do it at Mount Hope, we can do it here."

"But what if—?"

"It's decided. You were prepared to stand up for us so we're going to stand up for you. You've not done anything wrong. If it hadn't been for you, Mr Kennedy would still be strutting around like cock of the walk."

"But I thought ..."

"You thought what?"

" ... well, that you and Mr Kennedy were ... friends."

"That's what I thought too. But turns out he was friends with a great many nurses. He promised so many of us a cottage to live in he'd've needed to own the entire estate if we'd all taken him up on it! I should've listened to everyone.

But I was stupid and naive. Flattered. And a sucker for a handsome face. But I'm not doing this to get back at him. It's just not right that you're being punished for his wrongs."

"But what if Dr Lockhart refuses to reinstate me and dismisses you all?" Helen said. "What will you do? I can't let you do that for me."

Nurse Millar laughed. "We're not doing it for you. We're doing it for ourselves. If they can do it to you – what with you studying for the Red Book and everything – what might they do to the rest of us?"

Helen considered her colleague's question. There was more fire in Nurse Miller than she had given her credit for.

ISABELLA

ANGUS WAS IN FINE FETTLE, going with Dr Norman from patient to patient and giving out copies of *The Passing Hour*. Each time he handed one over, his voice got higher. "Read and enjoy. It's published for your amusement."

Isabella turned to Miss Worthington. "He's very excited to finally be able to distribute it. He wanted to wait until you were here. I fear, however, that some of the readers may not be as enthusiastic about the magazine as he is."

"He's right to be," Miss Worthington said, eyeing the copy she was holding. "It's most engaging. A model of what such a publication should be."

"Thank you. It's gratifying to hear that our efforts – the asylum's efforts – are appreciated."

Isabella stopped a polite distance behind Angus and Dr Norman when they paused to speak to two elderly patients sitting knitting on one of the Blue Room's comfortable couches.

"Am I to take it, Mrs Lockhart, that you played some part in the development of the magazine?" Miss Worthington said.

"A bit."

"I thought so."

"Yes, I had one or two ideas about what might make

interesting pieces and Angus was kind enough to agree to include some of them."

Miss Worthington flicked through her copy. "'Cappelmuir Characters'. I imagine that was your idea? She turned over another few pages. "And this? The review of entertainments?"

"Guilty as charged."

"And this ..." Miss Worthington started to giggle. "... this must be your doing. I can't imagine the medical superintendent considering it suitable unless influenced by someone with, let's say, a greater sense of what might be entertaining to patients."

Isabella looked over the top of Miss Worthington's magazine to see what she was referring to.

"I mean, it's just wonderful: 'The Leghorn That Doesn't Love The Ladies'."

"Oh, that. Yes."

Poor Mr Smith. He would never see his words in print now.

Miss Worthington began to read aloud:

"When next that those two kitchen maids encounter him

On his ground, he'll find he's met his match;

And the other girls will all be in the jolly swim

When they set out this chanticleer to catch."

I think it's wonderful there are contributions from the patients."

Isabella leaned into her. "To tell you the truth, it did take a bit of persuading to have that one included."

Miss Worthington put her arm through Isabella's and laughed. "The sign of a good physician is one who's prepared to listen to the views of others and to accept that he doesn't always know what's best. Sometimes a little bit of humility is just what the doctor ordered."

Isabella tittered and Angus glanced round. A smile from her was enough to persuade him to continue his procession. He handed a magazine to a young woman sprawled on an armchair and sporting an extravagant feather hat. She stared at the cover then looked at him mischievously.

"That's a nice picture of the prison."

"Oh, that's not a prison, my dear, it's the asylum," he said.

The young woman, catching sight of Isabella, raised her eyebrows and pointed at Angus as if he were the insane one. Then she puckered her lips and looked again at *The Passing Hour*. "Thank you for keeping me right, Doctor."

Angus looked pleased with himself and carried on to the window, where Tilda White was sitting in the nook with old Mrs Shaw. Isabella swallowed but kept a smile fixed on her face. Tilda looked away then recovered her poise.

"Well, aren't we honoured, Nellie?" she chirped in an accent that sounded a bit more Irish than before. "Look who's come to see us? None other than the medical superintendent himself. Top of the morning to you, Dr Lockhart!"

Isabella caught Tilda's eye and, despite her bravado, saw fear. She stepped forward and introduced Tilda's companion. "This is Mrs Shaw, Miss Worthington. She's been here a good many years and could teach us all a thing or two. Isn't that right, Mrs Shaw?"

As the group's attention turned to the bewildered old woman, Isabella gave Tilda the tiniest nod of reassurance.

"Yes, that's right, Mrs Shaw," Angus said. "How many years is it now we've had the pleasure of your company?"

"Was it last year I came?"

"Come now, Mrs Shaw, it's been a tad longer than that."

"And I'm fed up sharing my bathwater with five others," she snapped.

"Ha! That doesn't happen anymore, Mrs Shaw! No." Angus turned to Dr Norman. "That doesn't happen anymore," he said seriously. He spun round again, flashed an insincere smile at Mrs Shaw, then thrust a magazine at Tilda. "Read and enjoy!"

She opened it immediately and held it in front of her face.

"And here's one for you, Mrs Shaw. That'll keep you

entertained for a while! Keep your mind off the bathing water, I dare say."

Old Mrs Shaw gazed at the magazine as if it were a precious artefact. "My goodness. I've never seen anything like this before."

"Indeed not. It's a first, and is published for your amusement and entertainment. Read and enjoy!"

Angus steered Dr Norman quickly on.

Isabella smiled at old Mrs Shaw, grateful for her inadvertent diversion. "Good day, ladies. Enjoy the magazine."

Tilda didn't look up from her reading.

Once every patient had been given a copy of *The Passing Hour*, Matron Campbell took the visitors to inspect the kitchens while Angus walked Isabella to the main doors.

"That went very well, don't you think? Dr Norman was most impressed. He's talking about starting a magazine at his own establishment. Didn't I tell you it would promote our reputation?"

"You did, yes. I'm very pleased it's been such a success for you," Isabella said.

"And despite recent unfortunate events, the esteem in which Dr Norman seems to hold us doesn't appear to have lessened any. In fact, if anything, he seems to have been impressed with how I've handled things. I wouldn't have believed it. It really couldn't have gone any better."

"No."

"But there you are." Angus gave a satisfied sigh. "Isn't it strange how things work out?"

"It is."

He rubbed his hands together. "Now, my dear, I have something to ask. As you know, I was considering staying overnight for the symposium. Now that we have the car, of course, the journey will be much quicker. However, it's been going so well with Dr Norman that I was thinking that it might be politic to stay over anyway. He's been talking about asking his establishment to fund a visit of physicians and he's hinted that I might be among those invited. Just imagine – Dr and Mrs Angus Lockhart travelling to America."

Isabella stared at him. "Dr *and* Mrs?"

"Yes. Dr Norman was most insistent. It seems I'm not the only one who's made an impression," Angus said, patting her arm.

"Well, it's certainly nice to be appreciated by someone."

"Anyway, they'd like to see a bit of the city the day before the symposium so I was thinking of offering my services as a guide. It wouldn't do any harm to spend more time with them. In the interests of the asylum. So what I was wondering was whether or not—?"

"You want to stay away overnight?"

"Only if you don't mind being alone in the house. I'd be back on the Monday evening."

"Well, I …"

"You could always invite Effie to stay," he said. "For some company."

"I suppose I could."

Isabella turned her head to hide her smile. If Effie were to stay at Cappelmuir, she wouldn't pass the night in her own dwelling and wouldn't be counted in the census. Her husband could truthfully complete the form saying he was the only person there. Enumerators wouldn't be calling at Isabella's, because the asylum was submitting an institutional schedule compiled by the house secretary. And he would be far too busy counting the patients and staff to realise there was a guest at the medical superintendent's house.

She turned back to Angus. "Oh all right. I suppose you're right. It would make perfect sense."

"Are you sure, my dear?"

"Of course," Isabella said. "If it's in the interests of the asylum, then it's in my interests too."

JESSIE

WHEN JESSIE SKULKED into the laundry, Miss Wilson suggested she work in the dispatch room for the day.

The head laundress didn't have to say it twice. The prospect of facing questions from the other maids about her father's disgraceful performance at the concert distressed her. Not because her colleagues would be unsympathetic, but because they might be too sympathetic. While anger, teasing and sarcasm Jessie could cope with, pity she could not.

Matilda, however, was far from content at being removed from the bustle of the wash room, and had been griping about it non-stop.

"Can't I go back? Will you ask Miss Wilson?" The disgruntled patient cast a pile of folded shirts into a trolley.

"Don't throw them like that. They'll get creased again."

How could she be so self-centred? She'd witnessed the stramash at the concert and knew Jessie was sore in both body and heart.

"And no. You can't." Jessie began to sort the garments, irked. "I've told you before – where I go, you go. That's how it works. It's not that long ago you were saying you wouldn't work with anyone else *but* me."

"But it's boring in here. I want to go back to the wash room."

"It's only for today," Jessie snapped. "Just make the most of the peace and quiet for a change."

Matilda lifted another pile of shirts. "Well, it doesn't really matter anyway. I won't be here much longer."

"What do you mean?"

"I'm being discharged soon."

"What?" Jessie took a bed sheet and handed one end to Matilda. "When did Dr Forbes tell you that?"

"She hasn't."

"Dr Lockhart, then."

"He hasn't either. But they will." Matilda grinned. "Soon."

Jessie tugged the sheet. "Help me with this." She had enough to be getting on with without being drawn into any more of this patient's games.

"You should get away from here too," Matilda added. "He'll never leave you alone."

They came together to fold the sheet, then Jessie dropped it in the trolley. "They won't be long bringing the next load. Then we can get on with our rounds."

Matilda continued undeterred. "You don't need to put up with him. You should go somewhere he won't find you …"

Jessie thought she had.

"… somewhere away from town where no one knows you. You could get a position somewhere else easily. Don't let him control you."

Jessie went into the corridor to avoid having to engage in the conversation. "What on earth's keeping these girls?"

"He won't change, you know. Take it from me. No matter what you do. Once a drunk, always a drunk."

Jessie marched back to Matilda. "Shush! People will hear you."

"They don't need to hear me to know what he's like. Not after the other night. It's as plain as the nose on your face."

Jessie glowered at her charge. Was it worth risking instant dismissal to slap Matilda to shut her up? Probably not. "Thank you, but I think you've got enough on your plate without giving anyone else advice."

"That's exactly why I can give advice. Let me guess – at first it was just occasionally, after a few drinks too many. Then it became more regular. Then it was every time he had a drink. And now it's all the time. I'm telling you, get away before it's too late. Trust me."

The maids from the ironing room appeared with a bundle of fresh laundry. Jessie took their inventory and checked the items off as Matilda put them into the trolley.

"Good, that's everything. Come on. Push."

She led Matilda along the trail of paths, dropping off newly-laundered bedding, clothing and towels at each designated point.

The last destination was the men's hospital ward, which generated such never-ending loads of soiled items that it really ought to have its own laundry. For every job that came from the women's wards, there were three from the men's – it was like living with her father and brothers.

When Jessie turned left at the fork in the path that would take them to the courtyard at the rear of the ward, Matilda carried straight on.

"This way," Jessie said, correcting the direction of the trolley. "The linen goes to the back courtyard."

Matilda instead veered to the front of the building. "Nurse Elliot's up there. I need to ask her something."

Jessie pulled the trolley again. "Never mind Nurse Elliot. This way. Come on."

Matilda let go the trolley and marched off.

"Come back! You've work to do. Don't be bothering people," Jessie called after her.

Matilda ignored the instructions and went up to Nurse Elliot, who was overseeing four bedridden patients on the verandah. Jessie hadn't seen her for a few days, as Nurse Haggarty had been escorting Matilda to the laundry. Maybe Nurse Elliot had been asked to look after the patients in the hospital because she knew more about bodily illnesses. Though, Jessie had once heard Miss Wilson say that Nurse Elliot had 'nothing to do all day except stick her nose in a book. A day at the laundry would show her what hard work was.'

Whatever the reason for Nurse Elliot's absence from the ladies' wing, Jessie hoped it wouldn't be for much longer. She was one of the nicest nurses and always gave the time of day to the laundry maids.

After chatting to Matilda for a moment, Nurse Elliot accompanied her back. "Here she is, Miss Purdie."

"I'm sorry about that." Jessie frowned at Matilda. "It won't happen again."

"It's quite all right. I know what she can be like."

"Thank you. Well, we won't keep you from your duties any longer, Nurse Elliot." Jessie nodded at Matilda. "Go on, then."

"Miss Purdie – your father's out on the verandah, if you'd like to see him."

Jessie stepped back. "No."

"It's all right. He's not—"

"No!"

"He can't hurt you. He's very drowsy. The medical superintendent's given him a sedative."

Jessie shook her head.

"You should go and see him," Matilda said. "If only to say goodbye. Then take your chance and go. Before it's too late."

"It's the first bed on the left as you go up the steps. I'll supervise Matilda if you want a few moments with him."

Jessie looked over to the ward. *Take your chance and go. Before it's too late.* Too late for what? If her father were to die tomorrow, she wouldn't grieve. She'd already mourned the man he once was. Matilda was right, though – as long as he lived, he'd never stop pursuing her.

Jessie plodded over to the verandah, stalling to admire the decorative red line that ran along the newly painted white railings. The patients had done an excellent job. She paused and looked over her shoulder. Nurse Elliot gave a sympathetic smile, Matilda a swish of the hand. There was no going back.

Jessie slowly went up the steps and approached the first bed on the left.

The contrast of his yellow skin against the crisp white of the bedding was stark. She swallowed. An old man. A skeleton with neatly combed hair and a stubble-free chin. More grandfather than father. Fingernails the cleanest she'd ever seen them.

His eyelids flickered and she swayed back.

"Annie."

Her mother's name.

His hand, a stranger's, floated up. Jessie moved out of reach.

"Annie?"

She leaned over and spoke into his ear. "Annie's gone."

He moaned and moved his head to one side.

"Dead."

His hand drifted back down and Jessie caught it, intertwining her fingers with his until it settled again on the bed.

"And Jessie's gone too." She shook his shoulder roughly. "Do you hear me? Jessie's gone too."

KATHERINE

KATHERINE WALKED the short distance from the railway station to the conference hall, carefully dodging the puddles from the previous night's rain.

In her best tweed suit, cream silk blouse with matching scarf (the one from Cree & Co she'd treated herself to twelve months before but had yet to wear) and the dark grey leather boots she kept for formal work occasions, the last thing she wanted was for her appearance to be spoiled. Dr Lockhart would never forgive her if she turned up looking anything less than professional.

It ought to be a proud moment, hobnobbing with eminent physicians from home and abroad. It would likely benefit her career in as yet unanticipated ways. But was it worth having let Mr Smith down so badly?

His case was officially closed, Dr Lockhart's assessment having been endorsed by both the General Board of Lunacy and the Procurator Fiscal. *Objective and reasonable.* That's what they'd agreed Dr Lockhart's conclusion had been. So he was right about trusting the system – after all, it had trusted him.

But what sort of system was it? Was it right that she was about to woo the gentlemen of her profession when, if she'd put her patient first, Mr Smith might not be dead? Could she even, on soul and conscience, still call herself a doctor?

She paused outside the venue to read the poster pinned to the door.

The American Psychiatric Association Proudly presents a symposium on *THE TREATMENT OF ACUTE INSANITY*

Lectures include: *The Pathological Significance of Mental Symptoms, Employment of Women Nurses on the Men's Wards in Hospitals for the Insane, Studies in Heredity with Examples, Borderland Cases of Insanity & the Voluntary Patient*

Chaired by Charles F. Norman, MD, Medical Director of the State Asylum, Massachusetts. Speakers include Dr Angus D. Lockhart, Cappelmuir Asylum …

The medical superintendent would be cock-a-hoop about his name being mentioned in such distinguished company. They'd never hear the end of it back at Cappelmuir. And in truth, it was a little thrilling.

She went into the foyer and scanned the huddles of men for Dr Lockhart. As she peered into the lecture hall, she spotted Dr Cowan and ducked. She hadn't replied to the question on his postcard yet – what if he asked her about it? She skulked out of his line of sight, taking cover behind a trio of delegates who were discussing Dr Lockhart's imminent lecture.

"Lockhart's signal success is due to his keen insight into a woman's nature. He who best knows a woman's heart obtains best results from a woman's service."

"Well, I think he's making a great mistake. Cases of degeneracy are better in the hands of the attendants. As are cases of strong homicidal and suicidal tendencies better under male control. Not to mention those having strong erotic and animal desires – they should not be nursed by women under any circumstances."

Katherine edged away from the group. What was she doing lurking on the fringes? She knew more about the employment of women nurses on men's wards than almost anyone in the hall, which hopefully she'd get the opportunity to demonstrate.

As for Dr Cowan, of course he wouldn't ask her about the message on his postcard. Not here, with all these people present. She was behaving like a schoolgirl. Was the danger of succumbing to matrimony making her befuddled?

Katherine took a deep breath to calm herself. It was just as well she hadn't been introduced to anyone yet. With her foolish behaviour, she was hardly making a good case for employing women in hospitals for the insane.

"Ah, Dr Forbes, you're here. Excellent."

"Dr Lockhart, sir, good morning. I trust you're well?"

"I'm quite excellent." He gazed around the foyer. "Isn't this wonderful?"

"It is, sir, yes."

"This is going to be a turning point, Dr Forbes, I can feel it."

"Let's hope so, sir."

"Shall we go in? There are seats with our names on them at the front."

He steered her through the gathering crowd. As they reached the entrance to the lecture hall, a man in a dark suit stepped in front of them. He pushed Katherine to one side and stood chest to chest with Dr Lockhart. "Remember me?"

Dr Lockhart stumbled back, peering at the man. "It's Noakes, isn't it? William Noakes."

"Correct."

"Mr Noakes ..." Dr Lockhart tried to sidestep him but Noakes stood his ground. "What are you—?"

Noakes took a revolver from his trouser pocket and fired

three shots into the medical superintendent. Katherine screamed as Dr Lockhart slumped to the floor. She dropped to her knees beside him.

"I want that quack in the witness box again to wring the truth out of him! I lost hundreds of pounds over him. He ruined me." Noakes fired two shots into the air.

Katherine cowered into Dr Lockhart, expecting the worst. When something cracked on the floor, she opened her eyes. A black and silver revolver lay just inches from her.

"Take the fool to hospital!" Noakes roared. "He's a—"

A gang of men rushed him to the ground and held him down.

"It's all right, I'll come quietly," Noakes said as he was dragged away. "I'll not cause you any bother. I've done what I came to do and given him the message. I've got a licence to use the revolver so it's all legal. I know I'll get six or eight months but I just want him back in the witness box."

Dr Lockhart was oozing blood from his chest. Katherine removed her scarf, covered the wound and pressed down on it. She put her ear to his face and felt a wisp of warm breath on her cheek.

"He needs to go to hospital. Now!" she shouted at the gawping onlookers.

One man lifted him by the shoulders, another by his feet. Then they carried Cappelmuir's medical superintendent out of the building.

Katherine stared at the dark blotches on the carpet where he'd lain. There were a few smears of blood on her blouse too. She closed her eyes, her body suddenly leaden.

She shuddered, then froze, as she felt a hand on her shoulder. Had Noakes evaded his captors and come back to shoot her now?

"Dr Forbes?" Fingers around her wrist. She held her breath. "It's all right. Let me help you up. Take my arm."

She opened her eyes. Dr Cowan was looking down at her

kindly, encouragingly, while a circle of men behind him seemed to be staring at her in judgement.

She could feel the tears coming. But she mustn't cry. She was as able as any man to deal with what had happened.

"It's all right. You're all right," Dr Cowan said, gently helping her to her feet.

"Thank you. I just need a moment to …" She wiped her bloody hands on her skirt. *Don't cry.* She turned back to him. "Where are they taking Dr Lockhart?"

"The City Hospital."

"I have to go there."

"All in good time. He's in good hands. There's nothing you can do for him just now. Let's get a cup of tea, or something stronger, to—"

"To what?" Katherine snapped. *Do not cry.* "Settle my nerves?" She brushed herself down. "It's quite all right, Dr Cowan. I've seen traumatic flesh wounds before."

"Of course. But with it being someone so close … anyone would—"

"I am a doctor, you know?" She eyeballed the watching group of men. *Do not cry.*

Dr Cowan gripped her arm. "Yes, you are. But you're a human being first."

"But, I—"

"Let me help you, please."

Katherine's eyes welled up. She looked at her feet. Then she let him usher her away, tears streaming down her cheeks.

HELEN

THE MEN MIGHT all be sleeping but Helen was restless. Ordinarily she'd be glad of the lull in activity, of the fact that none of the patients needed assistance or attention. However, any occupation, no matter how foul, was preferable to having the time to dwell on where she might end up once she was relieved of her position at Cappelmuir.

Staying at the town's inn for any more than a day or two would make short work of her savings. And if she wanted a room in a private dwelling, she'd need to secure another position without delay. But without a recommendation, no asylum or hospital would have her.

It was even doubtful if any reputable household would offer her a domestic role, with no one to vouch for her except the insane. And even the insane mightn't, were they to discover her neglect of Mr Allan.

"Nurse Elliot?"

Helen sprang to her feet. Never would she have thought Matron Campbell swooshing into the ward would be a welcome distraction.

"You're wanted by Dr Dorsie."

"What?"

Matron Campbell swept back out. "Come."

Helen skipped to catch up with her, then continued briskly along the corridor to keep time with her superior. "Do you know what he wants?" He'd never asked to see her before.

Matron Campbell marched on. "A gentleman has arrived claiming to be Matilda's husband and seeking her discharge."

Helen paused, then got back in step with the matron. "Really?"

"Yes. And with Dr Lockhart and Dr Forbes at the symposium, Dr Dorsie wishes a word with you, since you've been close to the patient."

"Of course."

Was Matilda's friend finally coming to rescue her?

What if it was her husband instead and she was discharged into his care only for him to do away with her?

Helen would just have to take her lead from her patient. As usual.

Matron Campbell stopped outside the Admissions Room and knocked once. The doctor came out.

"I'll wait with the patient," she said, going in and closing the door.

Dr Dorsie looked at the floor and rubbed his bald head. It was a mystery to Helen that he'd ever thought to become a doctor. Perhaps he came from a line of medical men. But he would've been better suited to a different profession. Preferably one which had no need to interact with people.

"Nurse Elliot, is it?" he mumbled without looking up.

"Yes," Helen said, more eagerly than she'd intended.

He edged back. "You're familiar with the Irish woman, Matilda?"

Helen's hands began to tremble. She clasped them behind her back. "Yes, Doctor."

"Are you aware of any medical reason why she shouldn't be discharged into her husband's care?"

Helen's heart raced. "None at all." Her words came out

high-pitched. She cleared her throat and moderated her tone. "The patient's bodily signs are normal and her blood shows no sign of disease or infection. She is—"

"Thank you," Dr Dorsie said. He flapped the back of his hand against the door and Matron Campbell came out. "Bring Mr Murphy along now, please, Matron. And, Nurse Elliot, you supervise the patient."

"Certainly ..." Helen was hardly over the threshold when he closed the door on her. "... Doctor."

Matilda was sitting on the cane chair. Helen took her by the wrist and led her to the window. "Is this him?" she whispered. "Your friend?"

"Of course it's him." Matilda jigged on the spot. "Who else could it be? Didn't you read the letter?"

"No, I didn't."

Matilda dug her nails into Helen's arm. "You did send it, didn't you? I know you said you did but you haven't been on the ward so I wondered if something had happened. Someone said you wouldn't be back so I was worried. Are you leaving?"

"Never mind that. Yes, of course I sent it." (Well, she'd given it to Mr Thomson, and if she was any judge of character he'd'd've been as good as his word.) "I told you I had."

Matilda loosened her grip. "Thank God."

"Your friend, is his name Mr Murphy?"

Matilda threw her arms around Helen's neck and hugged her. "Yes! That's the name we agreed. He's from the Emerald Isle, don't you know?" she said, putting on her Irish accent.

"Really?"

Matilda laughed. "No."

"Of course not."

"But just for today he's Mr Murphy, a Belfast tailor who comes across the water every few months to buy tartan and tweed. He and his wife had a terrible misunderstanding and she left home. But she couldn't cope on her own and with the emotion of it all, she lost all sense of reason and ended up taking a trip over the sea, thinking she would end herself. He heard about the Irish woman who got pulled from the river, recognised the description and has come to get her. He'll even have a photograph of the two of them to confirm her identity. And poor Mrs Murphy, she's going to be overjoyed because it was all a big mistake and she's happy for him to take her home."

"You've got it all worked out, haven't you?"

Matilda crossed the fingers of both hands. "Let's hope so."

Dr Dorsie came back in, followed by a man of about thirty with dark curly hair and blue eyes. In his black suit, with its slightly worn cuffs and turn-ups, Helen wouldn't have taken him for a tailor. But Dr Dorsie was unlikely to think anything about the man, let alone notice how he was dressed.

Matilda rushed over to him. "Peter! I'm so sorry! I should never have left." Her Irish accent thickened. "I don't know what I was thinking. I'm so glad you're here."

Peter shushed her and gently stroked her hair as she clung to him.

Dr Dorsie looked extremely uncomfortable. "Em, Mr Murphy?" He pointed to a piece of paper on the desk. "You need to sign that, stating that you're receiving your wife into your care of your own free will."

"Of course." Peter scrawled something illegible, while Matilda rocked back and forth. "There we are." He reached into his jacket pocket, took out a small brown envelope and put it on the desk. "And there you are. This is what you're owed. It should cover the costs of my wife's care."

"Thank you. I'm sure—"

There was a knock on the door. Dr Dorsie nodded to Matron Campbell to open it.

"I'm sorry to disturb you, Matron, but—"

"Mr Johnstone. What on earth are you doing here? Dr Dorsie and I are with a patient." She went to close the door.

"But Matron, they sent me with this letter that's just

arrived. They thought it might be important. It's about the woman who … well, the Irish woman … the one that …"

Helen glanced at Tilda, who was rigid.

"Oh for goodness sake, let me have it!" Matron Campbell snatched the letter from Mr Johnstone and closed the door in his face. She read the front and back of the envelope then handed it to Dr Dorsie. He gave a start and looked at it quizzically. "It's been opened by the office. Perhaps you should take a look in Dr Lockhart's absence?"

"Oh, yes. Of course, of course."

While he read the letter, Helen looked at her feet. She could hear Matilda breathing and Peter tapping his shoe on the floor.

The tick of the wall clock reverberated around the room, the pause between every second seeming to get longer. Was this it? Was Matilda finally going to be exposed? And if she was, who knew what she might say to try and deny it?

"Right then." Everyone stared at Dr Dorsie in anticipation. He took an eternity to fold the letter and manoeuvre it back into the envelope. Then he slowly slid Peter's brown envelope over to Matron Campbell.

"Em, is everything in order, Dr Dorsie?" she asked.

Helen held her breath. Matilda closed his eyes. Peter bit his lip. The clock ticked.

"What? Yes, yes, Matron. It was just a letter advising that one of the leads Dr Lockhart was following up has come to nothing. Which is hardly surprising now that we know this is Mrs Murphy. Is it?"

Helen could feel Matilda and Peter trying to contain their relief, just as she was.

"Right. That's that. Everything's concluded," Dr Dorsie said briskly. "Nurse Elliot will see to you now, Mr and Mrs Murphy. Matron Campbell? Please come."

When the door closed, Matilda fell into Peter's arms. "Has he gone? Am I safe?"

Peter glanced at Helen.

"It's all right. Nurse Elliot knows everything. She sent the letter. So has he gone?"

"Yes. I watched him get on the Liverpool ship myself. And it says in the newspaper that the liner set sail for New York as scheduled. He's gone."

Matilda hugged Helen. "Thank you, Nurse Elliot. You've saved my life."

"I think you would've found a way, with or without me."

"Probably."

"Anyway, don't waste time here. Get yourselves going. The next post will be here in a couple of hours and who knows what it might bring!"

"Yes, yes!" Matilda turned to Peter. "Have you secured lodgings?"

"I have."

"Write the address down for Nurse Elliot."

He tore off a piece of the blotting paper that was on the desk.

"Could you give it to Miss Purdie for me?" Matilda said. "It's always good to have somewhere to go if you're running away."

Helen took the scrap from Mr Murphy. "It is indeed."

ISABELLA

WHEN ISABELLA WOKE from her afternoon nap, Tipper was cooried in beside her, snoring quietly. She glanced over at the wall clock, then sat up when she realised it read five thirty. Where had the afternoon gone? She'd only intended to shut her eyes for half an hour or so, just long enough to give her an energy boost after the very late night she and Effie had had.

She shoved Tipper onto the floor, ran a hand over the bedspread to flatten the creases, then went to the dressing table to check her hair in the mirror. There were a few loose strands, but once they were pinned back up, Mrs Drummond would be hard-pressed to see that Isabella had been sleeping. The fewer opportunities for disapproval, the better.

Mrs Drummond never said anything, of course, but she always made it known – a subtle glance here and a tiny gesture there – that she didn't think Isabella good enough for the medical superintendent. (Or, more charitably, that she thought the medical superintendent too good for Isabella.)

The housekeeper wasn't alone in that view. On the occasions Isabella accompanied Angus to Board functions, there were plenty who looked down their noses at her too.

Even Angus sometimes seemed to think she was getting above her station.

She put her hand over her mouth to stifle a giggle; imagine if he'd seen her and Effie's census-night shenanigans! What would he have thought of her then?

Effie had started it. 'So what if it's just the two of us? Who says we can't have a house party?' And once she had an idea in her head, it was nigh impossible to shift it.

After a quiet dinner, the evening began sedately enough with a few games of whist and some bridge practice. But Effie's suggestion that they take a snifter of Angus's scotch to toast the Women's Freedom League quickly led to them reading aloud from *The Vote*, in such impassioned a manner that Charlotte Despard herself would've been proud. That then led to singing. (Their off-key rendition of 'The March of the Women' might even have been heard up on the wards.)

Isabella drew the line at getting out Angus's violin but she couldn't stop Effie going outside at two in the morning to roller skate along the drive. 'If they can do it in London, we can do it here!'

Then they marched up and down the drawing room in their own mini-rally, before partnering each other in a few dances and heading off to bed around four. It was a wonderful evening. A purposeful evening.

Isabella glanced in the mirror again – the state of her hair might be the least of her worries, for Mrs Drummond couldn't but have heard their high jinks. Hopefully, however, despite her disdain, the housekeeper would know *her* place. Although Isabella might not count for much in her eyes, the wife of the medical superintendent did. So if the medical superintendent's wife wished to snooze fully clothed on top of her bed in the middle of the afternoon, so be it.

"Right. Come on, Tipper." Isabella smoothed down her dress. "Let's face the music."

He bounded downstairs to the hall, almost colliding with

Mrs Drummond as she scurried from the back of the house to answer a rat-a-tat-tat on the front door.

"Tipper! Here!" Isabella called. "I'm so sorry, Mrs Drummond. And it's all right, I'll get it. It sounds like Mr Gillies's knock."

Hopefully it was him and not a census enumerator coming to double-check who'd spent the evening in the house. Isabella giggled again at her minor flirtation with civil disobedience.

She opened the door. Dr Forbes was standing in the vestibule. "Oh. Hello. I thought it was Mr Gillies. You're back from the symposium early."

"Good afternoon, Mrs Lockhart." The assistant medical officer's face was pinched. She was faintly trembling.

"Is everything all right?"

"May I come in?"

"Yes, of course. Is there something wrong?"

"Can we sit down?"

"Where's Angus?"

Dr Forbes put her arm round Isabella. "I'm afraid I have bad news."

Isabella's stomach lurched. "What?"

Dr Forbes guided her into the drawing room. Isabella took a deep breath as the doctor sat next to her on the settee. Tipper jumped up, too, and padded across their legs.

"Mrs Lockhart, I'm sorry to have to tell you this ..."

Isabella's heart began to race.

"This morning at the symposium, a man – a former patient of Dr Lockhart's – shot him."

"What?" Isabella couldn't have heard that right. "*Shot* him?"

"Yes. Three times before he was apprehended. They carried Dr Lockhart to the City Hospital ..."

Isabella lowered her head and leaned forward, fearing she was about to faint. There was ringing in her ears, spots before her eyes.

"... and while they were able to remove the bullets, I'm afraid—"

"No!" Isabella sat back up quickly.

"—one of them pierced a main artery. He lost too much blood and ..."

This couldn't be happening. Dr Forbes must be mistaken. "No!" *How could Angus have been ...*

"I'm very sorry, Mrs Lockhart. Dr Lockhart died from his injuries."

Isabella slumped to the side and banged her fist on the arm of the settee. "No! No! No!"

"I'm so sorry. Everything possible was done for him but he was too severely wounded. Mercifully, it was quick. He didn't suffer."

"How do you know he didn't suffer?" Isabella spluttered, tears running down her face.

Dr Forbes rubbed a dark red stain on her jacket with a fingernail. "I was there. I was beside him when it happened."

"No ... this can't be true ... there must be a mistake. Are you sure? No. No."

Tipper whimpered, then licked Isabella's hand.

"Mrs Lockhart, it might be a good idea if one of the nurses comes to look after you. And maybe spends the night. In case there's anything you need. You've had a terrible shock." Dr Forbes looked as if she wanted to comfort Isabella but didn't quite know how. "I can prepare a sleeping draught, if you'd like."

Isabella wiped her cheeks with the back of her hand. The room was out of kilter. Everything was out of kilter.

When she'd last seen Angus, she hadn't given him the fond farewell of a loving wife ... she'd rushed him out of the house as quickly as possible, her heart singing that she was going to have time without him to be her true self.

"Nurse Elliot. I'd like Nurse Elliot to come."

"I'm afraid Nurse Elliot leaves us tomorrow. But I'm sure whoever comes will be most proficient and—"

Isabella grasped Dr Forbes's arm. "I want Nurse Elliot! She's a—"

"But—"

"—good nurse. Angus thinks so too."

"Yes, she's a very good nurse. But I'm afraid she's been dismissed."

"But not because she wasn't a good nurse."

"No, that's true." The assistant medical officer thought for a moment. "All right. I'll put it to Dr Dorsie. Although I don't know what he'll think."

Isabella sniffed. "I expect he'll think whatever Matron Campbell tells him to think."

"Well, I …" Dr Forbes shifted uncomfortably. "Yes. In the circumstances, I'm sure Nurse Elliot can remain for a few more days. Of course. Yes." She got up. "Once again, Mrs Lockhart, I'm so very sorry. I'll go and make arrangements for Nurse Elliot to come immediately. I'm sure Mrs Drummond will sit with you in the meantime. I'll see myself out."

As if on cue, Mrs Drummond appeared and put a glass of brandy on the table. "Madam, I'm so very sorry."

Isabella stood, then fell into her housekeeper's open arms, weeping. The world she knew was changed forever.

JESSIE

JESSIE TOOK off her regulation maid's shoes and put them on the floor next to her folded uniforms. Then she spat on her Oxfords and rubbed them to a polish with her shawl. Her mother's shoes felt unfamiliar at first, but after pacing the room a few times, the strangeness faded.

She slid her hand under the mattress to retrieve her cloth bag. With the last few months' wages added to what she'd already saved, she almost had four pounds – more money than she'd ever had for herself. The pin clasp on her Band of Hope medallion was still attached, albeit loosely, and if she could keep it safe until she got to the city, she'd finally get it fixed.

She went over to the chest, where Mary's books remained. What would happen to them when someone else was allocated the room? Mary was unlikely to be back after having been away for so long now and Miss Wilson would probably just throw them out.

Jessie opened the top drawer. It was empty, with not even a mark to suggest it had ever contained anything untoward, let alone the corpse of a newborn. She shuddered, then opened the drawer underneath and took out the books. Mary would surely rather a friend took them than they were destroyed. She dropped them with her other belongings into the sack she'd filched from the store. Then she left the room for the last time.

The door to Miss Wilson's office was ajar. Jessie rapped twice and waited.

There was some rustling before the head laundress called out. "Come."

Jessie waited in front of the desk while Miss Wilson folded a newspaper and put it to one side. "Here are my uniforms. And I've counted and I'm due three days' wages."

Miss Wilson put the clothes on the chair behind her. "Just let me check."

She reached for the hefty wages book and sighed. "It's terrible about Dr Lockhart, isn't it? Such a shock. I don't know whether I'm coming or going. He was such a wonderful man. He did wonders for this place. Always saw us right and always able to persuade the Laundry Committee to invest in new equipment. He'll be sorely missed. They should hang the man who did it. I hope he rots in hell. And poor Mrs Lockhart. What's she going to do? She was a school teacher before she married Dr Lockhart, you know? Did very well for herself. She'll be lucky to find another one like him."

Miss Wilson picked up a pencil and wrote some figures in the wages book. "Yes, you're right, three days. Initial here." She turned the book round for Jessie then took a metal box from one of the desk drawers and counted out some money. "There you are. I think you'll find that's correct."

"Thank you."

"And I've something else before you go." Miss Wilson handed Jessie a piece of paper embossed at the top with the asylum's name and address. "It's a recommendation. You've been a good worker and good with the patients. I can't say that of all the girls who come through here. If you show that at any other asylum, you'll have no bother getting a position."

Jessie scanned the page: *conscientious ... trustworthy ...*

honest … no hesitation in re-engaging. "Thank you, Miss Wilson. Thank you very much."

"You could be a nurse if you wanted to. You've the right temperament for it and—"

"I don't think so."

"—it's easier than working in the laundry. They get their own bedrooms here, the nurses. Did you know that? While all our girls have to share."

"No, I don't think it's for me," Jessie said. "Even with a bedroom of my own."

"No. You're like me. An honest day's work for an honest day's pay. Where you can see and touch the products of your labour. There's something to be said for that."

Jessie turned the money over in her hand. Miss Wilson had never spoken to her like this before.

"Well, anyway, good luck to you wherever you end up. Do you have any plans?"

"Well, I …" It might offend Miss Wilson if Jessie admitted she had no intention of continuing as a laundry maid. And after what had happened to Mary, domestic service in a private house had little appeal. "… I'm just going to see what comes along. But at least I know I'll be able to find another position with this." She held up the recommendation. "Thanks again, Miss Wilson."

Before leaving, Jessie paused to enjoy the fresh smell of the laundry complex. Then she put her wages in her cloth bag and swung the sack by her side as she went down the sweeping drive towards the gates.

She slowed as she approached the medical superintendent's house. Every curtain was drawn. Poor Mrs Lockhart. She'd been kind and caring – Jessie wouldn't forget that.

The vestibule door opened and Nurse Elliot came trotting down the path. "Miss Purdie, wait!"

Jessie went to meet her at the garden gate.

"I'm glad I spotted you. There's something I need to give you." The nurse reached into her apron pocket.

"Are you seeing to Mrs Lockhart?"

"Yes."

"I know it's not my place, and it probably won't mean much to her anyway, but could you tell her I'm very sorry about Dr Lockhart. It's terrible what happened to him."

"Of course. I'm sure she'll appreciate your condolences." Nurse Elliot handed Jessie a scrap of paper. "Matilda asked me to give you this. It's her address."

Jessie peered at the smudged writing. "Her address?"

"She said it's in case you need somewhere to go."

Jessie swallowed. "Is she safe now?"

"Yes. And I know she'd be happy that you're leaving. She was very grateful for what you did for her."

Jessie slotted the piece of paper behind the pin clasp of her Band of Hope medallion. "It turned out she helped me too. And you did as well, Nurse Elliot. And about Mrs Lockhart … could you also thank her for the typing and everything? And tell her I'm sorry about what I said to her in the laundry about Miss Anderson. I didn't mean anything by it."

"I think the less said about all that, the better."

Jessie delved into her sack and brought out *Jane Eyre* and *The Channings*. "And perhaps she could have these returned to Miss Anderson, if she knows where she is. If not, she should probably keep them herself. She likes books. And she's a teacher. Maybe now that she's … well, Dr Lockhart's … anyway, they'll be better off with her than me."

Nurse Elliot took the books. "You're doing the right thing, leaving."

Jessie glanced towards the asylum.

"Don't look back. Go and make a life for yourself."

When Jessie reached the entrance gates, Mr Gillies was opening them for Thomson's Aerated Water cart. Mr Thomson nudged the lad to pull up the horses. "Hello, lass. D'you want a lift anywhere? If you wait till I've finished my delivery, I can take you. Where are you heading?"

Jessie looked to the road beyond the gates. "Would the railway station be all right?"

"The railway station would be just fine, miss."

KATHERINE

With his bulbous nose, spidery blood vessels and glassy eyes, Ex-Provost Easton, Chairman of the District Lunacy Board, was the picture of a man who took a good drink.

It troubled Katherine that people in important positions were frequently so unimpressive. Perhaps in the boardroom, holding court over the twenty other members, he was dynamic in steering them towards key decisions. But sitting at the mahogany table in the medical superintendent's meeting room informing two shocked assistant medical officers of the interim arrangements which had been agreed, he was anything but.

Granted, it wasn't a pleasant task, but it wasn't as if he'd been there when Dr Lockhart had been shot. Nor was he going to worry for the rest of his life (which was probably not too long, judging by the yellow tinge of his skin) about former patients with a grudge killing him in cold blood.

She shifted in her seat. The subconscious was truly phenomenal in its capacity to record every detail of a transient incident and then transform it into an extended saga that played back in one's mind's eye at the most inopportune moments.

There was William Noakes again in his charcoal grey suit,

the collar of his white shirt peeking over the left lapel and the knot of his black tie slightly skew-whiff.

There was his hand on her arm, firm and steady, steering her out of the way. His other hand moving in and out of his trouser pocket in a single motion.

There was the flash of his gun, silver and black. A terrible bang. Then another, and another.

There was Dr Lockhart on his back, head to the right, eyes shut. Katherine beside him, crying out.

Blood.

Noakes so close his legs brushed her shoulder. Sharp crease in his trousers, loose thread at the seam.

A terrible bang. Another.

Katherine curling up: *Our father, who art in heaven, hallowed be thy name; thy kingdom come; thy will be done, on earth as it is in heaven.*

Noakes's voice. Passionate. But controlled. 'I want that quack in the witness box again to wring the truth out of him.'

The gun. A scrum.

Blood. White shirt turned red. Silk scarf from Cree & Co.

All fingers and thumbs.

Breathing. Thank God. 'He needs to go to hospital. Now!'

DYING DOCTOR CARRIED TO HOSPITAL, the headline in the paper the day after.

OUTRAGE UPON A LUNACY EXPERT, the day after that.

"So …"

Ex-Provost Easton was finally bumbling towards the point of the meeting.

"… the Board's decided that pending the final appointment, Dr Dorsie, as first assistant medical officer, will obviously be in charge, and the Board will supply a locum to work with you, Dr Forbes. We're very lucky to have Dr Stirling on the Board and he's kindly agreed to step into the breach. He'll stand down from the Board, of course, for the duration, but will remain as an elected member of his county. We hope to fill the medical superintendent's position as soon as possible. We're aware of some very fine up-and-coming young men who might fit the bill. Including, it goes without saying, yourself, Dr Dorsie. As first assistant medical officer, I presume you wish to throw your hat into the ring?"

Dr Dorsie spluttered something or other.

"Excellent. The Board wants to ensure that whoever takes over from Dr Lockhart continues the objective of having Cappelmuir in advance of every asylum in Scotland. Dr Stirling is free to start immediately and can report to you tomorrow morning, Dr Dorsie, so you can brief him on the duties of the first assistant medical officer."

"I beg your pardon?" Katherine said.

"I'm sorry, my dear. Was there something you didn't follow?" Ex-Provost Easton smiled at her and Dr Dorsie looked out the window. "It would be perfectly understandable. Indeed, I must say, I'm surprised to even see you here. I thought you might be resting. In fact, in the circumstances, the Board would understand if you felt that continuing in your role was too much."

Katherine clenched her fists under the table and dug her fingernails into her palm. "I thank you and the Board for your concern, sir, but I'm quite able to continue my duties. I want to assist the asylum through this very difficult period in any way I can."

"As you wish. Now, Dr Dorsie, as you'll be acting in a more senior capacity, you will of course be—"

"Excuse me, sir. Might I just confirm that Dr Stirling will act as *first* assistant medical officer?" Katherine said.

"That's correct."

"With respect, sir, I've worked here under Dr Lockhart and Dr Dorsie and know the institution and its ways, not to mention its patients, very well. Might it not be—"

"Dr Stirling's an excellent fellow. I'm sure he'll be most

willing to take advantage of your knowledge of the asylum and work with you accordingly."

"Sir, respectfully, I—"

"There's no doubt you're an excellent physician, my dear. Dr Lockhart spoke highly of you at the Board on many occasions. But we feel that your current position is the correct one for you." Ex-Provost Easton stood up. "Now, Dr Dorsie, let's you and I take a walk around the policies and I can brief you on Board matters. Board liaison is one of the medical superintendent's most important duties."

Katherine winced when the legs of Dr Dorsie's chair screeched on the floorboards. She should screech too; put her case to Ex-Provost Easton; leave him in no doubt she was best qualified to step up to the role of first assistant medical officer; assure him they wouldn't find a better doctor to do so if they scoured the length and breadth of the country. But just as she'd been helpless when they'd carried Dr Lockhart away, she was helpless as Ex-Provost Easton led Dr Dorsie out. And this time there was no one to help her to her feet, no one wise and kind who respected her for who she was and what she did.

For all his wisdom, though, Dr Cowan wasn't quite right about one thing – she may well be a doctor and a human being, but to the world she was more a doctor and a woman.

She gazed out the window. Mr Johnstone was coming up the drive, swinging his satchel. Katherine banged the table and got to her feet. If she wanted to be sure to catch him on his way back from his rounds, she'd better be quick writing her two letters. One, her notice of resignation; the other, to Dr Andrew Cowan.

HELEN

JUST BEFORE THE pallbearers carried Dr Lockhart from the house, Helen stepped outside and took her place alongside the others lining the path. She lowered her head as the bier passed by, glancing sideways to watch as the coffin was positioned inside the elegant glass-sided hearse. One of the black horses snorted and the feather plume over its ears quivered. Helen held her breath until silence descended again.

Mrs Lockhart appeared at the front door, supported by her friends, Mr and Mrs Buchanan. In her plain black dress, face covered by a tulle veil, the medical superintendent's hunched widow looked older than her years.

The three mourners stopped to bow before the coffin, then were escorted by the undertakers to the carriage behind the hearse. Helen was relieved when Mrs Lockhart got in and the door was closed behind her. Only an hour earlier, it wasn't certain she'd attend her husband's funeral such was her emotional state, which had deteriorated rather than improved each day since his death.

At first she was composed, busying herself with writing lists of chores. However, at the suggestion that a nurse was no longer needed in the house, Mrs Lockhart replaced the practicalities of death with the emotions of grief, consulting Helen about numerous bodily reactions that were troubling her. Then, reassured such symptoms were normal, she took up position beside the coffin in the front room and sobbed over how smart Dr Lockhart looked in his best suit and tie. It was a relief, therefore, that she'd succeeded in suppressing her emotions in order to navigate the first part of this harrowing day.

As the hearse set off, the undertakers fell in on foot behind. Mrs Lockhart's carriage came after, followed by the one transporting the Chairman of the District Board, Doctors Forbes and Dorsie and Reverend Fulton.

The cortege made its way slowly down the long drive, and when it reached the gates, Mrs Drummond was first to turn away. "I'd better get back inside. I need to prepare the food for after."

"Of course," Helen said. "Thank you for your assistance in the last few days."

"I'm just glad you were here. I'd've been no good trying to comfort Mrs Lockhart on my own."

"I'm sure you would've been fine."

Mrs Drummond flicked away a speck from the sleeve of her black dress. "I don't have a nurse's training."

"You don't need any training for this kind of thing."

"Be that as may, I'll just stick to running a household, thank you very much. Dr Lockhart was my third medical superintendent. I hope the next one's as much of a gentleman as he was."

"I'm sure whoever's appointed will find you as invaluable as Dr and Mrs Lockhart did."

"Thank you, Nurse Elliot. And good luck with whatever you do next. I'm sorry you're leaving us and I know Mrs Lockhart is too." Mrs Drummond went up the path and straightened the black crepe under the door knocker before going inside.

Matron Campbell was still at the garden gate, most likely waiting to escort Helen from the grounds now the unanticipated extension of her duties had come to an end. As Helen approached, however, Matron Campbell set off towards the asylum.

"Walk with me, Nurse Elliot," she called.

Helen nipped through the gate and trotted after her.

"Tell me – why didn't you report Mr Kennedy as soon as you suspected there was something amiss with Mr Allan?"

There was no point in concealing the truth now. If Helen had learned anything from what had happened, it was that secrets were debts that eventually had to be paid off.

"Because he said he'd tell the medical superintendent I was behind a petition by the nurses for better conditions."

"And were you?"

"No. I didn't start it and I wasn't behind it. But I did support it and I was involved with it. And I should never have been ashamed of it being known. It's the worst mistake of my life."

"Oh, you're still young. There's time yet for many more mistakes." Was that the hint of a smile from Matron Campbell? "Anyway, talking of petitions – a strange thing. Dr Lockhart received one the day before he … Nurse Millar handed it in."

"Oh?" So Nurse Millar had done it. Helen was taken aback.

"Yes. And all I'll say, Nurse Elliot, is that you must be very highly regarded by your peers if they're prepared to lose their jobs for you."

"But it's not about me, that's the thing. It's about what can happen to people like me. To any of the nurses."

Matron Campbell stopped. "In any community, there are mostly followers, with just a few leaders. You, Nurse Elliot, are a leader."

Helen laughed. "I don't think so, Matron. I don't put myself up to be followed or to tell people what to do. I just keep myself to myself. Well, I try to … but sometimes …"

"There are many ways of leading – yours is by the example of hard work and good judgement. Well, generally speaking, that is." Matron Campbell walked on. "There are going to be changes whoever becomes the new medical superintendent. I want those changes to be for the better and for the nurses to feel their work is properly valued and suitably rewarded. If I'm to persuade the new medical superintendent to review their hours and wages, I'll need the support of influential nurses." When Helen stopped, it took Matron Campbell several paces to notice and turn back. "Do you understand what I'm saying?"

Helen hesitated. She thought she did but … dare she hope?

"What I'm saying Nurse Elliot is …"

Helen's heart began to race.

"… if you wish, you may stay on."

Helen gasped. "Do you—"

The matron set off again. "I will, of course, understand if you prefer to leave. And if you choose to do so, I'll provide you with a recommendation. However, I hope not to have to put pen to paper."

Helen ran to catch up with her again. "But will Dr Dorsie allow me to stay?"

Matron Campbell looked puzzled. "Dr Dorsie?"

"I mean, isn't he in charge now?"

"Oh, I see." Matron Campbell chortled. "Yes, of course." She pushed her shoulders back and her bosom forward. "And I'm sure Dr Dorsie, if he were to notice, would have no issue with my decision."

Helen stifled a giggle.

"I'll leave you to think it over, Nurse Elliot. Please let me know when you've decided." The matron went into the main building and disappeared down a corridor.

Think it over? There was nothing to think over.

Helen closed her eyes, dropped her chin to her chest and let out a sigh of relief.

She would never have believed Matron Campbell would save the day. If ever there was a leader, it was her.

"Nurse Elliot? See what I got!"

Helen looked around and grimaced at the dead rodent Roddy The Rat Catcher was holding by its tail.

"It was in the laboratory stealing the guinea pigs' food."

"I see. Well, good job. I'm sure Dr Forbes will be delighted when she hears."

He beamed, then swung the rat around. "I've seen you in the hospital wards the last few days. Is that where you'll be working from now on?"

Helen glanced over to the ladies' wing. "No, Roddy. I'm pleased to say that Matron Campbell wants me back where I belong."

ISABELLA

ISABELLA WENT to the table by the front room window and opened the leather-bound family Bible at the birth records. There it was – the last on the list, the last of the line: *Angus Nelson Lockhart, June 2, 1881.* She covered his name with her thumb and gazed into the garden. She wasn't related by blood to any of these people, hadn't known any of them; and now she had no living connection to them either. Nor were there any children to pass down Angus's possessions to. She was the last of the Lockharts.

Except … was she even a Lockhart at all? As a Muir, she'd been a daughter, a scholar and a teacher, but she was no longer part of her father's household. As a Lockhart, she had a household, but now it had no head.

She toyed with her black onyx pendant. She had to take the Bible with her. Of course she did. How could she have countenanced otherwise?

She put it under her arm and glanced around the room for a final time. It looked no different to when she'd moved in, with the same furniture and household items provided by the Board. The only things Isabella was taking from the medical superintendent's house were her clothes, wedding presents, gifts from Angus and a few knick-knacks they'd acquired as a married couple: bedside lamps, a Persian rug and the mirror over the fireplace in the drawing room. To that extent, she was fortunate, for leaving a house was less of a wrench than leaving a home.

She went into the hall and put the Bible in her rose-patterned carpet bag along with her jewellery box, legal documents and letters of condolence.

Effie came out of the drawing room, Tipper at her heels. "Is that everything then?"

"I think so. If I've left anything behind, I'm sure Mrs Drummond will send it on to me."

"Good. The cart's gone on ahead with the trunks. And I think that might be …" Effie opened the front door and looked outside. "Yes, that's the carriage pulling up. It's so very kind of Mrs Huntly-Sykes to help out like this. But remember that if she gets too much, you're always welcome to come and stay with Robert and me until you can move into the house."

Isabella puffed her cheeks. "I can't get used to it being my house now. And to having tenants. It still seems unreal. Angus dealt with all that. Obviously."

"It must," Effie said. "I can't begin to imagine how—"

"Anyway," Isabella said, cutting sympathy off in its tracks, "I appreciate your offer but Mrs Huntly-Sykes said it herself, she has lots of room. I'm getting my own wing in her house, you know?"

"She'd better watch in case she can't get rid of you when your tenants go." Effie started to laugh, then stopped abruptly. She put her hand on Isabella's shoulder. "Ready?"

Isabella closed her eyes for a moment. "Ready."

"Let me take that, Mrs Lockhart," Mrs Drummond said. She lifted the carpet bag and headed out the door.

"She can hardly wait for me to go," Isabella said. She clapped the side of her thigh to attract Tipper. "She probably thinks it's about time I went back to where I belong."

"Don't be silly, Izzy. She's been a great support these last few days. Very caring."

"She cared a lot for Angus, that's true."

"And for you," Effie said. "If you're going to feel sorry for yourself, at least make it about something that's actually true."

Tears pricked Isabella's eyes. Effie was right – she was being unfair.

She carried Tipper to the door, which Mrs Drummond had helpfully left ajar. The fewer obstacles she had to negotiate, the better.

Now all she had to do was walk the thirty yards to the end of the path and get into the carriage. Such a simple thing, yet the hardest thing she'd ever had to do. At least when she left the house to attend Angus's funeral, she knew she'd be returning. Isabella took a deep breath. "Let's go."

She counted every step along the path: forty-two to the gate.

Mrs Drummond was already at the sleek black and plum carriage, standing next to the coachman, smart in his black uniform and top hat. He lowered the foot tread and opened the door, which had the initials 'H-S' painted in elegant letters on the side. "Madam."

Isabella handed Tipper to Effie, then, holding onto the coachman's upturned hand, used all her strength to climb into the cabin.

Mrs Huntly-Sykes patted the cushioned red bench. "Mrs Lockhart – please sit next to me."

Isabella took Tipper from Effie and pulled the silk blind next to her halfway down. Once Effie was inside, the coachman went to close the door. Isabella raised her hand.

"Stop. Please. Mrs Drummond?" Her housekeeper's head appeared round the carriage door. "Thank you for everything."

"Goodbye, madam. And good luck." Mrs Drummond stepped back and bowed her head.

Mrs Huntly-Sykes put her hand on Isabella's. "Are you ready, dear?"

Isabella peered below the blind for a last look at the house, then nodded.

When the carriage reached the main gates, they were already open. Through the front window, she caught a glimpse of Mr Gillies by his box, holding a salute. When she noticed his black armband, she buried her face in Tipper's fur.

After she'd counted to one hundred in time to the clip-clopping of the horses, she raised her head. Effie had her eyes closed and Mrs Huntly-Sykes was stroking Tipper's back paw. Isabella raised her blind. The spires of the town's churches were getting closer.

"There's something I need to know," Mrs Huntly-Sykes said, "if you're to be a guest in my house." She ruffled Tipper's head. "Did you ever get a licence for this dog?"

"Actually, I did not." Isabella smiled. "And do you know what?" She kissed Tipper's ear. "I have no intention of doing so."

JESSIE

"Miss Purdie? Could you come here a moment before you leave?"

Jessie glanced up at the large wall clock. It was after six, so surely she wasn't getting a ticking-off for leaving early? She turned and went back to her desk.

"Yes, Mr Quinn?" The manager looked rather stern. "Are the letters I typed all right? I checked them for mistakes."

"Yes, yes," he replied, dismissing her concern with a swish of his hand.

Jessie curled her lip – she surely couldn't have made a mistake writing out the accounts. She'd gone over them three times to make sure she'd copied the figures correctly.

"It's nothing like that." Mr Quinn twiddled one of his cufflinks. "In actual fact, your work since you joined us has been of a very high standard."

"Oh … thank you, sir."

"Now, I won't insult you by denying that I wasn't sure about taking you on at first. We've always had office boys and if the school had been able to suggest a suitable one, you wouldn't be here."

"No, sir."

"But I have to admit, my misgivings were entirely misplaced. So I'd like to end your trial period and take you on properly. If you'll accept the position, of course."

Jessie beamed. "Of course, sir. Yes!"

"You'll still be on ten shillings a week, mind. But carry on like this and there might be another shilling in it for you soon enough."

"Thank you, sir."

"Excellent. Well, I'll see you in the morning. Eight thirty sharp. If not before."

"Yes, sir."

Jessie went as casually as she could from the clerks' room. As soon as she reached the corridor, she punched the air and sprinted out of the building. She had to get home to tell Matilda and Peter the good news.

When she burst through the front door of their terraced house, Matilda was at the stove attending to a pot of soup and Peter was at the table reading the newspaper.

"Guess what? They've made me permanent. I'm officially the office girl! The office *girl*."

Matilda propped the ladle up inside the pot and hugged Jessie. "Well done! I knew you could do it."

"My wages'll still be ten shillings a week but Mr Quinn said there might be another shilling in it soon if I carry on the way I am."

Peter glanced up. "I might need to put your rent up."

"Peter!" Matilda slapped his shoulder playfully. "Ignore him. We're more than happy with you as a lodger, Jessie."

He laughed. "Just as long as you keep paying your rent on time."

"Get back to your reading, you." Matilda went to the Welsh dresser and lifted an envelope. "I've some news, too. You have a letter."

"What? How? No one knows I'm here," Jessie said.

"Don't look so worried. Nurse Elliot thought you might be here. Or that if you weren't, I might know where you were. She put this in with a letter to me." The envelope Matilda handed over had Jessie's name on it but no stamp. "It's from Miss Anderson, Nurse Elliot says."

"Mary Anderson?"

"Yes. Apparently, she's back at Cappelmuir. And look. Nurse Elliot sent me this." Matilda held up a copy of *The Passing Hour*. "So we can read about what's been happening." She opened the magazine. "Listen to this: *We were sorry to say farewell last month to Dr Katherine Forbes, who left to take up a post at a medical mission in India. If she is as good a wife as she is a doctor, her husband-to-be is a very lucky man. She has promised to dispatch regular news from Bombay and we look forward to publishing it in future editions.*"

"India? That's on the other side of the world!"

"And listen to this: *Our congratulations go to our own Nurse Helen Elliot who has gained promotion to senior nurse. Her gentle ways and sympathetic nature have endeared her to everyone among patients and staff and we are sure she will excel in her new position.*"

"Goodness!"

"I'd've made her matron," Matilda said. "We've a lot to thank Nurse Elliot for." She handed Jessie *The Passing Hour*. "Here. That'll be something new for you to read."

There was a picture of the Cappelmuir cricket team and some supporters on the cover. Jessie recognised a few of them. There was Roddy The Rat Catcher and Old Nellie Shaw. Mr Johnstone and Mr Gillies. And Clara Brodie with one of her amazing hats! She didn't know any of the attendants. It would probably all be different now, with Mr Kennedy in prison.

"Tea'll be five minutes, if you want to read your letter before then," Matilda said.

Jessie went to her room and sat on the bed. Although she

knew the letter couldn't be from her father or brothers, her hands were still trembling. She tore open the envelope and quickly checked the signature at the bottom of the page. *Your friend, Mary (Anderson).*

Thank heavens.

Cappelmuir Asylum
August 1911

Dearest Jessie

I pray this letter will get to you. I wasn't in a good state when I went away and I never thanked you properly. When I came back to Cappelmuir and discovered you'd left, I was upset I wouldn't be able to tell you how grateful I was for everything you did for me. But Nurse Elliot said there might be a way of reaching you and I only hope she's right and I can finally say what I've wanted to say ever since it happened. Which is that I can never thank you enough, Jessie. I wasn't in my right mind and not everyone would've been so understanding. I didn't deserve such kindness but I'm truly grateful you were my friend.

After you put me on the train, I was met by two very caring ladies. They took me on as a domestic, although their house didn't need another maid. The work wasn't hard and they treated me with warmth, which helped me recover. After the terrible thing that happened to Dr Lockhart, Mrs Lockhart had to move away from Cappelmuir. She went to stay with a good friend of my mistresses, a Mrs Huntly-Sykes, a very grand lady, with a very grand house, who then asked me to be Mrs Lockhart's maid.

Mrs Lockhart was very nice and I enjoyed serving her for a while. She kept me busy with this and that and even got me

*involved with her campaigning for the vote. She had me
typing up her writing. I wasn't very good at it. I went with
her for a stay on the Clyde, where she was protesting on the
street! A gentleman shouted out that she should be locked up
and she shouted back that it wouldn't make any difference
because women were already prisoners! I could hardly believe
my eyes and ears!*

*I have to admit, though, to being a bit lonely and missing the
company of a roommate and the other laundry girls. So when
Mrs Lockhart moved into her own house, I was happy to come
back to Cappelmuir.*

*I share a room with a girl called Janet now. She used to work
at Mount Hope and says that Cappelmuir's much better. We
get on very well. Miss Wilson's the same as ever and is
hoping the new medical superintendent will build another
room at the laundry. I've never seen him but they say he's a
kind man. Oh, and I must thank you for keeping my books
safe. Mrs Lockhart gave them back to me and also gave me
some of her own books when I left her service. Janet and I read
them in the evenings.*

*Well, that's all my news. I'm very happy where I am, thanks
to you. I'll never be able to repay you, Jessie, but, if you're
ever in need of anything, I'll do anything and everything I
can to help you. I hope we'll see each other again.*

*Your friend
Mary (Anderson)*

Jessie stared at the letter. Good for Mary. Back at
Cappelmuir with Nurse Elliot, a senior now. And imagine Mrs
Lockhart, out on the streets with her placards and pamphlets.
And Dr Forbes – getting married and going all the way to

India to work. Jessie had never known anyone who'd left the country before.

She fell back on the bed, clutching the letter to her chest. How strong and determined these asylum women were. How strong and determined they'd helped her become. Wherever she was, whoever she was with, she would never forget them.

HISTORICAL NOTE

Cappelmuir asylum is based on Stirling District Lunatic Asylum (SDLA) in the early 1900s, the archives of which are held by the University of Stirling.

The procedures and practices of Cappelmuir reflect those of SDLA, which was a forward-thinking institution for its time and which pioneered the employment of female nurses in male wards.

The characters in the novel are fictional. However, many of them are based on real individuals who appear in the patient records of SDLA.

The character of Dr Katherine Forbes was inspired by Dr Isabel Hutton (neé Emslie). While Dr Hutton is best known for her wartime service, after graduating from the University of Edinburgh she worked at SDLA. Her book *Memories of a Doctor in War & Peace* (1960) tells of her time there.

The storylines are fictional too, although they are based on real life contexts. Actual historical events and publications are referenced in the novel, which means that some of the beliefs of the characters and the language they use are not what would be considered appropriate today.

The inspiration for the shooting of Dr Lockhart was the

shooting of Dr John Carswell in Glasgow in 1907. Dr Carswell, shot twice in the hip by William Purves, survived. Purves, who pleaded not guilty, was found guilty and sentenced to seven years in prison.

The Red Book refers to the *Handbook for Attendants on the Insane* published by the Royal Medico-Psychological Association, 1908.

The Passing Hour was SDLA's magazine and the references to it in the novel are authentic.

ACKNOWLEDGEMENTS

Thanks to loyal beta readers Fran, Lesley and Susan for their feedback and input. And as always, to my husband, Hamish, proof-reader, red pen brandisher, tea maker, chief cook and bottle washer.

The Rescue Sisters

A tale of blackmail, kidnap and terrible secrets. Of children being sent abroad and of women trying to do the right thing at a time when they were second class citizens.

Stirling, 1900 – reeling from a family tragedy, Jane Knight volunteers at Gowanlea Children's Home in Stirling, run by upstanding pillar of the community, Eliza Frew. Before long, though, Jane discovers that everything isn't as it seems with a boy who's been sent to Canada and with Eliza Frew herself. While Jane sets off to Quebec on a rescue mission, Eliza faces a reckoning from her past that could ruin her.

To right a wrong and to settle a score, how far will Jane and Eliza go to protect the ones they love ... and save themselves?

<u>Praise for *The Rescue Sisters*</u>

'It isn't very often that a book comes along and quite literally takes my breath away, but Rescue Sisters did just that. An absolutely stunning, powerful

book that gave me goosebumps and tells you that 'girl power' was alive and kicking even in the late 1800s.'

'A powerful piece of historical fiction that pulls at the heart strings and brings a new appreciation for so many unnamed and unspoken women of the past.'

'I would highly recommend this well-written book and am looking forward to the author's next publication. In my opinion, this book would make an excellent film or TV series.'

'From the very start I was hooked! I could not put the book down. It really seemed to capture my imagination immediately and I felt like I was right there witnessing events unfold in front of me.'

'This truly unique historical account of a part of our history that is truly questionable is brilliantly executed. The amount of research that must have gone into this is unreal.'

The Rescue Sisters

ABOUT THE AUTHOR

Elaine Whiteford is a writer of fiction and non-fiction who lives and works in Scotland.

Fiction

- The Rescue Sisters
- The Asylum Women

Non-fiction

- The Story of Stirling Golf Club
- Wild & Temperate Seas, 50 Favourite UK Dives (contributor)

~

For more information and updates
https://www.elainewhiteford.com

instagram.com/elaine_whiteford_writer